WAKE UP,
DARLIN' COREY

By M. K. Wren

WAKE UP, DARLIN' COREY
SEASONS OF DEATH
NOTHING'S CERTAIN BUT DEATH
OH, BURY ME NOT
A MULTITUDE OF SINS
CURIOSITY DIDN'T KILL THE CAT

WAKE UP, DARLIN' COREY

M. K. WREN

PUBLISHED FOR THE CRIME CLUB

BY

DOUBLEDAY & COMPANY, INC.

GARDEN CITY, NEW YORK

1984

The words from "Darlin' Corey," collected, adapted and arranged by
John A. Lomax and Alan Lomax TRO © Copyright 1941 and renewed
1969 Ludlow Music, Inc., New York, N.Y., are used by permission.

Library of Congress Cataloging in Publication Data

Wren, M. K.
Wake Up, Darlin' Corey

I. Title.
PS3573.R43W3   1984   813'.54
ISBN 0-385-19292-4

Library of Congress Catalog Card Number 83–16474
Copyright © 1984 by MARTHA KAY RENFROE
All Rights Reserved
Printed in the United States of America

First Edition

WAKE UP,
DARLIN' COREY

CHAPTER 1

Conan Flagg was dreaming of kites, and that should have made for pleasant dreams, but it didn't. The sound of the Pacific surf pounding only yards from his bed and the wind-harried rain hissing against the wall of windows colored his dreams with foreboding verging on fear.

Dragon kites, sinuous as water snakes, stretching endlessly on black winds; and the kites were black, too, but quite clear in the irrational vision of dreams. Conan didn't feel threatened by them; he didn't seem to be present. They sang dryly like raven's wings in flight, waiting for the phone to ring.

Conan came thrashing out of the depths of sleep and a tangle of blankets and lunged for the phone on the bedside table. When he remembered to open his eyes, the clock on the control console offered his present temporal coordinates in glowing code: 2:02 AM 11 27 SAT. Which was more than he wanted to know at the moment.

He managed a nearly intelligible "hello."

"Conan, this is Di." Then, as if his befogged tone indicated a need for the reminder, "Diane Monteil. I'm sorry, did I wake you up?"

That wasn't as foolish a question as it might seem. Conan was as likely to be awake at this hour as not, and Diane knew that. She was not, however, in the habit of calling him at this hour. Conan reached for the light switch, squinting at the sudden glare. "Di, what's wrong?"

"Well, nothing, probably. It's just . . ." An odd hesitation, then, "I wondered if Corey was there. I mean, I thought maybe she stopped by and decided to stay over."

Conan maneuvered a pillow between his back and the headboard, smiling wistfully. "Corey stay overnight with me? Oh, Di, that's a beautiful thought, but highly unlikely."

A brief laugh. "Well, actually I wasn't thinking—I mean, since Lyn is there . . ."

"Oh." Conan had for the moment forgotten that Lyndon Hatch occupied his guest room tonight. "No, Corey's not here." He searched for a cigarette, found a survivor in the pack crushed under a book. "Is she supposed to be?"

"No, I was just hoping . . . Conan, I'm not checking up on her. It's just that when you have a child to worry about, you never go anywhere without leaving a detailed itinerary. She should be *home* by now."

Conan absently applied a lighter to the bent cigarette. "Home from where?"

"She went down to Gabe Benbow's to talk to him again."

"*Alone?*" But of course she would go alone. Why not? "Did she take Kate's diary with her?"

"Yes."

"Good God, why would she—no, never mind." He took a long drag on his cigarette. "All right, when did she go?"

"She left home about eight. I put Kit and Melissa to bed, then I was going to wait up for her. I wanted to know what the old bastard had to say. But I fell asleep and just woke up a few minutes ago, and . . ."

And she was worried sick. Nor could Conan think of any reason she shouldn't be at this hour. Corey Benbow and Diane Monteil were close friends, business partners, and, most pertinent, both were single parents who took their responsibilities very seriously. It was not at all typical of Corey to be out of touch with Diane—and her son, Kit—for so long.

"Di, have you called Gabe?"

A sigh, then, "No. I didn't have the nerve to wake *him* up at this time of night. I thought I'd wake you up first."

"I'll call him. Anyway, I doubt there's anything to worry about. Corey probably just . . ." Just what? What was the rational explanation for Corey's absence that didn't include disaster in some guise? "I'll call you back as soon as possible, Di."

He rose and went to the chair by the windows where he'd left his robe. As he pulled it on, he looked out past the rain-streaked glass with eyes as black as the vista, the epicanthic fold evident with his lids nearly closed, gaze focused inward. The one light in the room limned the stark planes of his face and gleamed on straight, black hair. Below this second-story window, breakers flickered dimly in the glow of a street lamp at the beach access north of the house. The waves were foamwhipped and fast, but for all its bluster, this was only a typical Oregon coast winter rain.

He turned abruptly, went back to the bed, and delved into the drawer under the table for a slim telephone directory and a fresh pack of cigarettes. The directory included listings not only for Holliday Beach, but for four other rural exchanges. Gabriel Benbow was listed under the Sitka Bay exchange. Conan punched the number, trying to control the resentment inspired by the very name of the man whom Corey always pointedly referred to as her grandfather-*in-law*. She retained the Benbow name only out of respect for her husband's memory.

"For Lord's sake—who *is* this?"

"Conan Flagg, Gabe. I'm trying to find Corey."

"Don't you know what *time* it is?"

"I'm well aware of the time. Is Corey there?"

"No, she's not here. Everybody left hours ago. Why don't you call that—what's her name? Monteil. Wake *her* up in the middle of the night!"

"Corey *was* there, wasn't she?"

"Sure, but she left a long time ago. Now, you just—"

"When did she leave?" Conan crushed out his unfinished cigarette with angry jabs.

"A little after nine. I remember because I wanted to watch 'Dallas,' and I missed the first part of it."

Undoubtedly J. R. Ewing was Gabe's favorite television character. "She hasn't come home, Gabe. Diane Monteil just called me. Did Corey say anything—"

"I'm her grandfather, not her keeper. The good Lord knows, she wouldn't tell *me* where she chooses to spend the night. Now, leave me alone!"

With that, Gabe abruptly terminated the call, leaving Conan with a dead line. He cradled the receiver and lighted another cigarette. The trouble with talking to Gabe, he mused, was that he always let himself get distracted by annoyance. Gabe *couldn't* have watched "Dallas" tonight. At nine o'clock this evening, Conan had himself been watching television. Lyn Hatch had a dinner engagement in Westport with a man considering a sizable donation of land to The Earth Conservancy, and Conan, finding himself alone, had enjoyed a special on Luciano Pavarotti. He distinctly remembered the voice-over preambling the show: " 'Dallas' will not be seen tonight so that we may bring you the following special presentation. . . ."

Was the lapse simply attributable to age? Gabe *was* eighty years old. Still, he seemed clear enough otherwise; all too clear, sometimes.

"Conan, what's going on?"

Lyndon Hatch stood in the doorway, looking like a blond, bearded "David" in knit briefs. Perhaps it was only the way he was standing, one hand raised to hold the robe draped over his shoulder, that made Conan think of Michelangelo. Lyn's tough, subtly muscled body was that of a runner and swimmer, of a man who spent most of his life outdoors. Rodin. If Rodin had ever done a Viking warrior, he would have reveled in Lyn's narrow head and prominent bone structure, the deep eye sockets that made him seem older than his thirty-four years. No matter that his eyes were brown, not blue, they had always in them a glint of the berserker.

Conan picked up the receiver and punched a number, explaining, "Di called, Lyn. Corey went down to Gabe's this evening, and she hasn't gotten home yet."

Lyn was across the room in three strides, but Conan held up a hand for silence; the call was answered on the first ring.

"Holliday Beach Police Department, Sergeant Hight."

"Dave, this is Conan Flagg. I'm looking for Corey Benbow. She's hours overdue getting home."

The sergeant paused, then, "You, uh, know where she went?"

"Down to Sitka Bay to see Gabe Benbow. She left home about eight. I just talked to Di Monteil."

"Oh boy." Another long pause, then, "Conan, we got a call from Jim Roddy with the State Patrol a few minutes ago. A guy who lives up Dunlin Beach Road noticed the guardrail out at the south end of the bay where the road cuts so close to the bluff above Reem's Rocks."

Conan said tightly, "Yes, I know the place." He didn't look up at Lyn, but he could sense the cold fear that sheathed him in immobility. Conan felt it too.

Hight went on, "The guy stopped and took a flashlight out to look. He saw a car down in the water at the bottom of the bluff. It's about a fifty-foot drop along there. Anyway, the guy went home and called the patrol, and they got a winch truck and some divers over there. They don't have the car up yet, but a little while ago, the divers gave 'em a license number."

Conan had to prompt Hight: "And?"

"The car's registered to Corella Benbow and Diane Monteil, and since it was a Holliday Beach address, Roddy called Chief Kleber. Figured the chief would know them. You say you just talked to Di? Well, at least she's okay."

"Yes. Did he—where's Earl now?"

"Well, the chief was home when Roddy called. Said he'd get dressed and go on down to the bay. Damn, I hope nothing's happened to Corey."

Conan felt an aching weight forming under his ribs. He had to clear his throat before he could speak. "Dave, can you radio Earl? Tell him I'll talk to Di and bring her down to the bay. I'll see him there."

When Conan hung up, the silence around him seemed to close in like a chill fog. Lyn Hatch spoke huskily without succeeding in dissipating it.

"What happened?"

Conan told him, and Lyn seemed at first either uncomprehending or impervious to the words, except for the slow fisting of his muscular hands and the pallor that made his eyes seem dark pools in their shadowed hollows.

Finally he said in a hoarse whisper, "That bastard!"

Conan stared at him. "Who? Gabe?"

"If he hadn't shafted her so—"

"Gabe didn't shaft Corey, Lyn. He shafted ECon."

But the cold, berserker's fire was in Lyn's eyes. "Somebody should kill him. Put the world out of at least some of its misery."

Conan rose and crossed to the dressing room. "Lyn, I'm going after Di. If you want to ride with us, I'll take the van."

Lyn visibly shook himself out of his preoccupation. "No, I'll take my cycle. You better take the XK-E. It's faster."

Conan was busy pulling on clothes. He didn't point out that speed was undoubtedly immaterial now.

CHAPTER 2

The Dunlin Beach Road left Highway 101 four miles south of Holliday Beach and struck westward, skirting the south shore of Sitka Bay. Then it divided, the left-hand branch running another mile down the beach to provide access for a handful of houses, while the right-hand branch continued around the bay for half a mile and dead-ended at Gabe Benbow's house at the heel of Shearwater Spit. The latter section of the road and the span connecting it to the highway were paved, although it was only a narrow, county road. The beach road was *not* paved, and some citizens of Taft County were cynical enough to think that uneven treatment was related to the fact that Gabriel Benbow had for twenty-six years been a county commissioner, and the paving was done the year he left public office and a few months before he began construction on his "retirement home" on Shearwater Spit.

Conan was among those cynical citizens, but the paving of Dunlin Beach Road was far from the forefront of his thoughts now. Jack pines and rhododendron bushes flashed in and out of the headlights on his left; Sitka Bay was invisible in the darkness on his right. Diane Monteil occupied the passenger seat, outwardly calm, but she'd spoken few words on this drive, only staring ahead blindly. Her aristocratic profile seemed carved in alabaster, even the sweep of golden hair, ashen in the reflected glow of headlights.

Ahead, where the road curved north toward the spit, an island of light, as unreal as a stage set in a darkened theater. A line of red warning flares led inexorably to the cluster of vehicles blocking the right lane: two State Patrol cars; a winch truck backed to the edge of the road, where a flimsy wooden guardrail was broken; and the ambulance, that sterile harbinger of disaster. The white glare of headlights and spotlights, the spinning red and blue emergency lights, fragmented the stark scene. The rain had stopped, but the wet pavement mirrored the lights in long, wavering streaks.

In response to a patrolman's waving, red-sheathed flashlight, Conan pulled over onto the shoulder. A glance in the rearview mirror showed the Cyclops eye of Lyn Hatch's motorcycle swooping to a stop almost on his bumper. The patrolman leaned down as Conan lowered the window.

"If you've got business up the road, go on around. Otherwise, I'll have to ask you to leave the way you came."

"Officer, this is Diane Monteil. She's Corey Benbow's business partner."

"Oh. You must be Conan Flagg. Chief Kleber said you'd—Wait a minute, mister!"

That was for Lyn, who left his cycle and strode toward the winch truck at the center of this glaring tableau. Conan got out of the car. "Lyn! Officer, it's all right. He's a friend of Corey's. Lyn, you'd better stay with Di."

Lyn's head came around slowly, windblown hair and beard haloed with light. Conan wasn't sure Lyn had heard him, but after a moment, he went to the car and opened the door for Diane, then took her arm as they moved into the hectic lights.

Conan asked the patrolman, "Where's Earl—Chief Kleber?"

"Sergeant Roddy sent him up the road to get Gabe Benbow. He's the woman's grand—"

"Yes, I know." And he knew Roddy's timing was, to say the least, unfortunate, bringing Lyn Hatch and Gabe Benbow in proximity now.

The winch cables creaked and whined, the truck's motor grinding stolidly. Shouts from the officers at the black edge of the scene indicated that the car was nearly up. Conan joined Diane and Lyn to wait. The wind blew cold from the south, laden with fine mist, scented with pine and salt. The grinding of the motor was too loud for the sound of lapping waves to penetrate; the only hint of the existence of the bay was a strand of lights on the northern shore a mile and a half away.

It came up streaming water, gouging ruts at the graveled edge of the road: a sky-blue Volkswagen Beetle with a rainbow stripe a foot wide running from the middle of the front bumper to the middle of the back bumper.

"Oh, no . . ." The words a whisper on Diane's lips.

Conan realized that there had been hope until now: hope that someone had made an error about the license plate, that it wasn't Corey's car. Even now there was hope. Perhaps the car was empty; Corey had somehow gotten out before it plunged over the cliff.

Conan watched two paramedics in dark blue flight jackets leave the ambulance and move toward the car. He said, "Di, stay here," and followed them, drawing the attention of the State Patrol sergeant who seemed to be in charge, a rangy man on the far side of thirty with mouth set in a tense, horizontal line.

"Sergeant Roddy?" At the man's nod, Conan introduced himself and pointed out Diane, adding, "The man with her is Lyn Hatch. He's Corey's fiancé." That wasn't quite true, but it provided an acceptable rationale for Lyn's presence.

Roddy glanced over at Diane and Lyn, nodded wearily, then turned back to the car. The rear end was still off the ground, the winch easing it down. "We've got a mutual friend," Roddy observed absently to Conan. "Chief Travers over at the Salem Division. Damn, I hate these things, especially with . . ." His distracted gaze flickered toward Diane and Lyn. "Another DUI, I suppose."

Conan frowned. "Drunk driving? What makes you think that?"

"No skid marks. I know the pavement's wet, but we checked it with spotlights. Not a damn mark. How else do you explain somebody running off the road like that without hitting the brakes? We figure she must've been coming down that grade from the west, judging by the angle of the tracks in the shoulder where she went through the guardrail. It's a tight curve, and I guess she just didn't—"

"Sergeant, we got a body in here!" That from one of the officers by the car, which was firmly on the ground now. The winch truck's motor stopped to make that announcement all the more audible.

Roddy snapped, "Damn it, Jenkins!" He glanced again at Diane and Lyn as he strode toward the VW.

The words galvanized Lyn, and he, too, started for the car with a hoarse cry. "Corey!"

Conan intercepted him and almost had a fight on his hands. But after a moment, the tension went out of Lyn's body with a sigh that was nearly a moan. Conan said firmly, "Lyn, Di's going to need you. I'm trying to get some answers here. You'll have to stay with her."

Lyn only nodded and went back to Diane, who hadn't moved and seemed oddly detached, as if she were simply a curious spectator. Conan knew better. She was at this moment *incapable* of moving.

Conan thrust his hands in his pockets and approached the car. Only the window on the passenger side was open, and that a scant three inches; the interior was filled with murky water to the tops of the seats. The bonnet and front fenders were crushed inward, the windshield marked with a spiderweb of fractured glass, its focus just above the steering wheel, but the damage was slight in view of the fifty-foot drop from the bluff. Conan went to the edge of the road. The spotlights were off now, and he could see nothing in the blackness; he had to imagine the water waiting below and the obdurate basalt that had left this bluff and the three remnant pylons of Reem's Rocks intact, in spite of millennia of erosion. At high tide, or within an hour before or after, there would be enough water below to cushion the impact of the VW's plunge. The last high tide had been about ten o'clock tonight.

"Damn doors are jammed."

Conan turned. Sergeant Roddy was standing beside him, frowning as two officers pried at the door on the driver's side with crowbars. Conan asked, "When did you get the accident report?"

"About one-fifteen. Man named Harrington called it in. Said he lives down on Dunlin Beach."

"That road turns off this one about a tenth of a mile back. The only house up *this* road is Gabe Benbow's."

"Yeah, well, I guess Mr. Harrington missed the turn. Maybe he'd lifted a few too many, too."

"Too? Like Corey? Sergeant, it's so unlikely that Corey Benbow was drunk, it isn't even a possibility. She seldom drank at all. But you're probably right about Harry Harrington."

Roddy eyed Conan with a sidelong smile. "You know him?"

"Yes. He's one of the local . . . characters, to be charitable."

"I know what you mean. You got it, Jenkins?"

One of the officers manning the crowbars at the door nodded. "It's coming, Sergeant."

"Well, let the water out slow if you can."

With a screech and a thud, the door gave way, and Jenkins and the other man had to throw their weight into the door to restrain the sudden flood of water. Conan stared at the spiderwebbed windshield, relieved that from this angle he couldn't see into the car seats; he would have to face what the ebbing waters revealed soon enough.

"Sergeant, when you check the car and personal effects, keep an eye out for a leather-bound diary, about four by six inches, sort of reddish brown."

Roddy squinted curiously at Conan. "You sound like you're working on a case. Yeah, I know about your sideline. Steve Travers says you're a damned good PI."

"He's never said that in *my* hearing. Just habit, Sergeant. I'm not on a case now."

"Well, doesn't look like there's much of a case here to work on. Hello, Chief."

Conan's head came around abruptly. That greeting was for Holliday Beach Police Chief Earl Kleber, who approached the VW frowning, black hair rumpled like his hastily-donned civilian clothes, his square jaw even bluer than usual.

It wasn't Kleber who brought Conan up short—the chief even had a passably friendly nod for him—but Conan was looking beyond him at the man standing near the ambulance.

Gabe Benbow. Tall and big-boned, he seemed to have gone to sinew with age, rather than to fat. Even in the old sou'wester, his wide shoulders made strict right angles with his arms; bony hands with spatulate fingers thrust out, making his sleeves seem too short. His face always reminded Conan of a Lincoln grown old, *sans* beard and *sans* most of his hair, the latter loss hidden now under a knit cap. All of Gabe's eighty years were starkly evident in the furrows and pleats they had added to his face, but behind the thick bifocals, his cold blue eyes reflected a rapaciously alert mind.

Conan walked over to Lyn, who stood with a protective arm around Diane's shoulders, his baleful gaze fixed on Gabe.

Conan asked, "Di, are you all right?"

She was also staring at Gabe, but with none of Lyn's smoldering anger. She nodded, pushing her windblown hair away from her face with both hands.

"Yes, I'm all right. God, why does it take so *long?*"

Conan didn't try to answer that, instead turning to Lyn. "Whatever diabolical plans you have in mind for Gabe, Lyn, forget them. At least for now."

Lyn's mouth only tightened, and Gabe chose that moment to demand loudly, "What're *they* doing here?"

The question was addressed to Sergeant Jim Roddy, who had joined Gabe by the ambulance, and "they" clearly referred to Lyn, Diane, and Conan. Roddy, looking embarrassed, apparently tried to explain their presence, but stopped abruptly.

The paramedics were approaching, maneuvering a stretcher laden with a still form shrouded in a gray blanket. They stopped a few feet short of the ambulance.

The sergeant said, "Okay, Mr. Benbow, you'd better have a look. I mean, if you're—"

"Get *on* with it!"

Roddy leaned down to turn back the blanket, but hesitated, looking up at Diane as if she had spoken; she hadn't.

"Ms. Monteil?"

Diane acknowledged the diffident invitation with a nod and moved slowly toward the stretcher, with Conan holding her arm, Lyn, hesitating, a pace behind.

Conan thought absently, thank God she hadn't been in the water longer. Corey seemed at first glance only asleep, wet, dark hair lying in tendrils across her forehead and one cheek like blown ink drops. Hers had never been a beautiful face, but it was well-proportioned, a pleasant and simple face. What had made her seem beautiful was gone now: the wholesome color in her cheeks, the warm perfection of her smile, the blue-green of her eyes that was so much the color of the sea on a sunny May day, as lucid and as changeable.

> *Wake up, wake up, darlin' Corey,*
> *What makes you sleep so sound?*©

That song, Conan knew, would haunt him now. But he had no urge to try to waken her. There was no mistaking the quality of this sleep, even if the more fearful signs of death weren't evident. The only hint of trauma was a lacerated area on the right temple.

Perhaps Gabe made the identification. Conan didn't hear it, but he heard Diane whisper, "Dear God, how will I tell Kit? How will I tell him he's an orphan now?"

What a cruel irony, Conan thought, that Mark Benbow had also died in a car accident. But Christopher had only been a year old then. He was six now and old enough for grief.

Lyn Hatch had been staring numbly at Corey's body, apparently unaware of anything or anyone around him, but at Diane's words he roused himself and put his arm around her.

"I'll help if I can, Di. I mean, telling Kit. And Melissa. It won't be any easier on her."

Diane turned away, letting Lyn lead her toward Conan's car. Lyn said over his shoulder, "Conan, I better stay what's left of the night at Di's. I'll head back to your house and get my stuff together."

Lyn didn't pause when Gabe muttered testily, "Get me out of here. Earl! Take me back home."

But Lyn sent a backward glance at Gabe that should have struck terror in the old man.

CHAPTER 3

Conan Flagg had chosen the solitary life because inherent in solitude is freedom. Since he could afford it, he shaped his solitude to his preferences. His house was a case in point. It occupied a wooded lot sloping down to the seawall that was occasionally all that stood between him and the full force of storm-driven waves. Conan had made only one non-negotiable demand of the architect: that the west wall of every room must consist of a floor-to-ceiling span of glass facing the Pacific.

The architect had met the challenge and more, especially here in the living room. The west wall was an expanse of glass forty feet long and thirty high, with a beamed ceiling sloping back over the balcony on which the two bedrooms opened. The interior decoration was entirely Conan's own and grew in an eclectic fashion out of the things he loved and collected: Lilihan rugs; Haida masks; cases of netsuke, jade prayer wheels, and agatized Cenozoic fossils; a Ben Shahn tempera, Cassatt pastel, Baskin woodcut, two Klimt drawings, a Grover encaustic; and the Bösendorfer grand piano that was the centerpiece, literally, of the room.

But now he stood at the windows looking into the darkness beyond the rain-shattered reflections. He couldn't remember when the rain had begun again, but when he had left Diane at her house with Lyn and Mrs. Miller, her neighbor and baby-sitter—and the two children still asleep in their blissful ignorance—a fine rain had been falling.

It was four-thirty now, but at this latitude and so near the winter solstice, it would be two and a half hours before dawn finally ended this night. He knew he should get some sleep. He also knew that it would be futile to try.

The first time I saw darlin' Corey
She was standin' in the door.
Her shoes and stockin's in her hand
And her feet all over the floor.

Damn that song. He couldn't get rid of it. Corey had loved it, willingly identifying with the plucky moonshiner who met such an enigmatic end.

So many things that had once been amusing had turned poignant now.

The first time he had seen Corella Benbow, she *had* in fact been standing in a door: the door of the Holliday Beach Book Shop, whose continuance, despite the slings and arrows of outrageous dry rot and irrational tax forms, he considered his primary *raison d'être*. He'd been at the front counter while Miss Dobie took her lunch break, when Corey and Diane came into the shop on a rainy October day five years ago. Kit had been asleep in a sling on Corey's back; Diane's daughter, Melissa, at two, had discovered the delights of bipedalism and needed constant supervision. Corey introduced herself and company and breathlessly announced that she and Diane had just bought the Camber building.

She said it as if she'd just been handed a deed to the Taj Mahal, but she was talking about a two-story, frame building across Highway 101 and south of the bookshop; a building that had been shabby when it was built fifty years ago and hadn't acquired any charm with age. Then, with even greater enthusiasm, Corey explained that she and Diane planned to open a kite shop. Diane had training in design; she'd worked as display designer and coordinator at the Marine Science Center museum in Westport until her recent divorce. As for Corey, well, she'd worked in a kite shop near Coos Bay, among other things—which Conan later learned included a stint at the Bumble Bee Tuna cannery in Astoria, a summer on a Forest Service fire tower, and a year in Bandon as a PUD meter reader. The kite shop would be called "Rainbow Wings," and she described it so eloquently, Conan began to see the Taj Mahal latent in the Camber building.

And it had come to pass. With the arrival of spring, Rainbow Wings opened for business, and the Camber building was transformed, painted a warm, cerulean blue studded with stylized clouds, and, arcing across the broad, board canvas of the facade, a huge rainbow. On sunny days, the shop was festooned with bright windsocks and air-gulping, gold-spangled carp; a joy forever, or so it seemed.

Conan turned away from the window and went to the stereo console by the fireplace on the north wall to put on a record; the graceful passages of the Chopin "Ballade in G Minor" spun out into the shadowed recesses of the room, finding a union of cadence with the quiet surf. He paused to light a cigarette, then crossed to one of the Barcelona chairs facing the windows.

Corey, *you* were the joy forever, and I loved you for it.

And at times he had wanted to be *in love* with her. She brought something into his life so delightful, he wanted to capture it. But he was well aware that some things do not fare well in captivity, and when he considered the matter objectively, he knew he wasn't willing to assume the rigors of fatherhood—which Corey would expect of any man she loved; she and Kit were a package deal—nor was he willing to give up his hard-won and stringently maintained freedom.

Freedom, as many a philosopher had observed, has its price.

But Lyndon Hatch had been in love with Corey and willing to make her—and Kit—the fulcrum of his life. And Corey had been on the verge of lowering the barriers she had raised against that kind of love during five years of widowhood. Conan wondered if it would be any comfort to Lyn to know how close she'd come to reciprocating his love and expectations.

So many loose ends, when a life is cut off so suddenly. The pattern seems to unravel and become indecipherable.

Was that it? he wondered. Was it simply a sort of gestalt need for a pattern that nagged at him now?

. . . doesn't look like there's much of a case here to work on.

Sergeant Roddy was probably right about that. Probably.

Conan was a licensed private investigator, but he didn't advertise the fact. He didn't have to, thanks to the continuing success of the Ten-Mile Ranch; he had been sole heir to Henry Flagg's sagebrush empire. Conan considered the PI role an avocation, but then everything he did seemed to fall into that category. He had sought the PI's license simply because he'd had some excellent training at one time in G-2, and it seemed a shame to waste it.

That was, he knew, only a glib rationale. Perhaps his real motivation was simply curiosity: a compulsive dissatisfaction with incomplete patterns. There was that mental itch to get it right, to understand, to complete the pattern.

And now grief added a bitter impetus to that compulsion.

Begin at the beginning.

When was that? Not when he'd first met Corella Benbow. Perhaps later, when he discovered that both Corey and Diane were—as he was—members of The Earth Conservancy, an organization whose primary function was the purchase and preservation of land it identified as ecologically critical. ECon had during its relatively short history taken part in the preservation of two million acres in the United States, and it owned and managed nearly seven hundred sanctuaries and preserves. One of them was near Pendleton in Eastern Oregon, and its 8,500 acres had once been part of the Ten-Mile Ranch: the Annie Whitefeather Flagg High Desert Preserve. Conan could think of no better memorial to his mother.

He hadn't been surprised to learn that Corey and Diane were also ECon members. Diane had worked at the Marine Science Center in Westport and was as well grounded in earth sciences as in art. Corey had reached ECon through a love of natural things that was apparently innate, and her husband had been a marine biologist at the MSC.

Perhaps the beginning was the day, over a year ago, when Corey learned that her grandfather intended to sell Shearwater Spit to a California developer, Isaac Wines, who, under the corporate identity of Baysea Properties, planned to make the spit the centerpiece of a high-bracket resort/residential complex. Baysea, as the development was to be called, would take up nearly six thousand acres south and east of Sitka Bay, including nearly a mile of its southern shore, as well as the thousand acres of the spit, threatening the fragile ecosystems of one of the last nearly pristine estuaries left on the Oregon coast.

The Earth Conservancy had rallied to the cause and sent a field representative and habitat inventory team from Portland immediately. Lyndon Hatch was that field representative. ECon's legal department and land acquisition and fund-raising committees had also gone into action, and within a few months ECon was prepared to equal Baysea Properties's offer to Gabe Benbow of $3,000,000.

This undertaking had been to a great extent Corey's responsibility primarily because Gabe wouldn't so much as talk to anyone else he suspected of being remotely connected with ECon. But finally, after months of wheedling, arguing, begging, and cajoling, she had succeeded, only three weeks ago, in garnering from Gabe a verbal agreement that he would accept the ECon offer, with only the minor stipulation that the sale wouldn't be completed until after the first of the year. The delay had to do with taxes, he said.

Conan had held an impromptu victory celebration at his house, with Diane and Corey, Kit and Melissa, Jory Rankin—the teenager who worked part-time at Rainbow Wings—Miss Dobie, and even Mrs. Early, who simply happened to be working at Conan's house that day, as well as Lyn and two other Portland-based ECon members, who had taken part in the long campaign, all tipsy with triumph on nonalcoholic fruit punch.

That victory celebration had been—and he should have expected it, knowing Gabe—premature. And it was the conclusion of a pattern of events, not a beginning.

The beginning of the pattern that led to that unreal scene on Dunlin Beach Road tonight—rather, this morning—he could mark in retrospect as occurring only a day and a half ago. Nearly two days now, if the dawn ever came.

Thursday morning. Thanksgiving Day.

> *The next time I saw darlin' Corey,*
> *She was standing on the banks of the sea. . . .*

On the morning of Thanksgiving Day, Conan awoke to find his bedroom flooded with sunlight, warming the cool blues and browns that had for the last week assumed the gray cast of winter rains. He propped himself on one elbow and squinted out the west windows, and there a grimacing Oriental face looked back at him.

Conan only laughed and threw the covers back. He remembered to find his robe and pull it on before he opened the sliding glass door and went out on the deck. The kites were back, and if the event was not as predictable or as portentous as the return of the swallows to Capistrano, he was no less elated.

One of the profound contributions Corey and Rainbow Wings had made to life in Holliday Beach was the kite shows that blossomed on this beach every summer day when there was sunshine and wind enough, and on any suitable weekend the rest of the year. Purely crass commercialism, Corey had insisted, but Conan knew she'd have her kites up even in the dead winter of the tourist season if the wind were right. But for the last few weeks, she'd been inhibited by bad weather. This Thanksgiving Day display was a celebration not only of a four-day weekend that would bring people flocking from the inland cities, but of the clear, sunny day that seemed a misplaced fragment of summer.

With Jory Rankin's help, Corey was struggling with a huge, orange-and-blue Jalbert parafoil. Two more teenagers—volunteers, no doubt; there were always plenty when school was out—tended various lines, and another leaned into the wind, a line in each hand, maneuvering a stack of seven stunt kites, each a different color, making a bright rainbow, long tails describing exquisite, simultaneous arcs on the sky. Melissa had a golden butterfly with twin tails rising skyward, while Kit launched a winged box kite of colored Mylar that looked, when it caught and refracted the light, like a giant alexandrite.

Other kites were already airborne, strings anchored on any handy driftwood log or stump. Peacocks, dragonflies, butterflies, and eagles spread their wings to the sun, while fluttering octopus and dragon kites tugged at their bridles. Corey had taught Conan the names and history of the various types, and he took pleasure in identifying them. She had also let him try his hand at flying most of them, and he could sense now the rhythmic impulses of dragons; the sustained pull of delta wings or Eddy diamonds on the steady wind; the electric, darting tugs of Indian fighters; the smooth surges of a rack of stunt kites tracing out its graceful choreography.

He watched another dragon mounting into its element. They were his favorites: a hundred, two hundred, three hundred feet of shining color undulating in long, slow waves that gave substance to the unseen shapes of the wind. Perhaps that was the fascination of kites. They made visible powerful forces that were otherwise invisible; forces that had once been deities, who conferred something of their power on the kites that were their messengers or personifications. For as long as humankind had called itself civilized, kites had flown into its myths, legends, and ceremonies.

At length, Conan reluctantly went back into the bedroom. He dressed in nearly record time, then hurried downstairs to prepare a hasty breakfast, which he ate at the table in the window alcove off the kitchen. Finally, after only half a cup of coffee, he emptied the rest of the carafe into a thermos, donned a windbreaker, and, automatically locking the front door behind him, went out to the paved beach access north of the house. He made his way down an easy slope of sea-worn cobbles to the sand. Winter sand, even if the day seemed like summer; gray sand streaked with heavy minerals, blue-black and purple-green. And it wasn't a summer sea today, although the breakers weren't high. Still, there was power behind these rumbling white cataracts.

He surveyed the beach, a long, flat scallop enclosed between two wooded headlands, Hollis Heights on the north, Jefferson Heights on the south. Houses were packed with hardly breathing room between them along the beach, scattered more loosely on the headlands. The town of Holliday Beach could muster a population of no more than twelve hundred permanent residents, but in the summer and on holidays it housed up to ten thousand. The number of people already on the beach promised that this week-end Holliday Beach would be filled to capacity.

Corey was standing alone now, head tilted back to watch the kites. There always seemed to be something of the dancer in her, a honed grace in her carriage and in her long, supple limbs. She wore denims, sand-caked running shoes, and a red jacket that had gone pink on the shoulders. Her brown hair, if left to its own devices, would fall straight and shining to her waist, but she made an attempt to tether it with a ribbon at the nape of her neck.

She saw him coming, and her hands came out of her pockets for a semaphore wave. When he was near enough to hear over the surf roar, she shouted, "Conan! I've been waiting for you." She leaned down to pick up a kite lying at her feet, a four-foot diamond, and held it sideways to the wind.

"Waiting for me? Why?"

"The *launching!*"

"A new kite?"

"Yes. Oh—you brought coffee. You're an angel of mercy. I forgot." Then she added with a laugh, "But you knew I would."

"It's happened before." He twisted the thermos into the sand by a half-buried log. "Let's see the new kite. One of Diane's designs?"

Corey nodded, lifting the kite for him to see. "Di made it for me. Oh Lord, isn't it beautiful? How come she got all the brains and talent *and* the good looks?"

The kite was, indeed, beautiful, made of silky, translucent rip-stop nylon, the design appliquéd on a white background: a blue-bird, in profile, flying upward within a circular spectrum. Conan sighed. "Thank God for the inequitable distribution of human talents."

"I guess some things shouldn't be diluted. It was something I said that got her started on this design. At least us lesser mortals are good for inspiration."

"Besides, producers need consumers. One of the basic laws of nature. What was it you said?"

She shrugged and squinted out at the breakers. "Oh, something about how if you get high enough above a rainbow, you can see the whole circle. The bluebird—well, it's my personal bird. Back in Montana, Aunt Irene used to say whoever saw the first bluebird in the spring could make a wish and it would come true. I don't ever remember what I wished for, but I sure saw lots of bluebirds."

Conan smiled at that. "I'd have expected your bird to be the seagull."

"That's my second bird. Maybe bluebirds are reincarnated as gulls when they die. Anyway, let's get this kite launched! Kit! Lissa! Come on."

The children anchored their respective kites and came running, making an impromptu race of the short distance. Melissa was fortunate enough to favor Diane, her hair a paler gold, eyes the same grayed blue. Christopher apparently favored his father, fair-skinned and freckled, a grin that curled at the corners of his mouth, and a head of dazzling copper-red curls.

Both children shouted greetings to Conan, Kit adding, "Sure took you a long time to *get* here."

"Next time, you come on up to the house for me."

Corey interposed, "Don't give him ideas. He'll be prying you out of bed at dawn. Okay, let's get this kite up on her maiden flight. Kit, you hold the spool, and you can pay out the string, Lissa. I'll run with the kite."

Kit asked, "Why can't *I* run with the kite?"

"Because it's *my* kite. Besides, you're too short; not enough wind down there." She ran lightly up wind, lifting the kite high with one hand. "Come on—give me some slack!"

Kit picked up the spool, small hands easy on the handles, while the string spun out, and Melissa expertly payed it out, maintaining the proper tension, shouting in a piping voice, "Higher! Lift it up higher!"

Corey stretched upward, and Conan, watching her, felt the

wind take the kite from her hand as if reclaiming something of its own. For a moment, she stood poised, and it seemed that with a little more effort she might follow the kite as it leapt into the sky. Then she flung her arms out and ran back to embrace the children. "Look at her! Isn't she gorgeous?"

Melissa asked, "What are you going to name her?"

"Well, I'll let you two decide that." A heated discussion ensued, and Corey rose and went over to Conan. "What are you doing for dinner tonight? Di and I are having a proper turkey-day bash— bird and all. Want to help?"

"I'd love to, but I already have plans for the evening. I'm taking Miss Dobie out to dinner."

"Sort of an early Christmas bonus?"

"Bonus?" Conan made a show of looking around for listeners. "The management at the Holliday Beach Book Shop doesn't recognize the term."

Corey laughed. "Trouble is, at the Holliday Beach Book Shop, it's a little hard to figure out who's management."

"Oh, *I* know who's really in charge. That's why I'm taking her to dinner." He checked his watch; it was nearly ten. "And it's time I got to work. Take care, Corey."

A brisk two-minute, two-block walk east up Day Street's gentle incline brought Conan to Highway 101 and to the heart of Holliday Beach, if not its actual center. Like so many coast towns, it had spread in accretionary lumps both north and south along the axis of the highway. Conan paused at the corner and looked across to the east side of the highway, where the businesses were randomly separated and of varying vintages: a plumbing and hardware store, a fish market, a "boutique" that changed hands and inventory nearly every spring, Driskoll's Garage, and the jewel of the lot, Rainbow Wings, with multicolored windsocks flying against its jaunty facade.

On the west side of the highway, the buildings presented a more united front with little space between them, although they too varied in vintage. At the south end, the Post Office, then an antique store, an insurance agency, a beauty shop, the Chowder House restaurant, and at the north end, a Mom-and-Pop grocery. Between the latter and the restaurant was a haphazard, silver-shingled building with three large, windowed gables adorning its second story. This was the Holliday Beach Book Shop, which

Conan fondly regarded as a historical monument, a haven for the world-weary, his pride and joy, and, occasionally, the albatross around his neck.

The bells on the front door announced his arrival. Behind the counter across from the entrance, Miss Beatrice Dobie—auburn-curled, no matter what, and virtually unflappable—worked the ancient cash register to register the purchase of a stack of used books by a middle-aged couple.

"Good morning, Miss Dobie."

"Good morning, Mr. Flagg. Happy Thanksgiving!" She beamed as she meted out change for the customers, then slammed the cash drawer shut. "Yes indeed, a day to count our blessings!" She didn't add that the blessing she particularly enjoyed counting was the cash accumulating in the old register. The dark, shelf-lined nooks and crannies of the shop were crowded with browsing potential customers.

Conan nodded as he looked around, then, "Where's Meg?"

"Hiding. In your office."

The door behind and to the right of the cash register sported a sign reading "private," but it was open. Conan found Meg asleep amid a clutter of papers on the Hepplewhite desk. Meg always chose her surroundings carefully, and perhaps that was why she seemed to prefer this small but comfortably appointed room, with its wood-paneled walls adorned with paintings, and the ruby-and-maroon Kerman carpet that was her favorite claw-sharpening place.

Meg was a blue-point Siamese, and most of the regular customers at the bookshop recognized her as the ultimate management. She woke to look up at Conan with lucent, sapphire eyes, gave him a throaty greeting, and stretched luxuriously, as only a cat can. Conan sat down in the leather armchair behind the desk to give her the obligatory morning rubdown.

"Good morning, duchess. Yes, tell me about your night. How many mice did you catch, and where, in God's name, did you leave the bodies?"

The imperative jangle of the bells on the front door distracted him. He looked around, frowning irritably as the door slammed shut. Then he came to his feet.

Nina Gillies.

Nina had a tendency to dramatic entrances, and she was undoubtedly accustomed to second looks—even stares—especially from men. She had been born beautiful, and as she approached forty, she obviously had no intention of forfeiting that asset. Her blond hair was shoulder length and coiffed with skillful nonchalance; her faultless features were so artfully enhanced with cosmetics that the blush of pink in her cheeks, the dusky shading and velvety lashes emphasizing her green eyes, seemed integral to her. Her *ensemble*—and no one would make the error of calling that combination of velour, leather, and Glen plaid anything less—would be entirely appropriate on the streets of Beverly Hills, but was startling in Holliday Beach, where attire tended to jeans and T-shirts.

But Conan had become accustomed to Nina's taste in clothing in the two years she had lived here. What brought him to his feet now was surprise at seeing her in the shop—not to mention the unmistakable glint of triumph in her eyes. Nina Gillies was a real-estate broker with her own agency, Pacific Futures Realty. She was also local agent for Baysea Properties, Incorporated, part of the California-based conglomerate empire of Isaac Wines Enterprises.

And in relation to Shearwater Spit and Sitka Bay and to ECon, Nina Gillies was the enemy. At least, the local manifestation of the enemy.

Nina strode past Miss Dobie, high heels thudding on the wood floor, stopped in Conan's doorway, and said coldly—and loudly, "I thought you and your bleeding-heart ecology friends should be the first to know. You thought you had Gabe all wrapped up! Well, you were dead, damned wrong! He just signed the papers this morning. He's accepting *Baysea's* last offer—for *four* million dollars." The laugh that followed was, for all its lilting softness, decidedly nasty. *"So, have a happy Thanksgiving!"* And with that she turned and marched out of the shop.

Conan went to the office door, watching through the front windows as she got into her silver-blue Cutlass and departed with a flourish of squealing tires. Like everyone within earshot in the shop—which meant everyone on the first floor—Miss Dobie was staring at Conan.

"Well . . ." she drawled, "I bet little Miss Oregon was never voted Miss Congeniality."

Conan frowned, the sinking sensation of sudden disappointment vying uncomfortably with mounting anger somewhere in the region of his stomach.

He asked distractedly, "Miss who?"

"Congeniality."

"No. What was that about Miss Oregon?"

"Oh, well, Nina was a Miss Oregon years ago, and before that, either Rose Queen or one of the princesses at the Portland Rose Festival. But as they say, beauty is only—"

The ring of the phone mercifully cut her off. Conan snapped, "I'll get it," on the way to the phone on his desk.

It was Diane Monteil. "Conan, what happened? Nina Gillies was just here in the shop a few minutes ago looking for Corey. When I told her Corey wasn't here, Nina went flouncing out, and I just saw her drive away from the—"

"I'm not sure what happened, Di, but it looks like Gabe has just made colossal suckers of ECon and all of us. I'm going down to the beach to get Corey; I think we'd better have a talk with Gabe. Do you want to go along?"

She hesitated, then, "I can't leave the shop, Conan. Not today. Just don't let Corey do anything . . . dumb. She gets so angry when it comes to Gabe."

Conan laughed bitterly. "I'm the wrong person to ask to do the restraining. Don't worry, Di. Try not to."

When Conan reached the front door, he paused, frowning questioningly at Beatrice Dobie. "Miss Oregon?"

"Um-hmmm. That was before she married Randall Coburn— you know, the football player—and they went to Los Angeles. Randy had a contract with the Rams, and Nina was going to be a Hollywood star." A portentous sigh, then, "Things didn't quite work out for them. Nina—well, she was certainly beautiful, but I guess she couldn't act her way out of a paper bag. Randy got into drugs. There was quite a scandal."

"Nina's not using his name. Did she divorce him?"

"Oh, no, Randy died. ODed, maybe. Something like that."

"Well, maybe that explains a lot." Then he shrugged as he opened the door. "And maybe it doesn't. Miss Dobie, I'll be back in an hour or so. I think."

The black XK-E, trapped in a southbound caravan of camper vans and cars loaded with unhurried sightseers, throbbed futilely, reduced to a virtual crawl on the bridge spanning the narrow channel into Holliday Bay. Many of the caravaneers turned off there, and even more a short distance farther at Shag Point State Wayside. Conan's foot bore down on the accelerator as the highway angled southeast on the long curve around Sitka Bay.

Corey fidgeted in the seat beside him, alternately crossing her legs, then straightening them, folding and unfolding her arms. "Conan, he promised me—he gave me his *word*. I should've known, that sanctimonious bastard!"

Conan didn't comment on that. "The last time you talked to Lyn Hatch—did he think ECon could come up with more than three million?"

"No. He said Sitka Bay is what's known as a 'sexy' project: highly visible, attractive setting—something the corporate donors can relate to. But he said he didn't think ECon could top three million. Did Nina actually say Baysea offered Gabe *four* million?"

"That's what she said, loud and clear."

"I can't believe it! Yes, I can. For a Californian, that's probably peanuts. At least, for Isaac Wines. Oh, look at it, Conan."

He slowed down so he *could* look at it, at Sitka Bay, blue-green today, sparkling with whitecaps and peppered with rafts of scaups and scoters. In the shallows near the highway, islands of winter-brown sedge made still channels where coots and goldeneyes bobbed about like animate corks, and blue herons stood graceful sentinel. A mile to the west, ghostly in a veil of spindrift, lay Shearwater Spit, a narrow extension of beach like a long finger pointing north, enclosing the bay except for the outlet at the north end. The southern shore of the bay was shaped by a basalt uplift, crowned with spruce and jack pine, that continued around the curve to the spit, then sank into dune and finally into beach only a few feet higher than the water around it.

Sitka Bay was a misnomer. This was a tidal marsh, an estuary, and even now in the ebb-season of winter, it teemed with life, most of it invisible to the naked human eye, yet in some sense felt beneath the surface patterns of silver and blue, gold and green. It was a cradle for a multitude of marine species—many of which would become commercially viable in their adult stages—and a vital wintering ground for dozens of bird species. And Sitka Bay was unique because it was so nearly untouched by human hands. There were few estuaries like it remaining on the entire Pacific coast of the United States. One by one the estuaries on this coast were being fouled and destroyed by human hands.

Conan looked on these resplendent waters with a poignant sense of foreboding, as he might look on the face of a beautiful child doomed by a terminal disease. The issue was, in his mind, a moral one. And it was epitomized by the swans—the swans he did *not* see gracing these waters today.

Whistling swans had wintered on Sitka Bay long before human beings had been here to note their presence, but in the last few decades, their numbers had gradually dwindled until finally, two years ago, some mindless idiot shot the female of the last pair. Its cygnets died, and its mate had never returned.

Such a small piece of the world, Sitka Bay. Was it so much to ask that it be left alone, that its living creatures be left to flourish in peace? Was it so much to ask that Isaac Wines make a few million dollars less this year? He literally would not miss them.

Corey said, "Look at the way the air shines over the spit. Can't you just see it bristling with ticky-tack houses down the whole length of it?"

"Considering what Isaac Wines will be asking for the lots, I doubt there'll be any ticky-tack built. Nothing cheaper than two hundred thousand, probably."

"Ticky-tack isn't a matter of money. And can't you see all the cute little motorboats roaring out of the big, fancy marina, dumping gas and garbage, killing ducks and—"

"Yes, Corey, I know."

"And it's such an incredible rip-off! I mean, for the people who *buy* Wines's lots. All it takes is a good storm on a high tide with a west wind behind it, and nothing will be left on top of that spit. It's happened before and—"

"I know, Corey."

"I *know* you know, Conan! I'm just—oh, Lord, why did Gabe have to do this? He's going to force me to . . ."

She seemed to run out of steam suddenly, or perhaps she had said more than she intended. Conan glanced at her, then turned his attention to the bridge over the Sitka River. As the highway curved southwestward, he asked, "He's going to force you to *what?*"

She pulled her knees up and wrapped her arms around them,

frowning out at the bay. "Oh, nothing. I mean . . . well, I'll talk to you about it later. After I talk to Gabe."

Conan saw a pseudo-rustic, shake-roofed building ahead on the right; a prominent sign identified it as the Blue Heron Inn. He shifted down and began signaling for a right turn at the junction just past the restaurant.

"Corey, you can't talk Gabe out of this."

"Probably not. But at least I'll have the satisfaction of telling him what I think of him. *Watch out!*"

That exclamation was prompted by the Rolls-Royce Silver Cloud barreling into the intersection from Dunlin Beach Road. The XK-E was, fortunately, small and quick enough so that Conan could avoid the collision that for a moment seemed imminent.

"Conan, did you see who that *was?*"

"Yes," Conan replied, eyes down to black slits, "I saw."

He'd had only a glimpse of the driver, but the car itself was identification enough; there were few Rolls Royces in Taft County. Leonard Moskin, who had always reminded Conan of a Middle Eastern potentate in impeccable Western attire—which had to be tailored to accommodate his enormous girth. Even his car, so the rumor went, had to be altered for his driving comfort. There were also rumors rampant about the means by which Moskin had acquired his apparent wealth, and Conan was inclined to believe some of them. Leo Moskin had been a power in Taft County politics for fifty years and had never been constrained by vagaries like ethics.

But what Conan found interesting about Moskin's appearance here at the junction of Dunlin Beach Road was that it was highly unlikely that he'd been visiting anyone on Dunlin Beach. The only other alternative was Gabe Benbow. Gabe and Moskin had been cronies since the thirties, and Moskin was at present chairman of the Taft County Planning Commission. The sale of any property to be included in the proposed Baysea development would be contingent on the approval of the Planning Commission.

Corey slumped down in the seat, mouth drawn in a tight, contemptuous line. "I wonder how much Baysea is paying Leo under the table to get their plans approved."

Conan laughed humorlessly. "Corey, you're too young to be so cynical."

"I'm not that young. Two years over the hill, and you haven't got that many years on me to sound so fatherly. And I'm *not* cynical. But I'm not stupid, either." Then with a sigh and another restless regrouping of her long limbs, "Maybe I *am* stupid, accepting a *verbal* promise from Gabe. Kate Benbow would've laughed in my face at that. She knew him. She . . . knew him inside out."

Conan glanced at Corey, noting the break in her voice. Kate Donovan Benbow had been her mother-in-law and more a true mother to Corey than her biological mother had ever been. And Kate and Mark Benbow had died in the same car accident five years ago. Conan focused his attention on the narrow road, dappled with shadows cast by the pine and spruce crowding the left shoulder. The road followed the contour of the south shore of Sitka Bay, shearing uncomfortably close to the edge of the cliff above a trio of monoliths called Reem's Rocks, then made a tight westward curve up a steep incline as it departed from the bay. An open metal gate marked Gabe Benbow's property line, then a northward curve down the slope toward the spit. The trees gave way to Scotch broom, salal, kinnikinnick, and finally to beach grass, and the road dead-ended in the parking area west of Gabe's house.

It was only eight years old, and Gabe modestly called it his retirement home, but nothing else about it was modest. Except, perhaps, the architecture. That Conan regarded as so lacking in imagination it hardly deserved the name. He was convinced Gabe had acquired the plans from a mail-order catalog. The house consisted of two rectangular wings joined in an obtuse angle with the apex pointing north—like two giant boxcars that had inexplicably collided atop this dune and had simply been left here, with the addition of huge expanses of windows on the north to take advantage of the view. That, at least, was magnificent. The house was at the heel of the spit and high enough above it to be safe from storms —and no doubt Gabe had considered that danger, even if Baysea's designers hadn't—and high enough to have an unobstructed view of the entire spit, like the flat of a knife blade separating the foam-scalloped waters of the ocean from the quieter waters of the bay.

The interior of the house, Conan knew, was no more imaginative than the exterior, but he gave Gabe credit for a respectable job of landscaping. That, however, must be attributed in part to the expert advice of Gabe's daughter-in-law, Frances, who considered her own gardens as much a status symbol—and therefore something to be pursued with assiduous determination—as her antiques, electrical appliances, designer clothes, and diamonds.

Conan was reminded of France Benbow at the moment for the simple reason that the maroon Cadillac Seville in the parking area belonged to her and her husband, Moses, and they were presently lounging on the deck fronting the west wing.

Corey had also seen them, and she didn't immediately leave the car after Conan turned off the motor, but sat glaring up at the deck. Or perhaps her baleful look was for Gabe, who was pruning the rosebushes in front of the deck. He straightened and looked toward the XK-E, but made no move toward it.

Corey muttered, "I should've known Moses and France would be here. She's probably going to put on the big Thanksgiving dinner for the *family*."

"You weren't invited?"

"What do *you* think?" She opened the car door and got out, slamming it behind her, and marched up the flagged walk toward Gabe. Conan followed, a pace behind. Gabe hadn't moved, nor had France left her chair, but Moses was standing at the edge of the deck, waiting and watching. Closely.

Conan occasionally felt some sympathy for Moses Benbow, Gabe's older son, and for all intents and purposes, his only son, since Jonas had departed Holliday Beach in 1955—after embezzling $20,000 in county funds—and vanished from Benbow ken. But Moses had stayed in Holliday Beach and made a success of his insurance agency and real estate investments.

Conan's sympathy stemmed from a perception of Moses as a man caught between a domineering father on one side and an ambitious wife on the other. But that sympathy was probably misplaced. At the moment, Moses Benbow seemed very much in control of himself and his destiny, looking rather like an English country squire, fit and tweedy and considerably younger than his sixty-one years. That was due in part to the fact that his hair was a youthful brown with only a touch of gray on his sideburns. He wasn't as tall as his father, nor as angular, but he had Gabe's pale blue eyes. In Moses they were enlarged by the thick lenses of his glasses, and he had always been capable of a direct, unblinking gaze that Conan occasionally found disconcerting.

France Benbow, like her husband, seemed younger than her years—fifty-eight, according to Corey. She was tall and thin enough to have been a fashion model, and she always seemed ready for a nonexistent camera. She sat now with her legs crossed, calves parallel, elbows resting on the arms of her chair, left hand raised to hold a glass of iced, dark-brown liquid and show off a cluster of spectacular diamonds. Today she was being casual in a wool walking skirt and Shetland sweater. Her black hair was drawn back into a bun secured with a bright silk scarf, the severity of the coiffure emphasizing high cheekbones and heavy-lidded eyes under thin, arched brows. That face was a conscious art object, expertly embellished with cosmetics, and Conan never remembered seeing her without her face very much on.

Gabe was smiling affably at Corey, which only added to the tension evident in her posture. Before she got a word out, he said blithely, "Well, Corey, it's nice to see you on a Thanksgiving Day. Where's that great-grandson of mine?"

"Don't give me that fond great-grandfather scam. I don't have anything to give thanks for *today*, and you goddamn well know it!"

Conan almost smiled. Gabe brought out the worst in Corey; at least, in terms of language. Except when speaking to or of Gabe, she seldom used words that wouldn't be appropriate in a Walt Disney cartoon.

Gabe frowned, shaking his head. "I just hope you don't talk like that around that boy. 'Thou shalt not take the—' "

"Stuff it, Gabe!"

His frown deepened as his eyes slid toward Conan.

"Flagg, y'know, what this girl needs is a man to keep her in tow. I thought for a while *you* might be that man."

To avert a real explosion from Corey, Conan moved up beside her and said levelly, "Gabe, we didn't come for a lesson in Pauline morality. Did you agree to accept Baysea's last offer for the spit?"

Gabe mulled that over, jaw muscles bunching. "Who told you that?" He glanced up to the deck at Moses and France. The latter was standing beside her husband now, glass still in hand, a cool smile shadowing her mouth.

Conan answered, "Nina Gillies."

Gabe pursed his lips, then shrugged and knelt to resume pruning the rosebushes. "Well, it doesn't matter. Hey, France, maybe the young folks'd like one of those . . . concoctions you mixed up."

France looked startled, then put on a gracious-hostess smile.

"Oh, uh, yes. Black russians. We discovered them when we were in Acapulco this fall. I *know* it's a bit early for the happy hour, but it *is* a holi—"

Corey ignored her altogether. "Gabe, *did* you accept Baysea's offer?"

He looked up at her, still smiling. "Y'know, I just never could understand why all you knee-jerk ee-cologists got so excited over this little piece of property."

"Of *course* you don't understand!" Corey retorted. "You don't even know what an estuary is. You're so pious, a damned pillar of the church, and you think God made heaven and earth just for your benefit!" She paused, shoulders slumping. "No, you don't understand, and you never will. And I don't understand you. I don't know where you're coming from. Gabe, *did* you accept the Baysea offer?"

Gabe had listened with mocking attentiveness, but now he turned his attention to the rosebushes, casually snipping stems as he replied, "Well, yes, as a matter of fact, I did. Signed the papers this morning. Now all I have to do is wait for the Planning Commission to pass on it—and they're meeting next Friday—then Isaac Wines is going to send me a nice check for *four million* bucks."

Corey stood pale and trembling, her hair blowing, unnoticed, around her face. "You gave me your word, Gabe."

He cut off a stem heavy with dead blossoms. " 'The Lord gave and the Lord hath taken away; blessed be the name of the Lord.' I changed my mind, Corey. And promises are cheap. Good lesson for you there. Promises are cheap."

Conan rested a hand on Corey's shoulder, not so much to restrain her as to occupy that hand with something gentler than smashing it into Gabe Benbow's face.

Gabe rose, looking toward the bay. "Besides, this Baysea is going to be a real nice place. There'll be a lodge and restaurants and shops; a golf course and marina. Even an airport. Look what it'll do for the county. The jobs—like for the construction. And afterward. They're talking about a full-time staff of three-hundred people. The taxes—"

Corey cut in, "You don't care any more about the economy of this county than you do about its ecology. You *used* ECon, didn't you? You used it to jack up Baysea's price!"

Gabe only laughed at that. "Well, now, I guess I did. It worked, too."

Corey took a step toward him, her hands in fists. *"Why?* Isn't *three* million enough? And don't tell me you were thinking about your heirs! You don't think about anybody but Gabriel Benbow! But what good is that extra million to you? The IRS will get most of it, and you're an old man, Gabe. There's no way you'll live long enough to spend the money you already have! So, what do you want with *more?*"

She apparently struck a nerve with that reference to his mortality. The maddening smile vanished.

"Get out! Both of you—just get off my property! And you, girl! If you ever figured on being one of my heirs—the ones you say I wasn't thinking about—well, you can just—" He stopped, distracted, glaring toward the road. "Who the hell is that? Harrington? What's he doing *here?*"

An old, once-grand Pontiac rattled into the parking area. Conan recognized it—as Gabe had—as Harry Harrington's. That Gabe and Harrington were engaged in a continuing feud was common knowledge, but apparently Harrington had a purpose here other than annoying Gabe. He had a passenger with him.

The Pontiac came to a coughing halt at the foot of the walk, and the passenger got out, opened the rear door to extricate a travel-weary suitcase, then cordially thanked Harrington for the ride. "Would've been a long walk, Harry."

Harrington departed, while his passenger, suitcase in hand, looked up at his attentive and puzzled audience. He was in his late fifties or early sixties, gray-haired, with tanned skin that bespoke a sunnier climate and showed his blue eyes to advantage. He had been a handsome man in his youth and still was, although there was a certain puffiness around his eyes and an unnatural flush to his nose and cheeks. He wore a three-piece suit of good quality, but a few years out of style and badly in need of pressing. If he'd put on a tie with the suit, it wasn't in evidence now.

The rattle of Harrington's Pontiac faded into the distant murmur of surf as the man squared his shoulders and started up the walk. A few paces from Conan and Corey, he stopped to put down his suitcase and looked at Gabe, then Moses, and finally asked, "Don't you recognize me? It's been twenty-seven years, I know, but—"

Moses breathed, "My God! *Jonas.*"

"Jonas?" Gabe pronounced the name uncertainly, then approached to get a closer look. "It can't be—*Jonas?*"

Jonas Benbow shrugged and gave a short laugh. "The prodigal returns."

A purplish flush colored Gabe's face; he cried hoarsely, " 'So a fool returneth to his folly!' I told you I never wanted to set eyes on you *again!* You killed your mother—you know that? And you nearly killed *me!*"

Jonas pursed his lips thoughtfully. "Well, y'know, Ma had cancer when I left Taft County, and it wasn't till five years later that she died. And you—well, maybe I made it a bit sticky for you in that next election, but as for killing you—no, Pa, I don't think so." There was an ironic light in his eyes with that, but it vanished as he sighed and added, "Look, I didn't expect you to bring out the fatted calf for me. It's just that . . . well, a man comes to a point in his life where he wants to make his peace with his family, with the people he once held dear."

Conan raised an eyebrow, aware that he was in the presence of a consummate actor. The spectrum of emotions spanned in those few words was remarkable. There was even a convincing portent of impending doom. Conan looked up at Moses and saw that he was not entirely convinced; his unblinking gaze never strayed from his brother, but, typically, he said nothing. France, convinced or not, was worried, glancing uneasily from Jonas to Gabe and back again. Gabe stood silent, weighing his prodigal son's words and apparently finding them wanting.

It was Corey who finally broke the silence. She offered Jonas a hand and a tentative smile. "I'm Corey—Corella Benbow. Mark was my husband."

"Corey?" Jonas took her hand eagerly, eyes full of solicitude and even a hint of tears. "Oh, Corey, I just heard about . . . well, the lady next to me on the bus, she was from Holliday Beach. She told me about Mark and Kate."

Corey stared at him. "You mean you didn't know they—about the accident?"

"No. I heard about my mother a couple of years after it happened, but Kate and Mark—well, I guess I was out of the country then or something. It . . . well, it hit me hard. I loved Kate, I really did, and Mark was my boy and—but that was a long time ago. I know it was a lot harder for you. Oh, Lord, I'm sorry, Corey."

Gabe cut in impatiently, "You got a *lot* to be sorry about, Jonas. So, what do you want here? You figure I'm good for a handout now after all these years?"

Jonas replied staunchly, "I don't *need* any handouts, Pa. I got a good job. Had it for six years. I know I can't change anything that happened nearly thirty years ago, but—"

"You got a job? What kind? Doing what?"

"Bookkeeper for Southwestern Investment Company in Phoenix, Arizona. I'm . . . on vacation. Sort of a si— I mean, a leave of absence."

Gabe's sour expression hadn't sweetened. "How long do you plan on staying around here?"

"Well, I guess that depends. I've had a lot of . . . extra expenses lately." Then before Gabe could comment on that, Jonas insisted, "But I'm *not* looking for a handout. I've got a return ticket and enough money to eat along the way. All I'm saying is . . . well, I was hoping somebody could spare me a back room somewhere. . . ." He looked past Gabe to the house. "But I don't want to shove in where I'm not wanted."

Gabe did not take the hint. He stood in his righteous silence, and Jonas shifted his inquiring gaze to France. Her chin came up, the incised parentheses bracketing her mouth deepened, but she was no more responsive than was Gabe. Neither was Moses, and something in the wordless exchange between the brothers betrayed years of unforgotten animosity.

Jonas smiled ironically. "Funny, isn't it, Moses, how some things don't change."

Moses' eyes flickered behind his thick lenses. "If you remember the parable of the prodigal son, you know it wasn't the older brother who brought out the fatted calf."

Jonas nodded and looked at his father, still obdurately silent, then with an audible sigh, he picked up his suitcase as if it were filled with bricks. "Well, I better get back to town and find out when the next southbound bus leaves."

Corey could contain herself no longer. "You Benbows! You know what Kate used to call you? A bunch of stiff-necked hypocrites! And she was right. Jonas, you can stay with me—if you don't mind putting up with a couple of kids."

"Well, if one of them's my grandson, I wouldn't—"

"Oh, for Lord's sake!" Gabe finally broke his silence, and after a baleful glance at Corey, conceded, "All right, Jonas. Like you said, it's been almost thirty years, so . . . okay, you can stay here. For a few days, anyway."

Jonas sighed and said soberly, "Thanks, Pa. It means a lot to me. I . . . well, I really appreciate it."

"You ought to. Come on, I'll show you to the spare room."

Corey caught Jonas's arm. "You're still welcome to come visit us."

"Thanks, Corey. I want to meet that Christopher."

"He looks so much like Mark, you'll . . ." She averted her eyes briefly, then, "I'll be home tonight. I live up on Hollis Heights in—well, *you* know the house. It was Kate's—I mean, yours and Kate's. . . ."

"I know the house. Corella, you're a lovely young woman, and I'm just grateful I got to meet you before . . . well, anyway, I'll sure take you up on the invitation."

"Kit and I will be looking forward to it. But, Gabe—" He was at the front door; he looked around at her as she added, "Gabe, we still have some things to talk about."

He said acerbically, "Nothing more that *I* know about."

"Don't count on it." And with that enigmatic admonition, she turned to Conan. "Let's get out of here."

They were in the car, and Conan was maneuvering a tight turn around the parking area, when Corey straightened from her boneless slump. "Oh, Conan, I didn't even introduce you to Jonas. That was just plain rude. I'm sorry."

Conan shrugged that off. He'd been too intrigued to notice any breach of etiquette. He glanced in the rearview mirror: the deck was empty; the Benbows had all gone inside. One big, happy family gathered for Thanksgiving Day.

He said absently, "That lady on the bus must've been quite informative. Jonas knew about Kit—Christopher, yet—before you mentioned him, and when you said something about a *couple* of kids, that didn't confuse him at all."

"Maybe the lady was a big talker. Maybe she told him about Di and Melissa and our odd household. You know, he's not at all what I expected. He just seems like a nice old man. Tired. Soul tired, not body tired. And maybe . . . sick."

Conan frowned as he negotiated the downhill curve toward the bay cliffs. "He's good. Damned good."

Corey's head came around abruptly. "What do you mean?"

"Just that Jonas is an accomplished con artist, Corey. Probably learned it from his father. I never had a chance to see Gabe on the campaign trail, but Miss Dobie tells me he was a cross between FDR and a born-again preacher. As a matter of fact, Gabe's father was an itinerant evangelist."

She laughed. "Yes, I know. So, you think Jonas is a con artist? Who's the cynic now?"

"Did I ever claim to be anything less than a cynic?"

"You're a skeptic, Conan, not a cynic." Then, with a sigh, "Jonas almost made me forget about the spit. I guess I'd better call Lyn Hatch. I wonder if he's in Portland now or out in the mountains somewhere."

"*Someone* in the Portland office should be notified."

"Yes, but I think Lyn should have the bad news first. Lord, I hate to have to tell him. He'll be so disappointed."

"Lyn's been with ECon too long not to be used to disappointments. Would you like me to call him?"

She considered that, then shook her head. "No. But I would appreciate it if—I mean, if Lyn decides to come down to Holliday Beach—which he probably will—could you put him up in your guest room?"

Conan didn't take his eyes off the road; to do so at the moment would invite disaster. But that request surprised him. On Lyn's previous visits to Holliday Beach, Corey and Diane had always made room for him at their house.

"Yes, of course, Corey. I've told him before that my guest room is at his disposal."

They were well past Reem's Rocks when Corey said, "I'm not mad at Lyn or anything like that. It's just the opposite, really. You know, sometimes you need . . . distance. I just—well, I guess I'm a little afraid."

Conan glanced at her and found her looking directly at him, her sea-hued eyes clouded.

"Afraid of what, Corey?"

"Are you going to make me say it? Then I can't pretend it away."

"That's up to you."

She looked out the side window, frowning faintly. "Okay, I'm afraid of what I'm beginning to feel for Lyn. Sometimes I have a hard time keeping myself centered. I mean, I get off on this guilt trip because of Mark. I keep wondering how he'd feel about Lyn and me."

And Conan wryly wondered how she expected *him* to feel about it. For a moment, he felt cut to the quick, relegated before his time to the role of father confessor. He didn't reply until they reached the junction with Highway 101, where he could stop and give her his full attention. And again he found those disturbingly direct eyes turned on him.

Then he smiled, realizing there was something to be said for the father-confessor role. "Corey, did Mark love you?"

She laughed softly. "Yes, of course he did, and I know he'd want me to be happy, and he wouldn't expect me to lead a nun's life forever." She sobered, pausing before she added, "I also know that whatever he would have thought is totally irrelevant. He's . . . dead. I'm on my own now."

"An admirably rational way to look at it. I assume it doesn't help a damn in dealing with your feelings for Lyn."

"Well, no. Not really."

"Give it some time, Corey. I know that's stale wisdom, but occasionally it's sound advice." And in the best father-confessor tradition, he thought to himself. "Anyway, Lyn is a very tenacious man. He'll wait."

Corey studied him, then nodded. "And you—you're really special, Conan. I'm grateful for that."

He felt a flash of heat in his cheeks and occupied himself with finding an opening in the holiday traffic so he could make a left turn onto the highway.

"Do you want me to drop you off at Rainbow Wings, Corey?"

"No, I'd better get back to the beach. We've got two or three thousand dollars' worth of kites in the air today. Conan—" She hesitated, looking past him to the glittering waters of Sitka Bay. "Tomorrow when—I mean, *if* Lyn comes down, there's something I have to talk to the two of you about."

"Something to do with the spit?"

"Yes."

"What is it?"

"Well, it's . . . complicated."

"All right, I'll wait until you're ready."

"Thanks, Conan."

Conan left Corey at the beach access by his house and the XK-E in the garage next to the Vanagon, and before he returned to the bookshop, he made a call on the private line in his library. The call went to the Duncan Investigation Service in San Francisco. His name got him through to Charlie Duncan immediately.

The call lasted twenty minutes, most of which were spent in conversation that had nothing to do with the reason for the call. Conan and Charlie Duncan had met in Berlin, where they were both on assignment for G-2, and Conan's feelings for Charlie were a great deal stronger than they might be for just another old Army buddy. Charlie had once saved his life in a back alley in Berlin.

The purpose of the call was disposed of in less than five minutes. Conan wanted a close background check on one Jonas Benbow, and he wanted results by Monday morning.

Then, as an afterthought, he asked for the same close—and fast —check on Nina Gillies. And he requested a particular operative. Sean Kelly had more than once proven to Conan that she had far more than good looks going for her. She was gutsy and inventive and endowed with infallible instincts. Nina Gillies was exactly Sean's kind of job.

Charlie had asked if Conan was on a case, and when that answer was negative, irritably asked why Conan was spending good money—and it would be a respectable sum—investigating those two people, when he didn't have a client to foot the bill.

"I'm just curious about them, Charlie. *Very* curious."

Duncan had sighed prodigiously. "Sure. Well, it's your money. You'll have a report early Monday morning."

CHAPTER 4

Conan awoke to a room full of gray light with his field of vision dominated by gray clouds and gray sea, painfully aware that however well designed it was for short-term occupancy, the Barcelona chair was not intended for sleeping.

Corey Benbow is dead.

The memory called forth an audible sound, an aching gasp as if he'd been struck. He was too preoccupied with memories to wonder what had wakened him, until he heard a cheerful, off-key humming from the kitchen.

Mrs. Early. This was one of her cleaning days, and her arrival meant it was nine o'clock. The humming moved into the passageway behind him, then into the living room. He marshaled his strength and came to his feet.

Mrs. Early unleashed a shattering shriek.

*"What in—who—*oh, for pity's *sake!* Mr. Flagg?"

She stood aproned and staunch, her wide, china-blue eyes fragmented by trifocals, white hair like a nebula trying to escape her head. That, however, was the way it always looked, and had nothing to do with her state of alarm.

"Mr. Flagg, you scared the living *day*lights out of me!"

He rubbed his stubbled face with both hands. "I'm sorry, Mrs. Early, I didn't—"

"Was you *asleep* in that chair?" She propped her fists on her hips, shaking her head. "You should *know* better—"

"I *do* know better," he muttered as he made his way to the spiral staircase.

"Oh, dear. It's Corey Benbow, ain't it?"

Conan didn't ask what she meant by "it." He continued up the stairs. "Mrs. Early, I'm going up to take a shower. Would you mind fixing a pot of coffee? The Kona, please, and make it strong."

It took her some time to tell him that she would fix the coffee, but he didn't stay for the accompanying motherly discourse. He went to his room, stripped off his clothes as he passed through the dressing room, and walked directly into the shower. As he adjusted the cascade of icy water to a more reasonable temperature, he wondered how Mrs. Early had known about Corey's death. The grapevine. Mrs. Early was on the main trunk, and little transpired in Holliday Beach that she didn't know about within hours.

By the time he finished showering and shaving, he felt passably alert and capable of focusing his eyes and mind. He dressed hurriedly—well-worn English tweed trousers and a vintage cableknit sweater—then sat down on the edge of the bed to face the telephone. He found a fresh pack of cigarettes in the drawer and lighted one, closing his eyes on a long drag.

Corey had been murdered.

That conclusion was a result of his contemplation of patterns in the chill hours before today's dawn. It was a solid conviction now, but he was well aware that he had very little to back it up. Only three pieces of evidence, and that was defining the word loosely. First, Gabe Benbow had lied about watching "Dallas" last night. Second, there were no skid marks on the road above Reem's Rocks.

Third, the diary. Kate Benbow's diary for the year 1948. Diane had told him that Corey had it with her when she went to talk to Gabe.

Oh, Corey, you naïve, gentle fool.

On Friday afternoon—yesterday? Yes. What a temporal chasm Corey's death had created between yesterday and today. Yesterday, on the other side of that chasm, the kites had been flying above the beach and Corey had been there to watch over them, but as soon as Lyn Hatch's red Honda appeared at Conan's house, Corey left the kites and joined Conan and Lyn on the deck off the living room. She held a small, leather-bound volume in her hands.

"About a month ago," she began, "a woman from the County Historical Society called me. She said she'd been a friend of Kate's and knew she kept diaries since she was fifteen years old. Mrs. Cummins is writing a history of Taft County, and she thought

Kate's diaries might help her." Corey looked down at the book, her brow flawed with a frown.

Lyn Hatch tilted back in his chair, hands clasped behind his head, his frown echoing hers, although there seemed to be in his probing gaze a preoccupation not with what she was saying, but with Corey herself.

She went on, "Well, I knew Kate's diaries were up in the attic at the house; I'd seen the box. But I'd never read them. They seemed . . . so personal, somehow. But I told Mrs. Cummins I'd look through them and see if I could find anything that might be useful to her—that wasn't *too* personal. What I found—well, it kind of blew me away."

Conan asked, "Something about the spit?"

"Yes." She opened the diary to the place marked with a slip of paper. "This diary is for 1948. Kate was engaged to Jonas—off and on—and she was working as a 'fee girl' in the county clerk's office in Westport. I guess her job was mostly recording deeds. This was during Gabe's first term as county commissioner, and Jonas was a bookkeeper in the assessor's office. Leo Moskin was managing a bank in Westport, and he was a notary public."

Lyn leaned forward, resting his elbows on his knees. "Moskin notarized the deed for the spit. We checked that."

Corey nodded. "Anyway, let me read this to you. The date on this entry is November 21, 1948:

" 'Marj Kilty announced her engagement today to that nincompoop, Charlie Hampstead. Oh, well. Wonder what I'll do about my sometimes dear Jonas. Marry him, probably, sooner or later, for better or worse. He *can* be so sweet. But Gabe—now, I wonder about him. He brought in an interesting deed today. Bertran Reem was the seller, and the property was the Shearwater Spit plus a few acres at the neck of it. Bert just died a couple of days ago. I always felt sorry for him, all by himself in that shack on the bay. Nearly the last of his people, though they say he was only part Indian. He sure took to the white man's liquor, though. The odd thing about the deed is that it was dated August tenth this year and notarized the same day—by Leo Moskin. That man thinks he's God's gift to women, but someday—I hope!—he's going to run into a woman who'll tell him in a way he can understand that he's no gift to anybody, even with a satin bow tied around his neck!' "

Corey paused there, smiling. "It's hard to imagine Leo as a

ladies' man, but he was really very handsome when he was young
—and a hundred pounds or so lighter. Kate had some snapshots of
the Benbows and various friends. Leo was in a lot of them."

Conan lighted a cigarette, sheltering the lighter from the wind
with his hands. "Kate's wish came true about Leo meeting a
woman who would clarify his worth—if the gossip about his ex-
wife is true."

Lyn cut in impatiently, "Go on, Corey. What else did she say
about the deed?"

Corey resumed reading. " 'What made me wonder about the
deed was the date it was notarized, because I know Leo was on
vacation then. He made such a fuss about going to Miami Beach,
and I thought then, in the middle of *summer?* Yes, I just checked
the entry for August fifth. Jonas took me to the party Gabe gave for
Leo the day before he left on his vacation. Leo *couldn't* have
notarized the deed on August tenth. He falsified the date. So, just
out of curiosity, I checked Bert Reem's signature against Gabe's,
and I'd swear Gabe *forged* Bert's name on the deed—the old
bastard. I mean Gabe, not poor Bert. But I don't think Bert has any
heirs, and this is one crooked deal that's going to backfire on Gabe.
He'll never be able to sell that land. Nobody in their right mind
would buy it—not to build on. I saw the whole spit covered with
water nine years ago in that big storm. Houses built on sand—that
would sure be it. I wonder if Jonas knows about this. Probably not,
and it doesn't matter. The only money anybody's going to make on
this deal is the taxes the county will collect—from Gabe. Too
bad!' " Corey closed the book. "That's all. There isn't another
mention of it from that time on. I guess Kate really didn't think it
would make any difference."

Conan sat motionless, stunned by that revelation, at length taking a puff on his cigarette and letting the smoke out slowly to be
snatched away by the wind. "Kate was not, unfortunately, gifted
with twenty-twenty foresight."

Corey laughed at that, but Lyn didn't seem to hear it. The
berserker light was in his eyes, straitly reined, as he surged to his
feet, went to the deck railing, and after a moment struck it a blow
that should have broken his hand.

"Damn him! That sh—" He clamped his jaw tight, apparently at
a loss for words; at least, for any he felt free to pronounce in
Corey's presence. "Gabe's going to collect four million dollars for a

piece of land he doesn't even *own!* A piece of land he got by forgery!"

Conan observed, *"Allegedly,* Lyn. Kate may have been wrong about the forgery. But we can probably prove that Leo misused his powers as a notary, which might make life rather difficult for him. There's a group in Westport circulating a recall petition to get Leo off the Planning Commission."

Lyn turned abruptly. "I don't give a damn about Leo! If we can prove that Gabe has no right to sell that property in the first place—"

Corey said, "I thought about that, Lyn, when I first saw the diary. But at that point, Gabe had—supposedly—agreed to sell to ECon, and I knew it would be a legal can of worms. He can't claim adverse possession, since he didn't do a thing on that land until he built his house eight years ago, but can we prove beyond a doubt that Bertran Reem's signature *was* forged, and even if we could prove fraud, then who owns the spit?"

Lyn responded impatiently, "It would revert to the state, since Reem had no heirs."

"Yes, but first there'd have to be a search for heirs, and even if none turned up—well, this is a relatively enlightened state when it comes to environmental issues, but I'm not sure I'd want to trust the fate of Sitka Bay to the bunch of politicians running things in Salem right now."

Lyn considered that, his frown of anger gradually changing into one of speculation. "Okay, it's a can of worms for ECon, but it's an even bigger can for Gabe."

Corey nodded. "Right. He doesn't want to go to court, even if he thought he had a chance of winning. It could be years before the whole mess is cleared up. He can't afford those years—unless he really *does* believe he's immortal."

Lyn had relaxed enough to laugh at that. "Besides, Isaac Wines won't wait that long. He's got to get his money out earning *more* money."

"Yes!" Corey replied, grim determination underlying her apparent enthusiasm. "ECon doesn't want to start a long court battle any more than Gabe does, but we can and will, rather than let Wines buy the spit—and Gabe knows that."

Conan put in, "So, you're considering a little polite blackmail in a good cause?"

She wasn't comfortable with that, but she didn't argue it. "I thought we could offer him a chance to change his mind again, to tell *Wines* how cheap promises are."

Lyn folded his sun-browned arms. "You mean let the last ECon offer stand, and if he doesn't accept it instead of Baysea's, we'll go to court with that diary."

She nodded. "Yes. Will ECon agree to that?"

"Well, I'll have to talk to the state director, but I don't think there'll be any problem." He straightened and squared his shoulders. "So, the next step is to talk to Gabe—to do a little blackmailing."

"Yes, I guess it is," she said, with no enthusiasm now, turning into the wind as she brushed her hair away from her forehead. "But *I* want to talk to him first. Alone."

Conan felt a silent alarm at that and voiced vehement objections. Some argument followed, and in the end it hadn't been definitely resolved. They would talk about it later. But not that evening; Lyn was slated for dinner with a potential land donor in Westport. And the wind had suddenly dropped—and most of the kites with it. Corey had made a hurried exit to aid in the rescue.

> *Last night as I lay on my pillow,*
> *Last night as I lay on my bed,*
> *Last night as I lay on my pillow,*
> *I dreamed darlin' Corey was dead.*

And now the dream was reality.

His cheeks were wet, and the inner aching was in no way diminished. Conan put out his cigarette and reached for the phone. He had to check the first page of the phone book for the number; it was a Westport exchange.

"Oregon State Police, may I help you?"

"This is Conan Flagg. May I speak to Sergeant Roddy?"

"Just a moment, I'll see if—yes, he's in his office."

A click, then Roddy came on the line with another offer of help. Conan identified himself again, then, "Do you have any more information on Corey Benbow's accident, Sergeant?"

"Well, the deputy medical examiner should arrive in Holliday Beach any time now—"

"On a Saturday? I didn't know MEs worked six-day weeks."

Roddy laughed. "We all get our share of those. Anyway, we've already gone over the car. Far as we can tell, Ms. Benbow was alone, and there wasn't a damn thing wrong with the car. I thought there was a chance the brakes were defective, since there weren't any skid marks. I guess . . . well, the ME will run the usual blood tests."

"And what if those tests show she *wasn't* drunk?" That slipped out, and Conan winced in annoyance; he didn't want to antagonize Roddy. "I'm sorry, Sergeant. I know a DUI is the obvious explanation, and it has to be checked out. Did you talk to Gabe Benbow?"

"Yes. He said Ms. Benbow showed up at his house about eight-thirty and left about nine. I asked him why she came to see him, and he said they'd had an argument Thanksgiving Day. Something about a land sale. She belonged to some local antidevelopment group."

Conan felt a rush of anger that tightened his grip on the receiver. "I suppose those were Gabe's words."

"Mm. More or less."

"He was talking about a nationwide organization with a hundred and thirty thousand members and permanent capitalization of around forty million."

Roddy gave a low whistle. "Well, I guess Gabe—Mr. Benbow has his own peculiar way of looking at things. Anyway, his story is that he and Ms. Benbow talked for a while, then she left. He also said . . . well, she didn't have anything to drink at his house."

Conan didn't comment on that. "Where was Jonas?"

"Jonas? Oh—Benbow's son. Well, he was at the Blue Heron Inn lifting a few. According to Mr. Benbow, his son has always had a weakness for booze."

"Did you check with the bartender at the Blue Heron?"

"No. Is there any reason we should have?"

"Maybe. Did Gabe say he was alone when Corey arrived?"

"Yes. He said it a couple of times, matter of fact."

Conan considered that, then, "When I called Gabe earlier—about two, I think—I asked him if Corey was there, and he said, '*Everybody* left hours ago.' If he was alone, who was 'everybody'?"

"Mr. Flagg, I don't know, and unless some evidence of foul play turns up, that is not any business of mine or of the State Police."

Roddy's patience was obviously wearing thin. Conan mentally added Gabe's slip of the tongue to his scant list of evidence for murder as he offered a placating, "You're right, Sergeant. I assume the body is at Ronson's Mortuary?"

"Yes. It'll be released after the ME checks it. The DA is trying to find a next of kin. I mean, a blood relative. Mr. Benbow thought she came from somewhere in Montana, but he wasn't sure where."

"Havre," Conan said dully. "Havre, Montana."

There's nothing between Havre and the north pole but a railroad track. All you could see was prairie and sky. But I was seamarked. Some people are, you know. . . .

Conan added, "Corey told me her father was a brakeman on the Union Pacific, and one night he boarded a train for his shift and just kept on going. Her mother left for parts unknown a few years later. Corey was raised by a great-aunt and uncle. Irene and Chester—damn, what was the last name? Bronson, I think. But I don't know if they're still alive."

"I'll pass that on to Culpepper. Thanks."

"Sergeant, I know Corey would have wanted her body released to Diane Monteil."

"Oh. Well, of course, that's up to the DA."

Conan refrained from comment on that or on Owen Culpepper. "What about the personal effects?"

"We sent them to the Holliday Beach Police Department. Chief Kleber said he'd take care of them, since he knows Ms. Monteil and the boy—the victim's child."

"Did you find that diary?"

"No, nothing fitting the description you gave me last night. Her purse was there. Billfold in it with about twenty dollars. She was wearing a fairly good watch, and she had a diamond ring on a chain around her neck."

But the diary was missing, and that ominous absence was something else to add to the list of evidence.

"Sergeant, I'd like to see the ME's report."

Roddy took a long time responding to that. "Well, Mr. Flagg, you know I'm not supposed to give out that kind of information without some sort of official request."

"I understand that." Conan reined his urge to argue further, waiting for Roddy's reply.

"Look, I . . . well, Chief Kleber will have the information as soon as I do. Maybe sooner."

Conan smiled. "I'll talk to him." And hope Earl was in a cooperative mood today. "Thanks, Sergeant."

Conan pressed the cradle button, but didn't hang up. He hesitated, then took a deep breath and punched out a number from memory. Lyn Hatch answered the call, and in the two syllables of his hello, Conan could hear his ragged weariness.

"This is Conan, Lyn. I won't ask how you are; I can guess. What about Di? And the kids?"

"Well, nobody got much sleep last night. I think maybe Melissa's finally asleep now. Kit . . . well, Di's with him. She's incredible, Conan. The patience. I don't know how she . . . holds everything together like she does."

"I suppose it's a good thing she has the kids to worry about now."

"Yeah, I guess so." Then, with an audible intake of breath, "Have you talked to the police?"

"Yes, I just called Sergeant Roddy. Corey's body is being held at Ronson's Mortuary here in town until the medical examiner arrives. That should be soon. After the autopsy, I assume the DA will release—"

"Autopsy? Why are they going to do an autopsy?"

Conan recognized the defensive tone; he'd heard it from survivors before, and he had always wondered why people found the dissection of the body of a loved one so repugnant. The body was no longer the person loved.

"In a case of unexpected death, it's usual, Lyn."

"Oh. Yes. I guess I'm not thinking too straight."

"Who is?"

Lyn tried to laugh at that, none too successfully, then, "Conan, you've got a private investigator's license—I know that, and I . . . how much do you charge?"

This turn in the conversation took Conan by surprise. He shook a cigarette out of the pack and lighted it, bracing the receiver against his shoulder.

"Why, Lyn? What do you want with a PI?"

"I don't believe that crap about Corey's death being an accident! I think she was *murdered.*"

Perhaps this turn wasn't so surprising after all. Conan thought grimly, that makes two of us, but he only asked, "Why do you think she was murdered?"

"Because it's just too goddamned *convenient,* her dying right now. And she *did* have the diary with her. Di saw her put it in her purse before she left the house. Look, Conan, whatever it costs—I can sell my cycle and stereo and—"

"Oh, for God's sake, Lyn! If there's a case here, I'm already on it. Who do you think murdered her?"

Lyn said with chill distinctness, "You know who I *know* murdered her! *Gabe Benbow.* He had it all: motive, opportunity, and—"

"And means?" Conan kept his voice level; Lyn was the last person he wanted to argue with today. "We don't even know what the means were, Lyn, and Gabe certainly wasn't the only one who wouldn't want that diary made public."

"But he had—" Lyn stopped, his tone rife with suspicion when he asked, "You say you're already on the case? Who hired you?"

"No one, Lyn. My client is Corey. And I won't take another client, especially not you. What you want is someone to prove your foregone conclusion. But I promise you this: I'll keep you informed on my progress as if you *were* my client. In exchange, I'll ask you to stay out of it."

Conan didn't like the feel of the long silence that followed. At length, he heard a sigh, and Lyn said, "Okay, Conan. So, what've you got so far?"

At that, Conan had to laugh. "You expect fast results. Well, Roddy couldn't tell me much, except Corey's car was in perfect working order, and he did not find the diary."

"Of course not! Gabe has it!"

"That's a possibility. Anyway, Chief Kleber will have access to the ME's report. I won't. But Earl might at least discuss it with me, so I'm going down to talk to him about noon, and I'll call you afterward. Now, will you please just stay put?"

Lyn managed a recognizable laugh. "Don't worry about me. All I want is justice. I don't care how I get it."

That statement did nothing to soothe Conan's nerves. He took a long drag on his cigarette and decided not to pursue the subject of justice for the moment.

"Lyn, tell Di we'll have to wait until the DA releases the body before any arrangements can be made."

"Okay. And I'll tell her you're, uh, on the case."

"For what that's worth."

"It'll mean a lot to her, Conan. Thanks."

In the kitchen, Conan found Mrs. Early hovering over a skillet crackling with bacon. She said in an uncompromising tone, "Set down. I'll have your breakfast ready in a jiffy, and before you say no, jest remember, you gotta feed the body to keep the spirit goin'."

Conan's first inclination had in fact been to decline food, but he was seduced by the heady odor of bacon and coffee, discovering to his surprise that he *was* hungry.

"Mrs. Early, you're a rare gem." He went to the side counter where the coffee steamed invitingly, filled a cup, then sat down at the table in the window alcove. Mrs. Early had laid a place for him replete with clean ashtray. He looked out at the beach dotted with holiday beachcombers, all feeling no pain, he thought enviously. The clouds were dispersing, exposing patches of blue sky and dappling the ocean with aquamarine.

Mrs. Early presented him with a plate as inviting as any restaurant chef could offer: mushroom omelet and crisp bacon served with toasted English muffins and her own jelly—wild trailing blackberry, a gift from summer, and worth its weight, she had informed him, in gold. He didn't doubt that.

"Chester is an incredibly lucky man," Conan said as he unfurled his napkin, "to have you cooking for him every day. Won't you have a muffin with me? At least a cup of coffee." Conan had an ulterior motive in that invitation, but Mrs. Early didn't need much encouragement.

"Well . . . maybe jest a cup of coffee. And half a muffin." She brought a plate, knife, and cup and settled across the table from him. "Trouble with cookin' for Chester is Dr. Heideger's got him on one of them no-salt, no-cloresterall diets. Takes all the fun out of cookin'!"

Mrs. Early did not mention Corey Benbow's death while Conan was eating, although it obviously required some restraint on her part. However, she was far from silent—Mrs. Early was incapable of that—but her conversation, a virtual monologue, concerned such subjects as the weather, the influx of holiday people, and more on the unfortunate Chester's restrictive diet. Finally, Conan rose to take his empty plate to the sink, poured fresh coffee for both of them, and sat down to light a cigarette.

Only then did he broach the subject of Corey's death. While

Mrs. Early listened avidly, he told her what had happened, without including anything she couldn't have heard on the local radio station, then he gradually maneuvered the conversation to peripheral subjects, arriving finally at the desired destination. "You know, Mrs. Early, I've always had a hard time understanding Gabe Benbow."

She had her plump elbows on the table, her coffee cup encircled in both hands. "Ain't nothin' hard to understand about ol' Gabe. He jest believes in openin' the door real fast when opportunity knocks. Besides, he's got a funny idea about what a good Christian's supposed to be."

Conan laughed. "I've noticed."

"Mm. Not too many people around here Gabe can call a real friend. I remember when he first come to Holliday Beach. That was about 1932. Lots of people headed for the coast when the Depression hit. Wasn't too cold in the winter, and you could eat off the beach or out of the woods. When Gabe first come here with his wife, Grace—nice woman, she was; can't imagine how she ever got hooked up with *him*—they was so poor, they didn't have a pot to pee in, but Gabe got in with the county courthouse bunch, and it wasn't more 'n ten years before he was right in the thick of politics and that sort of thing and a *long* ways from poor."

Conan listened and puffed at his cigarette while she chronicled Gabe and Grace's early years in Holliday Beach, finally forcing her to skip a few years with, "Jonas came back Thanksgiving Day, you know." She did know, of course. In detail. Conan primed the pump with a show of ignorance. "What's this I hear about Jonas embezzling some money before he left Holliday Beach?"

"He embezzled it from the county! 'Bout twenty thousand altogether. Nearly lost Gabe the next election. Y'see, Jonas was always Gabe's fair-haired boy up till then, and Gabe got him the job bookkeeping in the assessor's office. Jonas was married and had a son. That was Mark—"

"Yes, I know. Corey's husband."

"Right. Jonas was a heller 'fore he got married, but he settled down real good, 'cept for one thing. He *did* like the cards. *And* one-armed bandits and that sort of thing, and they never was legal in the state, but there was always plenty of 'em around here, if you knew where to look."

Like the local fraternal lodge, Conan added, but only to himself, since he knew Chester was a member, and gambling machines were still to be found within its hallowed, benevolent halls.

Mrs. Early continued blithely, "I guess Jonas got into debt way over his head and started 'borrowing' from the county. He got caught, and Gabe got mad. Said Jonas could jest go to jail, *he* wasn't goin' to lift a finger to help him. So, that's when Jonas up and disappeared. Heard he's been all over the world since then."

Conan nodded. "And Moses was the older brother who stayed home, while the prodigal lived it up in exotic lands."

"Well, Moses did all right for himself, stayin' home. He managed to stay home from the war, too, while Jonas got shipped off. I mean, World War Two. Somethin' about his eyes. Moses had bad eyes since he was a kid. Gabe sent him off to Oregon State, and that's where he met Frances." Mrs. Early took time for a swallow of coffee and an expressive sniff.

"Talk about your power behind the throne! France Benbow decided she was goin' to be queen around here, so, by golly, she had to make Moses king. Hadn't been for her, I figure Moses'd be happy tendin' to his insurance business—Gabe set him up in that —and never would've got into real estate. And believe you me, she's right there lookin' over his shoulder ever' move he makes. Smart woman; leastwise, when it comes to business. They done real well, you notice. Fancy house in that new development— what do they call it?"

"Sanderling Point," Conan supplied, which Mrs. Early accepted without a break in the pace of her discourse.

"Big cars and diamonds, trips to foreign countries. So, Moses done all right bein' the brother that stayed home. Cold fish, that Moses. Never can figure out what's goin' on in his head. I used to clean for them. France, well she was downright picky, but I never minded that. Moses, though—well, one time he got it in his head I stole some diamond cuff links of his. Me!" She pressed a hand to her bosom, pink face turning even pinker at the memory. "Why, you *know* I been doin' some of the best houses 'round here, and I *never* even thought about takin' anything that didn't belong to me! That Moses—he's got what you call a one-track mind. Nothin' puts him off a scent once he's on it. Well, turned out he found the cuff links. Mislaid 'em *himself*. But never a word of apology to *me*. So, I jest told France she'd have to find somebody else to do her cleanin'. I didn't want nothin' more to do with *that* household."

Conan shook his head in commiseration, then ventured casually, "Real estate isn't the best thing to have your money tied up in right now—not with interest rates so high and the economy taking so long to 'bottom out.'"

Mrs. Early nodded sage agreement as she took another swallow of coffee. "Lots of people 'round here been learnin' *that* the hard way—includin' Moses. But he's jest like a cat; always lands on his feet. Way I heard it, he's put all his eggs in one basket. That's not so smart, usually, but that basket jest happens to be in the south part of the tract where that new development's goin' in down on Sitka Bay."

Conan took a last puff on his cigarette and stubbed it out. "Yes, I heard he's contracted for a lot of property south of the bay. I didn't think he'd be foolish enough to put all his . . . eggs into it."

She shrugged. "Friend of mind is married to—well, he's on the board of the Westport Bank. That's where Moses does most of his bankin' business, jest like Gabe. And she told me her husband told *her* that Moses has near stripped himself for cash to put into—what's it called?"

Again Conan provided the name. "Baysea Properties."

"That's it. But Moses'll come out of that smellin' like a rose. The whole thing was hangin' on Gabe sellin' the Shearwater Spit—" She stopped, eyeing Conan suspiciously. "But *you* know about that! You and that conservation bunch was tryin' to stop Gabe from sellin' the spit."

"Yes, and you can see how far we got with it. So, Gabe's going to get his four million from Baysea, and it looks like Moses will probably do nearly as well."

"Oh, he'll do jest fine. Course, all his propitty's on contract, but he'll still make more 'n a few dollars on it."

But if the Baysea sale didn't go through, Conan mused, the contracts would still be due, and Moses—and his ambitious helpmeet, France—would find themselves with a very empty basket.

Conan rose to refill their coffee cups, and when he returned to his chair observed, "Unfortunately, Baysea Properties seems to be inevitable. The only hurdle left is approval by the County Planning Commission, and with Leo Moskin heading that, I can't see the development being turned down."

Mrs. Early gave a cackling laugh. "Not hardly! Leo and Gabe've been scratchin' each other's backs since the thirties, and Leo never turned down anything like this Baysea deal 'cept once that I know about. That was maybe ten years ago. Portland company, and they got on their high horse and wouldn't pass Leo any money under the table. And they never got to build even a chicken coop in Taft County after that. Course, since Leo got divorced, he's needed anything he can get over *or* under the table."

"Really? I didn't even know Leo had been married," Conan lied without a qualm, again priming the pump. He knew very little about that ill-fated union, and Mrs. Early was always happy to fill any informational gaps.

"Leo got himself married, all right! That was back in . . . oh, must've been about 1957. He was gettin' into middle age then, and Nora Carr was still in her twenties. He met her in Hawayah, I think, and Lordy, was she ever a looker. Ol' Leo always did have an eye for pretty women, but he never let any woman catch him. I mean, get him to the altar. Don't know how Nora managed it. Well, she stuck with him for ten years, and you have to give her credit. I don't figure Leo was any jewel to live with. One thing, though, he did keep on raking in the money, and maybe Nora figured he was ripe finally. So, she sued for divorce. You had to have grounds back then, but that wasn't hard. Leo never did give up chasin' after women, so Nora didn't have any trouble provin' adultery." Mrs. Early leaned back, chuckling to herself. "And I guess when it come to how much alimony Leo had to pay, the judge let him have it right between the eyes. Somethin' like a thousand dollars a month with some sort of arrangement for inflation. No tellin' how much it is by now. The judge was a woman, by the way."

Conan laughed appreciatively. "I'm sure that taught Leo a lesson or two. Where does all his money come from? Not all under the table, surely."

"Well, I don't know for sure, but I guess he went into real estate, too. He was always sort of a gambler at heart. Maybe he went into the stock market."

Neither of which could be termed dependable investments at this point in the nation's economic history. Conan looked out at the beach, watching a father and child launching a kite into the wind. "What happened to Nora? Did she go back to Hawaii?"

"Well, she probably does a lot of visitin' over there, but she don't let Leo too far out of her sight. She moved to Portland. Got herself a fancy condominium up on Vista Avenue, so I hear. Never married again, and why should she, when all she has to do is wait for the mail to bring Leo's alimony check ever' month."

"How old is Leo? Must be around seventy. I'm surprised he hasn't retired by now."

"He's gotta keep up them alimony checks somehow. But I guess he might have a hard time keepin' his job after the election next year."

"You mean he's finally getting some real opposition?"

"Yep. Young feller from south county. Can't think of his name. Then I heard there's a bunch in Westport want to get Leo recalled. Got a petition goin' 'round. Used to be, Leo never had to worry 'bout that sort of thing. He's a big muckymuck in the Westport Bank, and it was the only bank in the county for a long time. That meant there wasn't too many people didn't owe the bank money, or didn't have folks who did. *They* didn't sign no petitions—not if they knew what was good for them. But now—well, we got a bunch of Portland branch banks movin' in and a lot of new people who don't have any reason not to sign that recall petition. Times're always changin'." Then she frowned as she looked up at the clock on the range. "And time's a-flyin'. I gotta get to work, or I won't get nothin' done today." She began gathering the remaining dishes on the table—including Conan's cup and ashtray. "Oh, I noticed you still have that rib roast up in the freezer. Better let me cook it up for you. Ain't gonna get any better with age."

Conan rose. "I'd appreciate that, Mrs. Early. I guess I'd better get to work, too. At the bookshop, I mean."

She eyed him curiously. "Where *else* would you mean?"

CHAPTER 5

Conan did go to the bookshop, but if he hoped for a quiet place to while away the time—it was highly unlikely Kleber would have any information from the ME before noon—Conan was doomed to disappointment. Miss Beatrice Dobie believed fervently that the customer—whom she recognized as the ultimate source of the bookshop's solvency—came first, even to the point of peremptorily ordering Conan to tend the cash register while she went upstairs to help a customer locate a particular book.

The press of business had one advantage, however: Miss Dobie didn't have time to question him, with her usual maddening obliqueness, about Corey's death.

But there were townspeople among the customers who were not so preoccupied, and Miss Dobie was apparently detained upstairs with more customer queries, leaving Conan trapped behind the front counter for half an hour, while an incipient headache became blinding. Finally, when Mrs. Carmody asked him for the third time when the funeral would take place and where, Conan raised his voice to a penetrating bellow that even aroused Meg and sent her scuttling off the counter.

"Miss Dobie!"

She was at the counter within thirty seconds, and after expertly assessing the situation, she pushed him out from behind the cash register.

"Go home, Mr. Flagg."

"I can't. Mrs. Early's there."

"Then go to the Surf House and have a drink. Good morning, Mrs. Carmody. What's that? Well, I don't think the arrangements have been made yet. *Mr. Flagg . . .*"

"I'm leaving."

And he did. He gunned the XK-E away from the curb, ignoring an oncoming camper-van, but he didn't drive south to the Surf House, as Miss Dobie suggested—although he gave it serious consideration—but north, turning right off the highway after ten blocks. Another block brought him to the flat-roofed, one-story building that housed the Holliday Beach Police Department. It was only eleven-thirty. Conan sat in the car for a while with his eyes closed, waiting for the headache to abate, then went inside the station. The dispatcher looked up at him curiously.

"Oh hello, Mr. Flagg. The chief thought you'd be around today. Said for you to wait in his office."

Conan did not like being predictable, but he accepted pigeon-holing gratefully in this case. At least Kleber's message implied that Conan was welcome.

"Thanks, Dave. Where's the chief?"

"Down at the mortuary talking to Feingold."

"Who?"

"The new deputy ME. Works out of Westport, you know. First time there's been an ME this handy."

Conan cooled his heels in Kleber's office for half an hour, but he didn't object. It gave him time to think, to sort through the information available to him. The office was a mundane, businesslike place: brown linoleum floor; metal file cabinets and furniture; dull blue-gray walls; a desk piled with forms and file folders. Murder seemed too bizarre for these surroundings, yet it had been the subject of more than one conversation in this room.

Conan was standing at the window when Kleber's car turned into the parking area. The chief looked harried and preoccupied. Conan heard him in a brief exchange with the dispatcher, then Kleber strode into his office, carrying a white paper bag, which he emptied on his desk before he spoke. Lunch, apparently; a hamburger and milk shake. He sat down and took a bite out of the hamburger, chewed a while, then looked up at Conan.

"I figured you'd show up here today."

Conan went to the chair across the desk from him. "Sergeant Roddy told me you have Corey Benbow's effects. I thought you might be relieved if I took them to Di."

Kleber's black brows came together in a straight line as he eyed Conan, then he sighed. "Sure, you can take them. Over in that plastic bag there, on top of the file cabinet."

Conan only looked in the general direction of the bag and nodded. "Thanks."

Kleber wiped his beard-blued chin with a napkin. "So, I suppose now you want to know what Feingold had to say."

"Yes, I'd be interested. Has he finished the autopsy?"

Kleber masticated another mouthful of sandwich. "He didn't do an autopsy."

"What?" Conan came upright in his chair. "Why not?"

"Well, there didn't seem to be any question about the cause of death, and since it was just a simple accident case, he didn't see any reason to do a full autopsy. And I couldn't think of a good reason, either."

Conan was still staring at Kleber, torn between bewilderment and anger, but he kept his voice level. "I thought an autopsy was customary in a suspicious death."

"What's suspicious about it? When Feingold writes up his report, the cause of death will be listed as 'craniocerebral trauma and/or drowning.' That's the sort of thing that happens to somebody when they drive off a fifty-foot cliff and go headfirst into the windshield. She had a skull fracture—hit just above the right eye—and Feingold took out some glass fragments. He said he'd have to do a microscopic comparison with the windshield glass, but he was sure it would check out. The windshield was cracked, you know."

Conan closed his eyes briefly. "Yes. I remember."

"Feingold said that was probably enough to kill her instantly, and even if it didn't, it was enough to knock her out so she would've drowned in a matter of minutes. Damn, I don't know why they can't make a decent hamburger anymore!" He thrust the offending remains into the paper sack, crushed it irritably, and threw it into the wastebasket.

"I assume Feingold didn't find anything else unusual in his examination?"

"No. And he did a good job. I've seen a few MEs at work, and I know. He did a damn good job."

"What about blood alcohol? Did he check that?"

"Of course he did! Well, he took blood samples. Has to be done in the Salem lab. He won't get any results on that till Monday." Kleber delved into a desk drawer and brought out a cigar; when he got it lighted, he didn't seem to find it any more pleasurable than the hamburger. "Anyway, Feingold called the DA with his preliminary findings. Culpepper is releasing the body today."

Conan asked warily, "Releasing it to whom?"

"Well, he said he was on the phone all morning trying to find somebody in Havre, Montana, who knew the whereabouts of any of Corey's blood relations, but I guess they've all either left Havre with no forwarding address or died off."

"So, what did Owen in his infinite wisdom decide?"

Kleber frowned at his cigar. "Since he couldn't find a blood relation, he settled for a relation by law."

"Gabe Benbow?" Then at Kleber's nod, Conan came to his feet and went to the window. There was something inevitable about that decision, but it still rankled. "Why Gabe? Diane Monteil is the only one Corey would've wanted to—"

"Look, *I* didn't tell him to pick Gabe. It's the DA's decision, and I can't do a damn thing about it."

"I know, Chief. And I haven't the slightest doubt that Owen was influenced in his decision directly or indirectly by Gabe Benbow." He turned away from the window abruptly. "There *must* be a way to force Owen—or the ME—to order an autopsy!"

"You tell me what it is, then. You got any reason why Corey's death shouldn't be listed as accidental?"

"Yes. Kate Benbow's diary." He returned to his chair while he briefly explained the diary and its potentials. Kleber listened intently through veils of cigar smoke, but his skeptical expression didn't change.

When Conan finished his explanation, Kleber delicately tipped the ash from his cigar into an ashtray. "Flagg, you know that doesn't change a damn thing. Di Monteil can swear Corey had the diary when she left the house, but that doesn't prove Corey *showed* it to anybody. Besides, if you follow this out, you end up with Gabe Benbow killing her. Is that where you're headed?"

Conan thought of Lyn Hatch, who didn't find that assumption at all unreasonable. "Why *not* Gabe?"

"Damn it, I don't like Gabe any more than you do, but I can't see him forcing an able-bodied young woman to get into that car and drive it off a cliff."

"Maybe she didn't *drive* off the cliff. Maybe she was a helpless passenger, and maybe she wasn't able-bodied at the time."

"Well, there wasn't another mark on her except the head

wound, and that happened *after* she went off the cliff. Unless Gabe bashed her head into the windshield first. Now, *that* would be a little tricky, especially inside a Beetle."

"There are means of immobilizing a person that don't leave marks on the body."

Kleber paused thoughtfully. "Like drugs? Okay, but how would Gabe get hold of anything like that? I mean, on the spur of the moment. And if you figure that diary was the motive, it *had* to be spur of the moment. He didn't know about it before, did he?"

Conan shook his head. "No. What about barbiturates? Maybe Gabe takes sleeping pills."

"If anybody gave Corey any barbiturates, that'll show up in the blood tests. Feingold said he asked for a test on that along with the blood alcohol."

"Well, that's something."

"Not much if you're after a good reason to force Culpepper to order an autopsy. There isn't any proof of foul play to begin with, and if you start accusing Gabe—"

"I'm not accusing him specifically. All I'm saying is that Corey's death is incredibly convenient when you consider what was at stake. Gabe isn't the only one who had a very personal interest in the success of Baysea."

Kleber began shaking his head well before Conan concluded that. "Flagg, you're talking about motive like you already had the *corpus delicti*. The proof of the crime—remember? Give me some proof that a crime was committed, and by God, I'll take on Culpepper and anybody else—even if it's *not* in my jurisdiction. But I've got to have some evidence!"

Conan's shoulders sagged wearily. "I can't offer you any evidence." And the bitterest aspect of that admission was that an autopsy might provide the proof.

Kleber nodded wearily, then tilted back in his chair, his gaze focused somewhere beyond the window. "I've got a daughter, you know."

"Caroline? Yes, she's a regular at the bookshop."

"She's sixteen, and that's a hard age to be these days. When Rainbow Wings first opened . . . well, Caroline loved it. Any time she could get free, she was down there or on the beach with a kite. She used to say flying kites was a 'mystic experience.' Corey and Di spent a lot of time with Caroline, and she thought those two women were great, working like crazy to make their own way, and good mothers, too. The best kind of—what do they call it? Role model. You know what I mean. Well, this morning, I had to tell Caroline that Corey Benbow is dead. That . . . was hard."

Conan remained silent, aware that Earl Kleber had revealed something in himself that was intensely private. And at the moment, Conan didn't trust his own voice.

At length, Kleber leaned forward to knock the ash off his cigar. "I just hope it *was* an accident. I don't like thinking about what it means if it wasn't."

Conan nodded as he rose. "I hope it was too, Chief."

"But you don't believe it."

"Do you?"

Kleber shrugged. "I don't know, but there doesn't seem to be much I can do about it, either way. Of course, *you* can nose around —long as you don't break any laws."

That was a first for Kleber—actually encouraging Conan in an investigation.

"Oh, I'll nose around. You can count on that." He went to the file cabinet for the plastic bag that held Corey's possessions. "I'll take these to Di, Chief, and give her the bad news about the DA's decision."

"There's more bad news—maybe."

Conan turned. "What *else?*"

"Culpepper told me Gabe is thinking about trying to get custody of Kit."

For a moment, Conan could only stare at Kleber. It was an effort not to shout when he asked, "*Why?* What makes him think he's capable of raising—" Conan got himself in rein, then, "That will be up to a judge to decide, but I know Corey made a provision in her will for Di to have custody of Kit. Di made the same provision for Melissa."

Kleber sighed with obvious relief. "I hope you're right. Listen, if you . . . well, let me know if you come up with anything."

"Don't worry, you'll be the first to know if I discover anything remotely resembling a *corpus delicti.*"

As Conan passed the dispatcher's desk, he heard the phone ring, but it hardly registered. He was nearly out the front door when the dispatcher called to him, "Mr. Flagg, somebody wants to talk to you."

Conan frowned as he went to the counter and took the receiver. "Thanks, Dave. Hello, this is Flagg."

"Lyn Hatch, Conan. I couldn't get you at—"

"For God's sake, Lyn, I can't tie up this phone. Look, I'll be at Di's house in a few minutes."

Lyn didn't seem to hear that. "We just got a phone call a little while ago from Di's ex-husband, Norman. He's still her lawyer, you know. He called to tell her he heard something from Owen Culpepper. He's the DA—"

"Yes, I know, Lyn, and I know—"

"Gabe Benbow is going to sue for custody of Kit! That son of a bitch wants to take Kit away from Di!"

Conan's jaw went tight. "Where *is* Kit? Can he hear you?"

"God, no! What do you think I am? The kids are outside. Anyway, there's more. Di called Gabe to find out if it was true, and— damn that bastard!—he told her the DA had released the body. To him! To *Gabe!* He said he wanted Corey buried in the family plot next to Mark, and he's already scheduled the funeral. He's got no *right*—"

"Yes, he has, Lyn. Legally, anyway. When is the funeral going to be?"

"When! I don't—Tuesday. He told Di next Tuesday."

Conan leaned against the counter, eyes closed. "Damn. He doesn't give anyone much of a chance, does he?"

"A chance for what?"

"To convince someone to order an autopsy. Lyn, I'll—"

"To *order* an autopsy? I thought it was supposed to be done today!"

"I thought so too, but the ME and the DA and the State Police were all apparently satisfied with a superficial examination. The official line is accidental death."

"Accidental? What does that mean? That the police are finished with it? They aren't going to do anything to—"

"That's the situation at the moment. Lyn, I'll be there in ten minutes, and we'll discuss—"

"What's to *discuss?* I suppose the DA in this county is one of *Gabe's* pals!"

"Just wait till I get there. I'll explain the whole situation." There was an ominous silence in answer to that, and Conan said sharply,

"Lyn, did you hear me? *Lyn!*" Another silence, then a distinct click. Lyn had hung up.

Conan thrust the receiver at the dispatcher with a barely intelligible, "Thanks," then ran out the door.

CHAPTER 6

It was another misplaced summer day, and the holiday traffic enhanced the seasonal ambiguity. Conan impatiently tolerated the snail's pace as he drove south on Highway 101, but at the first opportunity he turned right and wound the narrow lanes of Hollis Heights, throwing gravel at every turn. At length he reached an old, two-story, silver-shingled house that commanded the highest point of the headland. Diane's yellow Rabbit was in the driveway, but, Conan noted, with feelings divided between anger and dread, Lyn Hatch's red motorcycle was conspicuous by its absence.

Diane waited for Conan at the front door. Her eyes seemed bruised, but the transcendent calm that had always graced her features was still intact. She said quietly, "Come in, Conan."

Melissa appeared at her side, reaching for her hand. Conan touched the child's golden hair. "Lissa, it's not fair for you to have to go through this. I'm sorry."

Melissa looked up at him with eyes as tear-bruised as her mother's. She said soberly, "We're gonna go stay with Grandpa and Grandma for a while."

Conan nodded, then, aware of the weight of the plastic bag in his hand, said, "Di, Earl asked me to give you these."

"Corey's things?" She put the bag on a chair in the entry hall, then hurriedly turned away from it and went into the living room, a sunny room full of comfortable old furniture and bright fabrics, scented with a profusion of plants. "Lissa, I need to talk to Conan. Why don't you go upstairs and start packing your things? Kit?"

The boy stood in a bay window methodically fitting wooden building blocks into the flat box open on the window seat. He didn't seem to hear Diane. Conan sat down near him on the window seat, trying to think of something to say. There was no hint of animation in those eyes that were so much like Corey's; the same sea hue.

"Kit, are you all right?" And what a meaningless question that was.

Kit carefully placed the last of the blocks in the box. "Lyn went away."

Conan glanced at Diane as she responded, "But he's coming back, Kit."

The boy asked, "When?"

She folded her arms against her body, mouth tight. "Lyn has *always* come back. Remember?"

Kit put the lid on the box. "Mom said *she* was coming back."

Conan winced as he reached out and covered Kit's small hand with his. "Kit, your mother *can't* come back. She would if she could. Lyn *can* come back, and he will." If he doesn't for this child's sake, Conan silently promised himself, I'll *bring* him back, one way or another.

If Kit was convinced, he gave no sign. Diane said to Melissa, "Maybe you can help Kit get his clothes packed."

Melissa nodded. "Kit? Come on, we gotta get our stuff ready to go."

He followed her listlessly, hugging the box to his chest. Diane watched them go, sighed, then waved Conan into the kitchen, where she poured two cups of coffee and put them on the table. She sank into a chair and leaned forward on her elbows, long fingers combing through her hair.

She said dully, "Kit's retreating, and I don't know how to reach him."

Conan sat down at the table and picked up his cup. "I wish I could help. What about Lyn? *Is* he coming back?"

She frowned, her composure shaken. "Damn him. Why did he have to leave *now?*"

"That's what I was going to ask you. Didn't he tell you where he's headed or when he'll be back?"

"No. All he told me is that he *had* to go. He had to 'take care of something.'"

"Gabe Benbow?"

"That's what I'm afraid of. The rational, enlightened scientist . . ." She shook her head sadly. "And underneath it, he's still heavy into the Western macho tradition. You and Lyn have a lot in common, really. He was brought up on a ranch in Eastern Oregon, too. Lyn's parents live near Brothers, and one of the first things his father taught him was how to use a rifle and how to hunt. He told me once he killed his last deer when he was fifteen, and something just seemed to turn over inside him. He hasn't touched a gun since. But there's still this thing about . . . oh, Conan, he's in so much pain, and he won't let himself do anything *unmanly* to ease it. Like crying. He's turning all the hurt into hate." She closed her eyes, then reached into the pocket of her Levi's for a handkerchief.

At the moment, Conan was hard put to feel any sympathy for Lyn. "Did he give you any hint of what he intends to do?"

"No. He doesn't own a gun now—that's some consolation—but he took his bedroll and backpack. He always carries basic camping equipment on his cycle. He could probably live off the land around here for months."

Conan tasted the steaming coffee gingerly. "Maybe a few days in the woods is what he needs now."

"Maybe it is. Did Lyn tell you Norman called about Gabe wanting custody of Kit?" Then, at Conan's nod, "Norman knows about the provision in Corey's will for Kit. He said he's sure that will carry more weight than any claim Gabe can make, but he suggested for Kit's sake—and mine—that we should go stay with my parents for a few days. They have a farm near Dundee. We'll be back Tuesday. For the funeral."

Conan asked, "Is that necessary?"

"Yes. I won't let Gabe turn it into a pious show. And I think for Kit and Lissa . . . you need some sort of ceremony, you know; something to separate the before from the after, so you can *deal* with the after. I *did* get my way—I mean, Corey's way—on one thing: her body will be cremated. That's what she wanted. She also wanted the ashes scattered at sea, but Gabe wouldn't go that far."

Conan stopped himself before bluntly repeating the word "cremated." His first inclination was to argue that cremation would end any hope of an autopsy, but there was no purpose to be served in discussing that with Diane.

He said, "I'm surprised Gabe agreed to cremation."

"I was too, but he didn't argue at all about it." She paused, frowning into her cup. "Conan, *was* Corey's death an accident?"

Conan hesitated over his answer only because he wasn't sure

how Diane would react. At length, he replied, "No, I don't think it was an accident."

"Do you think Gabe killed her?"

"I don't know. I'm going to try to find out."

"Yes, Lyn told me that. Can I help?"

"Well, one thing I have to be sure of is whether Corey told anyone about Kate's diary other than you, me, and Lyn."

"No, I'm sure she didn't. I was a little worried that she might tell Jonas, but I asked her afterward. She thought I was crazy to even suggest it."

"Jonas? When did she talk to him?"

"Oh, that was . . ." She frowned, pressing her fingers to her temples. "It was Thanksgiving Day. I mean, that evening. He came to the house and stayed about an hour. The kids and I joined in at first, then I thought of an excuse to leave Corey and Jonas alone for a while."

"Did Corey tell you what they talked about?"

"Yes. After he left and we got the kids in bed, she talked about it for a long time. She liked Jonas, you know, but she said you'd warned her about him." Diane gave Conan an oblique smile. "You said he's a con artist."

"I still say it. Corey didn't agree?"

"Well, she did, but I think she needed the warning. Anyway, Jonas told her he has cancer. A particular kind—osteoma, I think. Yes, that was it. He's been taking chemotherapy for it. He said he doesn't have any insurance, and he's nearly broke."

"And I suppose he needs an operation."

Diane gave Conan a sharp look, then laughed. "Yes. But cancer often *does* require surgery, and even con artists can get cancer."

Conan took a swallow of coffee. "*Or* osteoma—which is not a malignant condition. But it sounds right. Was Corey convinced?"

"Not really, although I think she wanted to give him the benefit of the doubt."

"What was he asking of her?"

Diane considered that, then, "Well, nothing, actually. He told her that Gabe—ever a forgiving Christian—promised to give him a cash payment of three hundred thousand dollars *in lieu* of any future claim on Gabe's estate. But it depends on the Baysea sale. The day Wines's check arrives, Gabe said he'll write a check to Jonas for three hundred thousand. God, isn't that typical? There's

no reason for it, except it's a power trip for Gabe. He could probably write a check for twice that amount any time and not even
miss it."

Conan's eyes were down to black slits. "Yes, it *is* typical, which
makes it entirely believable. It certainly gives Jonas a vested interest in the Baysea sale."

She picked up her cup, but only stared into it. "I wondered
about that—I mean, considering what Kate's diary would mean to
the sale. But Corey said it didn't even cross her mind to tell Jonas
about the diary, because she knew he'd go straight to Gabe with it,
and she hadn't talked to you and Lyn about it then. But she said
Gabe told Jonas she'd been spearheading ECon's campaign, and
she'd caused a lot of trouble and delays. She thought that was
funny. Gabe never seemed much troubled by anything she or
ECon did, and the only delay we caused was forcing Baysea to
obey the law."

"Which in Gabe's lexicon is defined as 'trouble.' So, she thought
Jonas was only worried about her causing more of the same kind of
trouble?"

Diane seemed to focus on her coffee and took a swallow. "Yes.
She said she was sure he didn't know about the diary—or about
Gabe forging the deed. I mean, she thought maybe Jonas had
either seen the diary—back before he left home, of course—or
Kate might have told him about the deed. But Corey said she was
sure he didn't know anything about it."

Conan didn't comment on that, and Diane nodded. "Yes, I
know, Conan. Corey wasn't very good at recognizing lies. Anyway,
her impression was that he just wanted her not to make any more
trouble. And she was having a hard time working it out. I mean,
she was wondering whether it wouldn't be better just to forget the
diary, the spit, the estuary—everything. But finally she said she
couldn't do that, not when she might have the means of saving it in
her hands. She said she couldn't spend . . . the rest of her life
with that on her conscience. And if Jonas really did need surgery,
there *had* to be other options open to him."

Conan tilted his chair back and crossed his arms. "Friday evening, did she call Gabe to let him know she was coming?"

"No. I think—well, she wasn't really sure she could face him.
When she finally decided she *had* to, I wanted to go with her, but
she said she thought it would be better if she talked to him alone.

She wanted to give him a chance to save face. If he knew what he was up against, maybe he'd give in without a fight, if he could make people think it was *his* idea. Oh, God, Conan, I should've called you and told you what she was doing! I should've—"

Conan reached across the table for her hand. "Diane, it was her choice to go, and you had no right to question or subvert it. You didn't know any more than she did the ultimate results of that choice."

After a moment, her grip on his hand relaxed. "I know that. I keep trying to remember it." She studied him for what seemed a long time, then, "You know, Corey loved you, Conan. In a very special way, she loved you."

"Yes, I . . . finally understood that." Then he rose, clearing his throat. "You'd better get yourself and the kids ready to go. It's a good idea, a change of scene."

She nodded. "I'll give you my folks' phone number, in case you need to reach me."

A memo pad was placed handy to the telephone on the sideboard. She wrote a number on it and handed the page to Conan, then opened a drawer and found a pair of keys on a metal ring. "These are the keys to the house. By the way, the rest of Kate's diaries are up in Corey's room."

"Thanks. I'll take them with me now. And I'd like to look at the . . . Corey's effects."

"You didn't need to ask my permission, Conan. Go ahead. I'd better check on the kids, and I'll get the diaries."

He nodded, frowning absently at the keys before he put them in his pocket. "Damn, that reminds me—Lyn went off with a set of *my* house keys."

She smiled at that. "He'll get them back to you—sooner or later."

Conan walked with her to the front hall, then when she went upstairs, he opened the plastic bag and removed its contents. Clothing. Jewelry, including Mark's diamond on its chain, a wristwatch, a Black Hills gold ring. A large, leather purse. A keyring with a Greenpeace whale medallion on it. The ribbon that had so inadequately bound her hair when he last saw her alive. He examined every piece of clothing, every pocket and seam; they smelled of seawater, and in some thicker folds hadn't yet dried. The contents of the purse were still soggy, and only illegible shadows remained in the small address book and check folder. He found nothing unusual or unexpected, and at length put everything back into the bag and left it on the chair, except for the billfold. The headache, which he pretended was only due to lack of sleep, was returning.

He heard Diane's steps on the stairs and met her halfway to take the carton she was carrying, and at the foot of the stairs put it down to look inside. It was filled with diaries of various sizes and designs, some with clasps, most marked with a year in gold.

Diane said, "There are thirty-six of them, beginning with 1940."

Conan pulled out a sheaf of envelopes thrust down at one side of the box. They were postmarked from cities all over the world, from Cairo to Sydney to Guadalajara to Ketchikan to Las Vegas. The addresses were typed, and there were no return addresses. They had been neatly cut open, but all were empty now.

He asked, "What are these?"

"Kate's secret benefactor." Diane knelt beside him. "Corey said Kate told her about them. They began arriving after Jonas left her in 1955. They came at odd intervals, and every one contained cash —anywhere from twenty to five thousand dollars. See—Kate marked the amounts on the backs of the envelopes."

"From Jonas?"

"Kate thought so, but there was never a letter with them or any explanation."

Conan raised an eyebrow, then lifted the box as he rose. "Well, I'll get out of your way. Oh—I didn't find anything of interest in Corey's things, but her billfold was there. I left it out on the table. There was about two hundred dollars in it. You may need it; you and the kids."

Diane frowned. "Two hundred—Corey didn't usually carry that much cash. . . ." She paused, eyeing Conan, then after a moment she nodded. "Thanks, Conan. I mean, for telling me about it."

"Does Lyn know where you're going?"

"Yes. Don't worry, I'll let you know if I hear from him."

"Please do. And tell him—never mind. Diane, take care. Call me if it'll help. Any time."

"I will. Good luck, Conan."

CHAPTER 7

Conan kicked the utility room door shut behind him; his hands were occupied with the carton of Kate Benbow's diaries. A heady perfume wafted from the kitchen: rib roast cooking. Upstairs, the vacuum cleaner roared over an off-key rendition of "The Battle Hymn of the Republic." He took the carton to the library, retraced his steps down the passageway to the kitchen for a cup of coffee, then detoured into the living room. At the foot of the stairs, he shouted up to Mrs. Early. She emerged from his bedroom, her anxious frown giving way to a smile.

"Mr. Flagg! Didn't figure to see *you* again today."

"You won't. At least, not much of me. I'll be in the library, and I am *not* to be disturbed. If the house catches fire, call the fire department."

She laughed, then her mouth made an "O" of consternation. "Speakin' of fire, I better check that roast!"

Conan was already on his way to the library, and by the time Mrs. Early descended the stairs, the three-inch-thick, carved-wood door had closed behind him.

It was a narrow room with a high ceiling sloping up to the obligatory west wall of windows. Across from the hall entrance, a sliding glass door opened onto a pine-shaded patio, but there was no other break in the bookshelves that lined the three walls, except the fireplace to the right of the hall door. To accommodate the art works he found essential in any room where he spent a great deal of time, the pattern of shelves was broken with niches for paintings or small sculptures. He paused, as he always did on entering this room, to look to the corner to his left, where a brooding, life-sized, armored figure looked back out of a skull-helmet. He had known the painter—she had all but died in his arms—and he knew the figure did not represent death *per se.* Yet today it was hard to see any other meaning in it.

He went to the desk near the glass door, sat down and lighted a cigarette, swiveled to get a Portland directory off the shelf behind him, then pulled the phone toward him. He spent the next half hour calling Earth Conservancy officers whom he knew to be friends of Lyn Hatch's. None had heard from him, but all promised to inform Conan if they did.

Conan's next series of calls went to Westport, but District Attorney Owen Culpepper and Deputy Medical Examiner Dr. Gregory Feingold were not within range of any telephone on this Saturday afternoon. Conan was left with no recourse beyond recording his name and number on various answering devices. When he called Gabe Benbow, he was so frustrated with recorded messages and unanswered rings, he was at first surprised when he got an answer. It was Gabe himself.

"This is Conan Flagg, Gabe."

"So? What d'you want?"

"Just some answers. About Corey."

"I got nothing to say about Corey. She's dead, Lord have mercy on her soul, and there's nothing anybody can do about it."

Conan thought, would you change that fact if you could? But he said levelly, "Unfortunately, there are still some unanswered questions about her death."

"There aren't any unanswered questions according to the *law.*"

"Oh yes, you certainly made sure of that."

A suspicious pause, then, "What do you mean by that?"

"Just that I've never known Owen Culpepper to act so expeditiously. And on a Saturday, too. Gabe, the law may be satisfied, but I'm not, and sooner or later you *will* discuss those unanswered questions with me."

Conan was treated to a fusillade of definitely unchristian commentary, then, "Flagg, you tend to your own damn business, and Corey Benbow ain't it! I got nothing to say to you about Corey or anything else—not now, not ever!"

With that, the line abruptly went dead. Conan took a deep breath and hung up. Obviously, prying any information out of Gabe required more leverage than Conan could bring to bear now. Jonas. There, if instinct served, was surely the weak link.

Conan leafed through the local directory, then punched out a number.

"Blue Heron Inn, may I help you?"

"Jeananne, this is Conan Flagg. Would you connect me with the bar? Who's on duty now?"

"Right now, it's Harry."

"You must be short-handed." Harry Jens owned the Blue Heron Inn, and Conan knew his aversion to bartending.

Jeananne sighed wearily. "Short-handed? About three people short, is all. Hang on, I'll ring the bar."

After a brief wait, a hoarse voice came on the line with an impatient, "Yeah?"

"Conan Flagg, Harry. Sorry to bother you, but I'm looking for Jonas Benbow. Do you know him?"

"Sure, I know him. He's spending most of his vacation here, looks like. But he's not here now."

"Damn. Who was tending bar Friday night?"

"Friday? You mean last night? *I* was. Flu! How come people always wait for a holiday to come down with flu?"

"That's one of the great mysteries of life in a tourist-based economy. Was Jonas there last night?"

"No. He was here in the afternoon, but I didn't see him last night. You want me to give him a message if he comes in today?"

"Uh—no. In fact, I'd rather you didn't tell him I was asking about him."

Jens replied equably, "Sure, Conan. Whatever. See you around."

Conan hung up, then leaned back, frowning. So now he had another lie from Gabe to add to his list of so-called evidence: Jonas had *not* been partaking of demon rum at the Blue Heron Friday night. But even if he had been home—and Conan wondered if Jonas would call Gabe's house home—Jonas couldn't have been one of the "everybody" who *"left* hours ago."

The carton of Kate's diaries waited on the floor by the desk, but Conan made no move toward it. Instead, he reached for the Portland phone book again. He was thinking of Mrs. Early's account of Leonard Moskin's unfortunate marriage. Under "Moskin" he found no likely listing, but under the Cs he hit the jackpot: "Carr Nora 2222 Vista Av Apt 858."

He waited through four rings, then a husky, feminine voice came on with a curt, "Hello!"

"Is this Mrs. Nora Carr Moskin?"

"No. This is Ms. Nora Carr. The *ex* Mrs. Moskin."

"Oh, I'm sorry, Ms. Carr. The listing—well, that's not important. I'm W. Cameron Kluzinovski of the Northwestern Credit Research Systems Institution, Incorporated, and I'd appreciate a few minutes of your time."

"You're *who?* What's this about?" Nora seemed to have begun the happy hour early; her sibilants tended to slur.

Conan repeated his fake identity, running the words together, then added, "We're conducting a routine inquiry on Mr. Leonard Moskin, and I understand you—"

"Oh, a credit check on Leo!" At that, she laughed loudly. "What d'you wanta know about ol' Leo? Just ask, buddy, and it's yours, that son of a bitch!"

Conan's surprised hesitation was genuine, but he maintained his crisp tone as he explained, "Well, Ms. Carr, we understand that since the dissolution of your marriage, Mr. Moskin has been making regular alimony payments in accordance with the court ruling in the case of—"

"Sure, sure. He's been paying, all right! Up till three months ago, anyway. And you can put this down in your records: ol' Leo is three goddamn months behind as of now! Y'know what that means? Nearly ten thou! How's he expect me t'pay my rent? Or my car payments, or my—"

"Mr. Moskin hasn't discussed his, uh, refusal to pay—"

Again, the harsh laugh. "Buddy, ol' Leo didn't *refuse* to pay. He's just busted right now—so *he* says."

"Then he *has* contacted you about—"

"Sure he did. Called a couple of days ago. It was Thanksgiving Day, yet. Says he's got some deal on the fire, and he'll send my money—*with* interest—by December tenth. He damn well *better*, or I'll have him back in court so fast, he won't know what hit him, and he'll be lucky to come out with the clothes on his back! Not that Leo without his clothes'd be a treat for anybody. What'd you say your name—"

"You've been very helpful, Ms. Carr, and we appreciate it. Good-bye." And he hung up, smiling faintly. Definitely Kate Benbow would have been satisfied that Leo Moskin had met in Nora Carr a woman who made his worth all too clear.

He leaned back, looking out at the cloud-studded sky; the sun shimmered silkily on the sea, its acute angle verging toward the early evening of winter. He considered Nora's belligerent revelations, particularly the dates of Leo's call to her and his promised delivery of the overdue alimony. Thanksgiving Day, when Gabe Benbow had signed the papers for the Baysea sale, and December tenth, time enough for a check—or perhaps his reward would come in the form of cash—to reach Leo from Isaac Wines after the meeting of the Planning Commission.

But again, Conan realized, he was thinking of motive, when he didn't yet have a *corpus delicti*, nor any reason to think Moskin might have been one of Gabe's "everybody."

But he had to start somewhere.

And he had to start somewhere on Kate's diaries. He arranged the volumes on his desk by year. He could understand Corey's reluctance to read them; they were as personal as any written account could be, and probably no business of his. That thought reminded him of Gabe, and he resolutely picked up the first volume. He skimmed through the years 1940 to 1946 hurriedly. The latter was the year that twenty-one-year-old Katharine Donovan first met Jonas Benbow.

Even in youth, Kate demonstrated not only a clear eye, but a sense of humor that let her accept the Benbows' foibles—including Jonas's—with amused equanimity. She provided insight into the relationship between the two brothers: Jonas, his father's spoiled favorite, charming his way out of every predicament, obligation, and punishment, while Moses had to work assiduously for every crumb of approval. After Pearl Harbor, Jonas was drafted into the Army and at the end of the war returned a self-styled hero, although Kate knew he had spent most of the war in Hawaii and seen no real combat. Moses, on the other hand, *volunteered* the day war was declared, but was rejected by the Army because of his severe myopia. He spent the war years at the University of Oregon, where he acquired a degree in business administration and a wife.

Conan had passed the portentous hiatus of 1948 and reached the end of 1952, when he realized that the reason Kate's small, neat handwriting had become so difficult to read was that it was nearly dark both outside and in. He rose stiffly, then made his way through a blessedly empty house to the kitchen, where the roast was warming in the oven. He spent some time preparing his meal and selecting a Sokol Blosser Vineyards Cabernet Sauvignon. Then he took the sandwich and bottle back to the library and began 1953.

Corey had assured him that there were no further references in the diaries to Shearwater Spit, and before the evening was out, Conan had verified that. The diaries were simply a remote possibility that had to be explored, but the process became particularly painful after 1975, when Mark Benbow married Corella Danner. Corey became as vital a part of Kate's life as Mark and, after 1976, Christopher. The last entry was dated September 11, 1977, and its final paragraph read: "Corey and Mark are having a birthday dinner for me tomorrow. They're so dear and thoughtful. Mark's so lucky to have Corey, and I'm so lucky to have them both!"

Mark and Corey had been living in Westport at that time, and for Kate's birthday dinner, Mark had driven to Holliday Beach to pick up his mother, then that night driven her back home. Neither of them survived that short trip.

"Damn." Conan began piling the diaries back into the carton, but paused to study the envelopes that had contained Jonas's anonymous contributions. Or so Kate had believed, and Conan found that assumption reasonable. Jonas had shown at least some concern for her when he departed so precipitously. He had not only changed the deed to their house, making her sole owner, but left a thousand dollars in cash. Probably embezzled from the county, Kate surmised, but since she couldn't prove it, she decided, after much soul-searching, to apply it to tuition at the Oregon College of Education. All that had been carefully detailed in the diaries.

The envelopes had come at irregular intervals. Jonas apparently did well in Cairo in 1968. There were four envelopes that year, one—according to Kate's notation on the back—containing five thousand dollars. The last envelope came from Phoenix, Arizona, and the post date was August 10, 1977—a little over a month before Kate and Mark were killed. Conan considered it for a moment, frowning, then delved into his pants pocket for the paper on which Diane had written her parents' phone number.

Only after he heard the first ring did he remember to look at his watch, realizing that eleven was a late hour for farmers. Perhaps that explained why it was Diane who answered.

Conan identified himself, then, "I hope your parents aren't light sleepers."

He heard a brief laugh. "No, and they're upstairs where they can't hear the phone. So are Lissa and Kit."

"How are they?"

"Better. Especially Kit. The change of scene *is* good for them, and Mom and Dad are expert at spoiling grandchildren. Conan, have you heard from Lyn?"

"No, and I assume you haven't."

"Not a word."

"Well, I've alerted some of his ECon friends in Portland. He'll turn up somewhere sooner or later. Di, I was looking at these envelopes from Kate's anonymous benefactor. Do you know if any arrived *after* Kate's death?"

"I don't think so. At least, I don't remember Corey saying anything about it. Kate made her executor of her will—I mean, an alternate; Mark was first. Anyway, Corey saw all the mail that came to Kate after . . . after the accident. And I was helping her, so if there'd been—wait a minute."

Conan paused with his cigarette a few inches from his mouth. "What, Di?"

"There *was* an anonymous envelope, but it was addressed to Corey, not to Kate."

"It was from Jonas?"

"Well, Corey thought it must be. Kate had told her about the others. It had around three hundred fifty dollars in it."

"Do you remember how the envelope was addressed? I mean, was it to Corey in care of Kate, or directly to Corey?"

"I'm sure it was addressed to Corey in Westport."

"How would he know her address? I suppose it was in the Westport newspaper when Kate and Mark died."

"Yes, but Jonas told Corey he just found out about Kate and Mark—"

"—from that talkative lady on the bus, yes. Makes you wonder, doesn't it? And it makes me wonder if Jonas didn't know more about Baysea than he's admitting. And it makes me wonder about his fortuitous arrival on Thanksgiving Day."

Diane said wearily, "Well, Conan, you pegged him for a con artist."

"True, but it's discouraging to realize your best hope for the truth is probably a habitual liar. Well, try to get some sleep, Di."

"You too, Conan."

CHAPTER 8

At noon on Sunday, Conan relaxed in a canvas chair on the front deck of Gabe Benbow's house. The north wind was astringently cool, carrying the scent of cold ocean currents; the sky was an intense blue, brushed with cirrus clouds; and the sea, under that blue influence, had the pellucid light of a milky aquamarine. Over Sitka Bay, gulls scouted the shallows, flashing white with every turn.

Conan had been waiting for half an hour, and the only living presences around him were indigenous to the place. Gabriel Benbow was where he always was at this time on Sunday: in the first pew of the Emmanuel Methodist Church.

Conan wondered what Gabe prayed for in that pew.

At length, he heard a muted rumble and turned to watch the stately approach of Gabe's Continental. Jonas was driving, and Gabe was in the back seat, as if he were being chauffeured. Jonas didn't turn into the garage south of the house; he was being prodded by Gabe, who had seen Conan's XK-E near the foot of the flagstone walk. Before the Continental came to a full stop, Gabe was out and storming up the walk, looking like a choleric pallbearer in his black, vested suit.

"Damn you, Flagg! How'd you get past that gate?"

Conan rose and thrust his hands in his jacket pockets. "What gate?"

"The gate on my property line!" Gabe's bony jaw jutted ominously. "The gate that was closed and *padlocked!*"

"Oh, yes. Hello, Jonas. We haven't been properly introduced, but I'm sure you know who I am by now."

Jonas had sauntered up the walk, tanned features crinkled in a bemused smile as he eyed Conan, but Gabe didn't give him a chance to speak.

"Flagg, this is *trespass*, and if you don't get out of here *now*, I'm going to call the sheriff!"

"Gabe, I'm no threat to you—not if you told Sergeant Roddy the truth about Friday night." Gabe's jutting chin pulled in, and his eyes seemed to retreat into slitted folds. Conan added, "You always claimed to care about Corey. So did I. Why do you refuse to talk to me about her death?"

Jonas restlessly rattled the keys in his pocket. "This sounds like a private conversation. Pa, the car's making a funny sound. Fuel intake, probably. I better have Rafe Driskoll look at it." And he set off down the walk with studied nonchalance.

"Jonas!" Gabe turned on him. "I know what you're up to! Nothing wrong with that car. You just want to go to the Blue Heron and swill *booze!* Can't you even stay sober on *Sunday?* 'Remember the sabbath day, to keep it holy.' "

Conan cut in, "What about bearing false witness, Gabe? Isn't that as heinous a sin on the sabbath? What about Kate Benbow's posthumous testimony? What happened to it?"

Gabe glared at Conan, but it was a moment before he got his bluster back in gear, and Jonas took advantage of the distraction to make his exit.

Gabe spluttered, "*I* don't know what happened to Kate's diary. I never saw the damn thing, and I—"

"Then how did you know I was talking about a *diary?*"

"You—you *said*—"

"No, I didn't use that word." Conan smiled coolly. "Who else was here—other than you and Jonas—when Corey confronted you with that diary Friday night?"

"I told you, nobody else was—*Jonas!*" He spun around, hands in fists, at the sound of the Continental's motor, but Jonas was by now well out of range of his righteous wrath.

Conan observed, "You'd think he'd show more filial respect, since he has three hundred thousand dollars at stake here."

Gabe turned slowly, pale eyes burning. "Who told you about that? My God, it's *my* business what goes on between me and my son! Get out of here, Flagg!"

Conan decided that this dialogue had ceased to be fruitful. At least he was sure now that Gabe *had* seen Kate's diary, and that he *had* agreed to pay Jonas $300,000.

Conan started down the walk. "I'll be back, Gabe—unless you decide to come to *me* with the truth."

"Get out! Get off my property!"

Conan was getting, but when he reached his car, he put his retreat on temporary hold. Another car was approaching: a silver-blue Cutlass. Nina Gillies.

Since the XK-E was parked next to the walk, Nina couldn't reach the house without passing him, but she made no attempt to avoid him. She wore a silk shirtwaist dress of pale blue, as if she had chosen it to match her car. Even the suede attaché case seemed part of the ensemble. Her smile was almost warm.

"Well, Conan, what brings you all the way out here?"

He returned her smile. "Oh, it's not so far. I just came down to talk to Gabe." He glanced back at the house; Gabe had gone inside, but one of the drapes was pushed aside a few inches.

Nina gave her lilting laugh. "You're not still trying to change his mind about the Baysea sale?"

"That seems to be rather a dangerous undertaking."

Her smile faltered. "What does *that* mean?"

He studied her, then looked seaward. "Poor Gabe, he just can't control his temper. Besides, he's—what?—eighty years old. Not as sharp as he once was, you know; lets things slip out now and then." Conan turned to face her. "Otherwise, I'm sure he'd never have mentioned *your* name."

Nina's chin came up with a skeptical lift of her eyebrows. "*My* name? I hope he had something good to say."

"Why wouldn't he? You and Isaac Wines are going to make him even richer. And I don't suppose the commission is going to hurt *your* bank account. What are you getting—a standard six percent? That's two hundred forty thousand dollars."

"As a matter of fact, I'm getting *ten* percent on this deal. What's your game? What do you really want, Conan?"

"I want the truth."

"The *police* are satisfied. Why aren't you?"

Conan was hard put not to smile. *The police.* Now he could be sure that what worried Nina about Gabe's bandying her name about had something to do with Corey's death.

"Nina, what's your version of what happened Friday night?"

Again the fluting laugh. "Friday night I was at home watching television."

" 'Dallas'?"

"What? I don't remember, and I damned sure don't have to tell you, even if I did." She turned and started to walk away, then stopped, her perfect features marred with unflattering lines of tension. "You've got a long nose, Conan. Just keep it out of other people's business!"

Conan watched her stride up the walk, the wind blowing her skirt around truly elegant legs. He sighed and got into his car, noting as he turned on the ignition that Gabe had the door open for Nina when she reached the house.

The Blue Heron Inn had a plastic/polyester anonymity that made its studied rusticity all the more distasteful to Conan, but the view of the bay from the west windows compensated for the decor. The dining room was noisily packed with Sunday diners, and the bar had few empty tables. Jonas Benbow had found one, however; a window table, in fact, where he slumped over a beer. He didn't seem surprised when Conan sat down across the table from him.

"Well, Mr. Flagg, did Pa finally drive you out?"

"Our conversation was short and *not* sweet. And you needn't be so formal. The name is Conan." He saw a waitress approaching and asked Jonas, "Can I buy you a drink?"

"Why, thanks, Conan." Then when Conan had ordered his Old Forester, Jonas said, "Double scotch rocks, Jeananne. Chivas Regal." He smiled at Conan and pushed his beer aside, then turned to look out the window. "Real pretty spot, here. Look, you can see the old man's house. Damn, he sure blew a bundle on that thing."

"Gabe can afford it."

Jonas gave a snort of a laugh. "Damn right. But I still remember the first house we lived in when I was a kid. A drafty old shack on a stump farm up the Sitka River. When it rained, I swear there was more water inside than out."

Conan laughed politely as he leaned back to light a cigarette. "I suppose things have changed a lot around here since you left."

"Yes, things have changed. Some things, anyway."

"It must've been quite a shock finding out that Kate and Mark were dead."

"A shock? Well, that's one way to put it." He loosed a sigh, his malleable features assuming a cast of regret. "Kate was the main reason I finally decided I had to come home and . . . make my peace. She was quite a woman."

"Yes, I know."

Jonas eyed Conan intently, but he was distracted by the waitress bringing their drinks. After she departed, he reverently raised his glass and sipped the whiskey. "Oh, damn, that's nectar of the gods. Did you know Kate?"

"No. I spent the afternoon and evening yesterday reading her diaries. Of course, one of them is missing. 1948."

Jonas's gaze flicked down to his glass. "Is it, now? Must've made interesting reading, anyway."

Conan took a long drag on his cigarette. "Not as interesting as I'd hoped. But you must've read some of them."

"Well, I admit I did take a peek at a couple of them when Kate and I were first married. She didn't mind."

"Then you knew about Gabe's doubtful claim to Shearwater Spit before Corey presented the diary Friday night."

Jonas only laughed. "Conan, I don't know what you're talking about. I didn't see Corey Friday night. I was here at the Blue Heron. You can ask the bartender."

"I did, Jonas."

He barely missed a beat at that. "Well, he can't keep track of everybody who comes in and out of here."

"You'd be surprised what a good bartender can keep track of. Besides, Gabe already let it slip about you and Nina being at the house."

Conan got no revealing reaction from that probe. Jonas only smiled as he raised his glass, putting down half its contents in one swallow.

"I hear you're a private eye on the side, Conan. I mean eye as in 'I,' and that stands for investigator. So, what are you investigating?"

Conan paused, then chose to ignore the question. "Corey Benbow was quite a woman, too, and she liked you, Jonas. She wanted to be your friend, and she wanted you to be a real grandfather to Kit."

Jonas squinted out at the bay. "Well, I'm glad to hear . . . damn. You know, she made me feel like—well, like she and Kit could be real family." Then he roused himself and faced Conan. "Is that what you're investigating? Corey's death?"

"Yes."

"I thought the police had settled it. I mean, they—"

"The police—and the DA—are satisfied. I'm not. Too many lies were told about Friday night, and too many people had too much to gain by silencing her. Including you. That three hundred thousand Gabe promised you is contingent on the Baysea sale."

Jonas considered that, then emptied his glass. "You sound like you're talking about *murder.*"

"Maybe I am."

For a moment Jonas was silent, then he leaned forward. "You know, Conan, you're wrong about that. But, like you said, I've got a lot to gain here. Maybe more than money, if the doctors—well, never mind. What I'm saying is, it doesn't look to me like it's in my best interests—financially, that is—to talk to *you* about this. I mean, seeing how my old man feels about you, and how that three hundred thou is coming from him."

That, Conan thought with a wry smile, was as nice a touch as he'd heard. He extricated a blank check from his billfold. "Have you heard of the Ten-Mile Ranch, Jonas?"

"Well, as a matter of fact, I have. Your father owned it, didn't he?"

"And I'm now majority stockholder. Do you have a pen?"

Jonas already had a ballpoint in hand. Conan began writing, adding, "I heard about your illness, Jonas. Hell of a thing, cancer, but they're coming up with new treatments every day. Expensive, of course."

"Conan, you wouldn't *believe* how expensive. But my doctor says if I can have this new operation . . ."

"Sure, Jonas." Conan slid the check across the table to him. "It's for thirty thousand dollars. That's only a tenth of your potential legacy from Gabe, but it should buy a damned fancy surgery."

Jonas's mouth went slack as he stared at the check; then he grinned broadly and glanced at his watch. "Conan, if there *is* a heaven, this'll send you straight there."

"No doubt. By the way, you'll notice I dated it December tenth." If that date was good enough for Leo Moskin, it should certainly be good enough for Jonas.

Apparently Jonas had not noticed the date. He frowned at the check, then shrugged. "Well, I didn't plan on leaving Taft County soon, anyway."

"Glad to hear that. Your glass is empty." Conan caught Jeananne's eye and signaled for another drink for Jonas, then reached for his cigarette and took a contemplative puff. "You were saying I'm wrong about Corey being murdered."

"Afraid so. Well, not afraid. *Glad* to say so." He secreted the check in his billfold and stuffed it in his back pocket. "But you're right, there's been a few white lies told here and there. That wasn't to cover anything like murder. It's just that Pa wasn't alone like he said when Corey came Friday night."

"I know that much. You were there and Nina Gillies. And . . . France and Moses." Those names were stabs in the twilight, if not total dark. He brazened it out with, "What was it, a victory celebration?"

"Well, more like a strategy meeting. And you missed one. Somebody *else* was there." He smiled enigmatically.

Conan had to ask. "Who else, Jonas?"

"Leo Moskin."

Conan took a moment for a bracing swallow of whiskey. "Why was Leo there?"

"Oh, they were talking about the Planning Commission meeting. I guess there's one commissioner they were worried about. But it *was* kind of a victory celebration, too. Anyway, you can understand why nobody wanted it spread around that Leo was there. Might look like he was a bit biased when the Planning Commission decision on Baysea came down."

"A bit. You were present all during this strategy meeting *cum* victory celebration?"

"Sure. Of course, this little party hadn't been going on more than half an hour before Corey showed up."

"When did she arrive?"

"Let's see, it must've been about eight-thirty. Oh, thank you, darlin'." That was for the waitress as she served his drink. He took time to taste it, waiting until she was well out of earshot before he went on. "Nobody seemed too happy to see Corey, and she didn't seem happy to see so many people there. It was funny, really, everybody walking on egg shells, being so damned polite. France fixed Corey a drink, just to be polite, and Corey drank it—part of it —just to be polite. Black russians. France acts like the damned drink was invented last fall when they were in Mexico—for *her* benefit. She fixed black russians for everybody that night. Except Pa. He doesn't drink—so he says. Anyway, Corey finally said she had to talk to Pa alone—something about the spit—but he was feeling ornery, as usual; kept saying he didn't have any secrets from the rest of us. They argued a while, till Corey got disgusted and said, okay, they could all damn well hear it."

"The diary? She read the November twenty-first entry?"

"Yes." A sigh, then, "She read it, all right."

"Did she let anyone handle the diary?"

Jonas shook his head and downed more scotch. "No. Well, she let *me* look at it so I could verify the handwriting; make sure it was really Kate's." He glanced at his watch again. "As soon as I gave it back to her, she put it in her purse."

"How did the others react to the reading?"

Jonas snorted and rolled his eyes upward. "The shit hit the fan then, everybody hollering and calling names. And France—damned if she didn't pick up Corey's drink and throw it in her face!"

Conan frowned. "She *what?*"

"Just like in the old movies—slosh, right in the face. Well, Corey went to the ladies room to clean up, and—"

"Did she take her purse with her?"

"Sure she did. She never let go of that thing once while she was there. Anyway, Corey went to the john, and Moses took France out to the kitchen for a little talking-to. God, she was mad. Not hysterical or anything like that; just mad as hell. That woman—I don't know how Moses has stood it all these years. But, you know, I think he loves her. Meanwhile, Nina got Leo and Pa calmed down. And me. Just for your information, I *didn't* know about that forged deed before. Must've read the wrong diaries back when Kate and I were together. Nina's idea was for us to go along with Corey; agree to anything, then later—well, maybe we could get hold of the diary."

It took some concentration for Conan to keep his voice steady. He asked, "Didn't anyone consider the possibility that Corey had made copies of the pertinent passage?"

Jonas shrugged. "Sure. Leo did the considering. Damn, the fatter that man gets, the more he worries. Ol' Leo used to be—well, he'd take chances just for the hell of it, just to see what he could get away with."

"What was the upshot of his consideration?"

"Not much. Nina had asked Corey if she made any copies, and Corey said she hadn't. Gabe told Leo—hell, I can still remember the words: 'Corey's such a damn fool, she *wouldn't* make any copies.' I figure he was right, too." He looked sharply at Conan, as if he hoped for verification.

Conan gave him nothing. He took a last puff on his cigarette and stubbed it out. "Perhaps Corey *was* a fool by Gabe's standards, but she did show the diary to other people, not all of whom are as naïve as she was. Go on with your story."

Jonas hesitated, no doubt thinking about the implied existence of copies, then took up his narrative again. "Let's see—oh, Nina went to the kitchen to tell Moses and France the plan. Then she told France she could at least fix another one of her damn drinks for Corey."

"You could hear what she said?"

"Not every word, but the kitchen doesn't have a real door; just those swinging, saloon-type things. Well, after a while, France and Moses came back to the living room, then Nina brought Corey's drink out a few minutes later and put it on the coffee table. And another drink for France. Nina said she figured France needed it, but that wasn't exactly a friendly gesture. Those two women don't seem to care much for each other. Too much alike, I think. Well, Corey came out of the bathroom, and everybody was real polite again."

"Where was everyone sitting at this point?"

"Sitting?" That took some study. "You know the way the furniture's laid out? There's the two couches facing each other and at right angles to the fireplace, then there's that burl coffee table between the couches—"

"And I assume Gabe's recliner is still at the west end of the table: the head of the table, so to speak."

"Where else? So, Pa was in his recliner, and I was on the couch to his left, closest to him, and Leo was at the far end. Corey sat down between us. On the other couch, France was next to Pa, then Moses, and Nina at the far end."

"Was that the seating arrangement from the time Corey arrived, or did it change at any point?"

Jonas seemed to find these questions odd, but he replied with the tolerance of the indebted, "Nothing changed. That's how we were sitting before she came, and she took the only open spot. After France gave her that Kahlúa shower, everybody just naturally seemed to go back to their old places. Of course, Leo and Pa and me stayed put the whole time."

"After Corey rejoined the festivities, what happened?"

"Nina said she'd talk to Wines and see if he wouldn't be satisfied with leaving the spit and bay shore for a preserve or whatever, if he could go ahead and develop the rest of the land to the south. Pa said he'd take the ECon offer for the spit, if Corey promised not to go to court with the diary. Conan, it was all BS, you know, just to buy time."

"But Corey believed it." That wasn't a question.

"Sure, she believed it, and she left believing it."

"She left then?" He raised an eyebrow, then at Jonas's nod, "Was she alone?"

Jonas laughed. "Of course she was alone. She hadn't made herself too popular, you know."

"Yes. I know. What time was it when she left?"

"Oh, maybe nine-thirty." As if the mention of time served as a reminder, he glanced at his watch, and Conan's curiosity was aroused; this wasn't the first time he'd seen Jonas check the time, as if he were worried about an imminent appointment.

Conan unobtrusively looked at his own watch—1:17—as he asked, "Did Corey finish her second drink?"

"Mm? Well, I don't think she *finished* it. Didn't seem to be much of a drinker."

"She wasn't. Does France load her black russians?"

Jonas shrugged. "No, probably a standard mix. Pony of Kahlúa to two of vodka."

"So, Corey consumed about three, possibly four, ounces of alcohol over a period of an hour. That might be enough to make her a little fuzzy, but not drunk."

"Oh, you're thinking about the DUI the police are trying to lay on her. She *did* seem—well, not too steady."

Conan studied Jonas's lined, tanned, oddly flaccid face. There was nothing he had said so far that Conan rejected out of hand; in fact, all of it had the solid feel of truth, and undoubtedly part of it *was* true. A good con artist always builds his edifice of fabrication on a foundation of truth.

"So, Corey left the house then, to die within a mile. What happened to the remaining celebrants?"

"There wasn't much celebrating. They muddled around, trying to figure out what to do about the diary. Didn't come up with much. They all left within half an hour."

"When was the conspiracy of silence evolved?"

"What do you mean?"

"The story about Gabe being alone when Corey arrived."

"Oh, well, not until after Pa found out about the accident. He figured with Corey dead, he didn't have to worry about the diary anymore, but he damned sure wasn't going to tell the police that Leo Moskin had been there. I think he went too far, saying *nobody* was there. But maybe he was right. This way, the police didn't question Moses or France or Nina. Or me. You get too many people involved, that just raises the odds on somebody slipping up."

Conan lifted his glass in a mocking toast. "So it does. And Gabe called the other conspirators after he told his story to the police Saturday morning?"

"Right. So, you see, this . . . conspiracy didn't have anything to do with murder. I swear to God it didn't."

Conan gave him a direct look, which he met staunchly. "All right, Jonas. What do Gabe *et al.* intend to do about the diary now?"

"What do you mean? The police didn't find it, did they? It's probably sunk in the mud at the bottom of the bay."

"I doubt that."

"Well, where else would it be?"

Jonas asked that with such earnestness, Conan had to laugh. "That's a good question." He started to rise, then, "By the way, that donation to the Jonas Benbow Surgical Fund has a few strings attached. If you try to leave the area without telling me, or if I find out you've lied to me, *or* if you tell any of the other conspirators about our conversation today, I'll stop payment before you can get to a bank."

Jonas nodded, unconcerned. "Conan, don't worry. You can trust me."

"That's why I came to you first." As Conan left the table, he saw that Jonas was again looking at his watch.

Conan left the Blue Heron, and even went so far as to drive two miles up 101 to the Sitka River road. There he made a U-turn and returned to the Inn, drove around the north end, and parked by the kitchen entrance.

There was a pay telephone in the restaurant's foyer. Conan had noted its location on his way out, and noted as well that it was near the corner of the short hallway into the dining room. A person could stand on the dining room side of the corner and easily hear what was being said into that phone without being seen by the caller. Conan planned to do exactly that. He entered the restaurant through the kitchen, where the cooks and dishwashers were too busy to notice him; the dining room staff was equally preoccupied, and Conan reached his chosen post without having to offer a word of explanation.

". . . sorry I'm late, Mr. Belasco. I, uh, got sort of hung up."

Conan leaned against the wall, trying to look like he was waiting for someone, and trying not to smile too broadly. He recognized the voice: Jonas Benbow.

". . . don't worry. Everything's going even better than I expected. In fact, I'll have part of it for sure by the tenth. Right. What? Well, I, uh, can't be sure when, but you don't need to worry, Mr. Belasco. Okay."

Conan frowned over that enigmatic conversation, then straightened when he heard the receiver click into its cradle. The next sound was a coin chinking into the slot, then within half a minute, Jonas's voice again: "France? I've got to talk to Moses—"

The connection was abruptly broken. Conan had stepped around the corner and pressed the cradle down. He smiled into Jonas's slack-jawed face and observed, "Jonas, you have just forfeited thirty thousand dollars."

Jonas's shoulders slumped with a long exhalation of breath, but after a moment he laughed and shrugged.

"Well, like they say, easy come—"

"—easy go, yes. What was that other call about?"

Jonas responded with a cold stare and the words Conan seemed to be hearing all too often lately: "That's none of your business." Then he added in a more conciliatory tone, "I mean, it's got nothing to do with anything here."

"Something in Phoenix, then?"

"It was my bookie," Jonas said with a sly smile. But the smile didn't last. "You want your check back?"

"Oh, you might as well keep it for a while. Who knows, you might even manage to redeem it. Come on."

"Redeem—what do you mean?" He caught up with Conan just outside the door and stayed with him around the north end of the restaurant, but when Conan turned the next corner, Jonas came to a halt. "Now, wait a minute—what's going on?"

Conan looked around and saw Jonas standing white-faced, his hands in fists. He was, quite simply, afraid.

Conan asked, "For God's sake, did you think I was going to redeem that check out of your flesh and blood? Damn, you must've met some interesting people on your many travels." He motioned toward the Jaguar. "My car. You and I are going for a drive down to Westport, and the only reason I'm taking you along is so I can keep an eye on you. No more phone calls, no conversations with anyone but me."

Jonas willingly got into the car when Conan unlocked the door for him. "Is this how I redeem that check?"

Conan got in and started the motor. "Well, it might at least be a beginning."

"All *right!* Damn, this car's a little beauty. They're collector's items now, you know."

"So are parts for it. But it's the hyacinth in my life."

"Yeah. How come we're going to Westport?"

"Oh, it's a nice day. Seems like as good a time as any to pay a friendly call on Leo Moskin."

CHAPTER 9

The twenty-five-mile drive down the coast to Westport was particularly pleasant on this warm, crystal-clear day, and Jonas proved an entertaining companion, regaling Conan with stories of his world travels. He had indeed met a number of "interesting" people, many of whom lived by codes not written in the laws of any land.

In Westport, Conan stopped at a gas station to ask the way to Leo Moskin's house. The attendant directed him to a gravel road striking west from the highway. After winding through Westport's outskirts, then a stretch of uninhabited pine woods, it ended at length at Moskin's house on a promontory overlooking the beach. Conan wondered if Leo hadn't also resorted to mail-order architecture. Like its owner, the house was large and imposing—a two-story, bastardized French Provincial. Apparently, Leo was having a party, judging from the number of cars parked along the circular drive.

Conan stopped the XK-E well away from the house, then said to Jonas, "Give me your shoes."

Jonas stared at him. "My what?"

"Your shoes. It's not that I don't trust you, Jonas, but if you do decide to hike out of here, stocking feet on this gravel should slow you down enough for me to catch up with you before you reach a phone."

At first Jonas seemed ready to argue, a flash of cold resentment in his eyes. Then he shrugged, even laughing as he removed his shoes. "Do I get them back shined?"

"Worry first about getting them back at all." Conan got out and locked the shoes in the trunk of his car. Jonas offered a smile and a wave as he departed.

On his way to the house, Conan saw the special license plates of a state senator on a Mercedes sedan. A political gathering, apparently. This was verified when the door was opened for him by an aggressively attractive woman in her late thirties, offering a white smile and the handshake that seemed reflexive in political circles. "Hi, I'm Lindsey Cross, the senator's campaign coordinator. Come in!"

Conan let her take his arm to guide him down a hallway toward a large living room in which a decorator had attempted to maintain the French Provincial motif. There was not, Conan noted, a single original painting on the walls. At least fifty people crowded the room, most forced to stand, drinks and canapés in hand, all with the unmistakable sleekness of wealth about them, and all talking, of necessity, loudly.

Lindsey Cross was still smiling. She shouted, "I'll tell the senator you're here, Mr. . . . ?"

Conan recognized the senator in a knot of supporters in the center of the room, but he was looking for the party's host. Leo Moskin, even in this crowd, was not hard to find.

"Sorry, Ms. Cross, but I didn't come to see the senator. I'd appreciate it, however, if you'd tell Mr. Moskin that Conan Flagg is here, and I'll either talk to him in private or here—in public."

Moskin opted for the former choice, and within five minutes, Conan was sitting across a desk from him in a room Moskin referred to as the library. There were a few bookshelves, some of which contained books in carefully matched sets, and there *was* an original painting here: a shiny seascape with breakers frozen forever in Kodachrome hues.

Moskin occupied a huge, leather-covered chair, dark eyes cold under heavy lids, his oddly childlike hands interlaced atop his belt. He asked tonelessly, "Can I offer you a drink?" He seemed relieved when Conan declined, and he wasted no more time on amenities. "What do you want, Mr. Flagg? I have guests, you know."

Conan crossed his legs and settled back in his chair. "Mr. Moskin, you have some influence with Owen Culpepper, don't you?"

"I've . . . known Owen for a number of years, and I think I can say that he and I are . . . friends."

"Then perhaps you can tell me under what influence Owen was acting when he ordered the ME to make only a superficial examination of Corey Benbow's body, and when he released the body to Gabe Benbow within hours after the examination."

Moskin's jowled face remained expressionless, except for a further lowering of his eyelids. "I assure you, Mr. Flagg, Owen's decisions in the line of his official duties are in no way influenced by our friendship."

"And can you also assure me that you were not at Gabe Benbow's house Friday night to hear Corey's reading from Kate Benbow's diary?"

One of Moskin's index fingers twitched nervously, but his control was otherwise complete. "I haven't even seen Gabe Benbow for months, except in passing at the courthouse or that kind of thing. I most certainly was *not* at his house Friday or any other night, and, quite frankly, that business about a diary is gibberish."

Conan nodded. "Well, that's a good line to maintain for public consumption, but I *know* you were there—along with France and Moses, Nina Gillies, and, of course, Jonas, the returned prodigal."

"Mr. Flagg, there is no way you could *know* something that isn't true."

"Or something you think I can't prove?" Conan met Moskin's unwavering gaze with grudging admiration. The man had nerve and amazing control. But those were prerequisites in politics, and Leo had survived in that arena for half a century. Conan shifted ground slightly. "I understand there's a petition for your recall circulating in the county."

That at least brought one eyebrow up. "Yes, I've heard that, too. I suppose you were one of the first to sign it."

Conan laughed. "No, there were quite a few people rushing in ahead of me to sign. At any rate, it occurred to me that the people circulating the petition might be interested in learning that you had once misused your power as a notary public to help Gabe Benbow forge a deed."

Moskin's hands unlaced and came down on the arms of his chair. "What the hell's your game, Flagg? Blackmail? Is that it? If so, you're going about it in a very amateurish way."

"Then you've dealt with professionals in blackmail? No, my *game* isn't blackmail. It's worse than that. I was a friend of Corey Benbow's. I cared very much about her, and I intend to see justice done. You can't buy me out of that."

Moskin pushed himself to his feet and said curtly, "Very commendable, Mr. Flagg, but you're either misinformed or deluded. Either way, I have nothing more to say to you. Now, there's a deputy here today—for the senator's security, of course. Will it be necessary for me to call him?"

Conan recognized the obdurate facade of a stone wall. He rose and preceded Moskin into the hall. "No, that won't be necessary."

"Good. I'll see you to the door."

"That won't be necessary either."

Moskin forged ahead down the hall. "I understand you're a private investigator, Mr. Flagg. Seeing you to the door—and *out*— is only a matter of courtesy." When he reached the front door and opened it, he favored Conan with a smile. "Have a good day, Mr. Flagg."

Conan was caught without a suitably clever rejoinder, and when the door closed quietly, but firmly, he gave it a rueful laugh. He had never been thrown out of a place so adroitly.

As he walked back to his car, he wondered why Moskin was worried about having a private investigator loose in his house. Undoubtedly, there were records and correspondence there that Moskin wouldn't want made public, but the only thing of interest to Conan now was Kate's diary.

After a little consideration, however, Conan rejected that possibility. And with some relief. He didn't relish the thought of trying to circumvent Moskin's security system—evidence of which was visible at every door and window—and he knew that if he were caught, Moskin would see that he was prosecuted to the limit of the law. Perhaps that was the real point of that needle. At any rate, the risk wasn't worth taking. If Moskin had ever had the diary, it would have been destroyed by now.

Jonas was peacefully asleep when Conan reached the Jaguar. Conan retrieved his shoes from the trunk, and when he got into the car, handed them to his awakening passenger. "Here. Your feet will get cold."

"Mm? Oh. Thanks. Any luck with Leo?"

Conan said coolly, "Piece of cake, Jonas. You just have to know what buttons to push with people like Leo."

Jonas's eyes narrowed. "I'll be damned. Well, can we go back to the Blue Heron? I left Pa's car there, you know."

"We'll check it as we pass. Next, we're going to see if France and Moses are home."

It was nearly three o'clock when they reached France and Moses' home in Sanderling Point, an exclusive subdivision occupying the headland north of Sitka Bay. France had hired a real architect, and a good one; the house was a satisfying union of planes of glass played against slabs of cedar shingles. The landscaping was impressive, and France had no qualms about putting out potted flowers from the local florist when winter left her no other option, which explained the bright borders of pompon mums.

Conan wasn't interested in architecture or floral displays now, but in the maroon Cadillac waiting in the driveway, while Moses escorted France toward it. They were dressed too well for a casual afternoon drive, and Conan wondered if they were on their way to Moskin's party. He deliberately parked the Jaguar across the driveway, while Jonas tried to squeeze down out of sight, complaining, "For God's sake, you can't park *here!* They'll *see* me!"

Conan got out of the car, commenting absently, "I'll tell them you're being kidnapped and held for ransom."

As Conan approached the Cadillac, France observed shrilly, "Mr. Flagg, you're blocking our driveway!"

Conan leaned against a fender, arms folded. France was managing to look down on him—literally—with the help of her five-inch heels. The shoes gave her even more of an advantage over Moses, but no doubt he was used to it and not at all intimidated.

Certainly, he didn't seem intimidated by Conan. Behind the thick lenses of his glasses, his eyes fixed coldly on Conan as he pronounced, "Move your car, Mr. Flagg. *Now.*"

Conan nodded. "I will. But first, I have to talk with you for a few minutes."

France threw up her hands. "Oh, this is too much! We're late already, and he wants to *talk.* Moses—"

"Be quiet, France. What is it you want to talk about, Mr. Flagg?"

"Corey Benbow."

"Oh. Yes, you *were* a friend of hers, weren't you? Well, it's a tragedy, her death, and we'll all miss her very much, of course."

France took her cue with an approximation of sympathetic regret. "We were all just *devastated.* She was *so* young and so—"

Conan cut in angrily, "Don't say another word, France!" Then he straightened, jaw muscles tight, and went on, "I assume you've heard from Gabe and Leo by now, and you know I'm not satisfied with the official ruling on Corey's death. I won't be satisfied until I get the truth about what happened Friday night at Gabe's house."

France said haughtily, "I have no idea what happened at Gabe's house. Moses and I were both at home that evening."

"Watching 'Dallas'?"

" 'Dallas' wasn't on last Friday," she replied with a complacent smile. "We watched the Pavarotti special."

At least she'd done some homework on her alibi. "Yes, I watched it too. I don't think I've ever heard *Vesti la guibba* sung better."

"Oh yes, that's one of my favorites. Just beautiful!"

"Then you must've been listening to a recording. Pavarotti didn't sing that particular aria on that program."

"Then I must be thinking of another aria."

"Or lying."

"My God, you're insufferable! Doesn't it occur to you that you might be *wrong*, that you have no right to—"

"I'm quite aware of my fallibility, but in this case I know I'm not wrong."

She uttered a parody of a laugh. "Look at this, Moses. A man who can't be wrong. Now, that's something for the *Guinness Book of Records.*"

Moses seemed satisfied to let France have her head now; he said nothing, his level gaze never leaving Conan's face.

Conan ignored her sally. "France, perhaps you're just confused. Remember Friday night? The night you and Moses and Nina and Leo and Jonas met at Gabe's house for your victory celebration; the night Corey arrived and spoiled the fun by reading that passage from Kate's diary; the night you threw a black russian in Corey's face."

She paled, with that substantiating the truth of at least part of Jonas's story. That thrust had hit home. Even Moses blinked at it. But he remained silent, and France was one of those people who rise to adversity. No high-strung histrionics now; she was suddenly calm and even dignified. "Mr. Flagg, that's a terrible thing to say. You want the truth? Ask the police. Just don't harass our family with your sick fantasies!"

Moses' gaze had at length shifted—to the XK-E. "Is there somebody in your car?"

Conan thought daggers at Jonas as he turned to look at the car. "I don't see anyone." And he didn't—now.

"I thought I saw a head sticking up." Moses' eyes shifted back to Conan. "Maybe we should go have a look."

Conan only shrugged. "Go ahead."

Moses seemed to consider that, then reached for the Cadillac's door. "We're late for an engagement. Mr. Flagg, you'd better move your car. I wouldn't want to put any dents in such a valuable machine."

Again Conan recognized an adroit heave-ho, and again he had no clever Parthian shot. Not that Moses or France would have heard it inside the car with the motor revving impatiently.

When Conan reached his valuable machine, Jonas was imitating a contortionist, with the lower half of his body squeezed into the footwell, while the upper half miserably occupied the part of the seat designed for the lower half. Conan managed to keep a straight face as he drove away. The Benbows, he saw, headed in the opposite direction, taking the more direct route to Highway 101.

"All right, Jonas, you can straighten up now."

"Are you kidding? I'm paralyzed for life! I'm an old man; I'm not up to—oh, damn, I can't even *feel* my feet." But after more shifting, groaning, and cursing, he achieved a normal riding position. "Well, did brother Moses and his lovely helpmeet have anything useful to say?"

The transmission snarled as Conan shifted down around a curve. "Jonas, I didn't bring you along as my Watson."

"Well, you can't blame me for trying."

Conan glanced at him. That had undoubtedly been Jonas's watchword since childhood: always testing the limits to see what he could get away with.

They were approaching the highway, and Jonas sighed with relief. "The Blue Heron—finally?"

Conan signaled for a left turn. "No. Nina Gillies."

CHAPTER 10

To assuage Jonas's concern about being seen in his company, Conan devised a disguise for him. Thus, as they drove north through Holliday Beach, Jonas sported a pair of Conan's sunglasses and an old watchcap pulled low over his ears. At Pacific Futures Realty—a glass and fake-shake building designed to last at least five years—Conan parked at one side where Jonas could feel relatively safe from observation.

Pacific Futures, like most businesses in Holliday Beach, was open on Sunday, but only one of its three agents was present, a fresh-cheeked young man who was a stranger to Conan, and who informed him that the agency's broker was also absent. Conan identified himself as John Upshaw of Los Angeles, a man with an avid interest in investment properties, by which subterfuge he eventually learned that Nina had gone home to her apartment.

When Conan returned to the car and informed Jonas of their destination, Jonas asked wearily, "Where *is* her apartment?"

"At the south end of town near Holliday Bay. Relax, we're taking the back way this time."

Across the highway from Pacific Futures, August Street angled southeast until it met Foothills Boulevard Road, which had been platted half a century ago when Messrs. Hollis and Day founded Holliday Beach. They had attached no "Road" to its name; they had envisioned it as a major north-south thoroughfare and a true boulevard. In the fullness of time, however, it had remained simply a narrow, graveled road, and eventually some county official added what seemed a redundancy, but more aptly described it.

There was little traffic and only a few dwellings along the way. Finally, as the road sloped down toward Holliday Bay, Conan saw a two-story block of apartments on the northwest corner of the first cross street they had met for some time. A weather-faded sign identified it as "Douglas." He turned right and parked well past the corner, so Jonas could avoid playing contortionist again. As Conan walked back to the apartment building, he saw Nina's car in the carport.

When she answered his knock, she made no pretense of surprise at seeing him and invited him in, if not cordially, at least with no open hostility. She was just out of the shower, apparently, clothed in a vermilion velour robe, with her hair in a towel turban. She sat down on a long, low couch, tucking her bare feet under her.

Conan took a chair near her. The room was full of hot, bright colors, and there *was* original art here: soft sculptures and bold graphics. It was an elegant room, yet it set his teeth on edge. Perhaps because nothing was natural, except the plants; it was all metal, plastic, and Naugahyde. There was not a piece of furniture made of real wood.

Nina took a cigarette out of the box on the end table; she held it between long, red-nailed fingers until Conan brought out his lighter, then she turned her head to blow out smoke. "I suppose you're here to talk about Corey."

"You've heard from Gabe *et al.,*" Conan commented with a wry smile while he lighted a cigarette for himself.

She laughed. "You've got them coming unglued, Conan. I suppose Jonas was your source of information."

"Well, don't be too hard on Jonas. He thought he was doing the right thing. I mean, he realized I wasn't going to back off until I had the truth, so he gave me enough to satisfy me—so he hoped."

She stretched her legs out on the couch, showing quite a length of sleek calf and thigh. "*Are* you satisfied?"

With a shrug, Conan said, "The problem is, Jonas doesn't strike me as the most dependable source of information. I might be satisfied if someone else would verify his story. All I've gotten so far is denials and advice."

She tilted her head, smiling. "Advice?"

"To mind my own business."

"Oh. Well, *I'd* be willing to verify Jonas's story—if I knew what he told you."

Conan took a long drag on his cigarette. "Why don't you tell me what happened Friday night, then I can judge Jonas's honesty for myself."

Nina thought about that, something cold and angry in ambush behind her lingering smile. Then she rose and went to a low cabinet that revealed its true function as a bar when she opened it. "Would you like a drink, Conan?"

"Yes, thank you. But not a black russian." Her back was to him, but he saw the tensing of her shoulders.

"I don't serve anything that fancy here. It's either scotch or gin or—what's this? Oh—brandy."

"That will do nicely."

Nina apparently decided brandy would do for her, too. She returned with two snifters, handed one to Conan, then sat down on the couch and crossed her legs. "I'm willing to verify Jonas's story, even if you won't tell me what he said. You're making waves, Conan, and until the Planning Commission has passed on Baysea, and all the money exchanged hands, I don't want the boat rocked." She sipped her brandy, eyes lowered, then flashing up again, coolly green. "Just remember one thing: I'm willing to satisfy you to keep you quiet, but if you expect me—or anybody else involved in this—to repeat the story for the police, forget it. We'll stand on what we—I mean, what Gabe told them—and it will be your word against six people."

Conan nodded. "Which of the six has the diary now?"

That stopped her, but only for a fraction of a second. "Well, I assume it was among Corey's effects."

He withheld comment on that. "All right, since you're in such a cooperative mood, tell me your version of what happened Friday night."

"My *version*?" She sent out a puff of smoke. "I'll tell you what *did* happen. Where do you want me to start? When Corey came?" At Conan's nod she began, "Well, I think that was about eight-thirty. I don't know who was the most surprised—her to find all of us there, or us to see her. Anyway, Gabe invited her in and told France to fix one of her *famous* black russians. There was a lot of small talk, and finally Corey got around to that diary *supposedly* written by Kate Benbow, yea, these many years ago."

"Didn't Jonas identify the handwriting as Kate's?"

"Conan, he hadn't seen her handwriting for twenty-seven years, and he doesn't qualify as an expert."

"And if a true expert never gets a chance to examine the diary, the question of its authenticity will remain moot. By the way, where was everyone sitting?"

Nina frowned, then with a shrug, "Well, Gabe was in that recliner of his at the end of the coffee table, and on the couch to his right, first France, then Moses, and I was at the other end. Jonas was on the other couch nearest Gabe, Corey was in the middle, and Leo at the far end."

"Did anyone handle the diary?"

"No. Well, Jonas did when Corey asked him to identify the handwriting. I still wonder if he wasn't shilling for her. But otherwise, the diary was never out of her hands. As soon as she read the one entry, she put it in that saddlebag of a purse, and she never let go of that."

Conan nodded. "After the reading, what happened?"

"Oh, a lot of shouting and name-calling. That's when France got hysterical and threw Corey's drink in her face. Corey retired to the bathroom to repair the damage, and Moses took France into the kitchen to calm her down. I was trying to get Gabe and Jonas and Leo calmed down meanwhile."

"Did any of them leave their seats?"

She thought about that while she flicked the ash from her cigarette into an anodized ashtray. "Well, maybe right after France threw the drink. Things got a little confused. But everybody was back in the same place when Corey came out of the bathroom. Yes, including me. What's your thing about seating arrangements?"

Conan ignored that. "What about Moses and France?"

"Moses came out of the kitchen first, then France a few minutes later with a drink in each hand—one for Corey, and one for her. We started talking about some sort of compromise that Corey—I mean, ECon—would accept."

Conan swirled his brandy, watching the liquid patterns of reflections in it. "If you didn't think the diary was authentic, why did you bother to discuss compromises?"

"Don't play so innocent, Conan. We just didn't want it to go to court. Isaac Wines wouldn't want it to go to court. There've been enough delays on this project already."

"But you thought he'd accept a compromise with ECon?"

Nina sighed, her mouth tightening. "Well, I wasn't looking forward to trying to talk him into it."

"But now that's one thing you don't have to worry about."

"Obviously. And I can do without the knife-turning."

He smiled at that. "Did Corey agree to a compromise?"

"On her terms. The spit and the south shore of the bay were to be left out of the development. Gabe said he'd agree to sell the spit to ECon, and I said I'd talk to Isaac about redesigning Baysea. She seemed satisfied with that, so she left. And that's it. End of story."

Conan tasted his brandy, and when he looked up at Nina, he made it clear that he expected something more. It was a long silence, but finally she said offhandedly, "I mean, that's all that was said about the spit or the sale. That's when Corey started complaining about feeling sick."

Conan managed to mask his shock with a nod and a faint smile, as if that were exactly what he'd been expecting.

"What did she say?"

"Well, I . . . can't remember exactly, but she decided to leave then." Nina watched him closely, undoubtedly seeking in his reactions clues to what Jonas had told him.

Conan tossed in a ringer with, "She *didn't* go back to the bathroom?"

Nina apparently decided she should agree with that. "Yes, I guess she did. Maybe her stomach was upset."

Conan took a sip of brandy. He wanted desperately to pursue the subject of Corey's sudden illness, but he was in uncharted territory now, and if Nina realized that, she could lie at will. Now she was confined to backing up what she guessed Jonas had said, and she could only assume he would stay with the truth as far as possible.

"Nina, who was with Corey when she left the house?"

A split-second pause, then, "No one. She was alone."

"What time was it when she left?"

"I don't know for sure. About ten, I suppose."

"When did *you* leave?"

"Well, we all left within—oh, I guess half an hour."

"When did you learn that Corey's body had been found?" He had worded that carefully, and it made her hesitate.

"When Gabe called me. That must've been about three-thirty in the morning."

Conan took a last puff on his cigarette before he put it out. "What's at stake here for you—beyond the commission?"

Her first reaction to that was not what he expected: she stiffened, something akin to dread flickering in her eyes. But a moment later, she uncrossed her legs and leaned forward to rub her calf, smiling coolly. "Oh, I guess . . . well, I've worked so damned hard on this Baysea project, and there's not much call for aging beauty queens who can't act." Then, still leaning forward so that her robe opened on a promising curve of breast, "Conan, I'm sorry you and I ended up on opposite sides of Baysea. I mean, I understand your reasons, but I have my own. I hope—well, maybe when it's all over . . ."

She was a better actor than she admitted, Conan decided, well aware that this beauty queen was aging very nicely. He finished his brandy and put the glass on the end table. "I'm glad you *do* understand my reasons, Nina. I'm trying to understand yours." He rose and started for the door. She didn't leave the couch, and when he reached the door and looked back, she was calmly lighting another cigarette.

She asked, "Are you satisfied now?"

"No. Not yet, Nina."

On the short walk to the car, Conan went through several stages of anger, most of it directed at Jonas, but when he got into the car, he was tautly calm. Jonas, however, had apparently reached the end of his patience.

"Damn it, Conan, I've about had it! You didn't *buy* me with that damn check. Probably a con anyway. If my old man finds out I spent the whole damn day with *you*—"

"Shut up, Jonas," Conan said curtly, turning in his seat to face him. "The check was not a con, but there were terms—remember? You broke one by trying to call Moses. You've broken another by lying to me, even if it was a lie of omission."

Jonas put on a pained expression, then decided that wouldn't work. He asked warily, "What did Nina tell you?"

Conan didn't answer that. "Tell me about Corey's unexpected illness."

Jonas went pale, and Conan could almost see the wheels turn behind the sunglasses. How much would Nina tell Conan Flagg? Nothing really damaging. Jonas managed a shrug. "It wasn't anything serious. I forgot about it."

"Did you? But your memory is returning, isn't it?"

"*No*, by God! You got the story from Nina, and that's all you're going to get! I'm *finished* spilling my guts for nothing!" And with that, he began fumbling at the door to get out.

Conan sighed and started the motor. "Relax, Jonas. I'll take you back to the Blue Heron."

Conan drove down Douglas Street two blocks to the highway, then turned left. During the four-mile drive to the Blue Heron, Jonas maintained a stony silence, and Conan didn't impinge on it until they reached the Inn. He parked beside Gabe's Continental, then turned to Jonas.

"I know I've treated you shabbily, and I hope it doesn't jeopardize your legacy from Gabe. But Corey did *not* die accidentally. I'm not through with this thing, and I won't back off out of consideration for you. I can't."

Jonas nodded as he opened the door and got out. "You want your check back?"

Conan shook his head. "Think about it. Maybe you'll decide to tell me the whole story and the whole truth."

"Maybe. Well, it was an interesting ride." He shut the door and started for Gabe's car, but when Conan turned onto the highway, he saw Jonas pass the car and go to the restaurant's front door and, no doubt, directly to the bar.

Only when Conan drove into the garage at his house did he realize that Jonas had walked off with a fifty-dollar pair of sunglasses.

Conan spent the evening at his desk in the library filling the pages of a legal pad with notes while the day's events were still fresh in his mind. When he came to Nina's admission—invention? —about Corey's illness, he absently penned an exclamation point in the margin, then, frowning, he reached for the phone.

He had intended to call Diane Monteil under any circumstances, and most of their conversation concerned the children. They were doing well, at least during the day. Last night had been a different matter, and Diane planned to sleep in their room tonight. She was fine. Subject closed. Her lawyer and ex-husband had called to assure her that she needn't worry about Gabe's custody suit, but she was not as confident. She knew Gabe Benbow, and she knew something about Taft County politics.

But she quickly closed that subject, too, by asking, "Have you heard from Lyn?"

"No. Of course, I was away from home and a phone most of the day." Then Conan hesitated, regretting the necessity of bringing up more reminders of Corey. "Di, was Corey feeling all right when she left the house Friday night?"

"You mean physically? Yes, of course. Why?"

"Just something I need to check out. Did she have a tendency to stomach problems, especially under stress?"

Diane managed a brief laugh. "Corey? No, she was healthy as a horse. She . . . used to say that. I've seen her under a lot of stress at one time or another, and the only problem she ever had was an occasional headache. I mean just a plain headache, nothing like a migraine."

Conan reached for his cigarettes with his free hand and shook one out of the pack. "Would there be any other explanation for a sudden illness?"

"If you're trying to ask tactfully if menstrual cramps were a possibility, the answer is no. Not last Friday. Did someone say she was sick?"

"Yes, but it's entirely unsubstantiated. Di, you'd better try to get some sleep. Give Kit and Melissa my love."

"I will, Conan. Thanks for calling. Thanks for . . . for everything else."

When Conan hung up, he sat motionless for some time. At length, he lighted the cigarette and turned his attention again to his notes.

> *The last time I saw darlin' Corey*
> *She had a wine glass in her hand;*
> *She was drinkin' that cold pizen liquor*
> *With a low-down sorry man.*

Damn that song!
And yet . . .

CHAPTER 11

At eight o'clock Monday morning, the sun hadn't yet topped the hills east of Holliday Beach, but Conan was already dressed and breakfasted. From the kitchen alcove, he watched the breakers, delicately tinted with dawn colors, while he smoked a cigarette with his third cup of coffee.

At exactly 8:01, he checked his watch and reached for the phone on the kitchen table. The call went to the county courthouse in Westport.

A chill, feminine voice announced, "Deputy Medical Examiner's office."

"Is Dr. Feingold in?"

She didn't answer the question. "Whom shall I say is calling?"

Annoyed, Conan replied, "Dr. Daniel Reuben." He had the temerity to use the state's chief medical examiner's name only because he knew him well enough to call him a friend.

It worked. "Oh, yes, Dr. Reuben. One moment, please."

The voice that came on after that moment was pleasant enough, but gave no clue to its owner's age. "Dan?"

"No, Dr. Feingold, I'm afraid I used Dan Reuben's name in vain. I'm Conan Flagg, and I must talk to you. Today."

There was a pendant silence, then, to Conan's relief, a laugh. "Flagg? Yes, Dan told me about you. Said I should look you up, but I've been so damned stacked up with work—in fact, I just dropped by the office to check a couple of reports. I've got a job up in Tillamook this morning."

"Can I meet you somewhere on the way? You'll be going through Holliday Beach."

"Well, I suppose . . . what's this about, Mr. Flagg?"

"Corella Benbow. You did an examination Saturday—"

"Oh, yes. Right. Car accident. What's the problem?"

Conan hesitated, then, "It's rather complicated, Doctor. Can I buy you lunch on your way back from Tillamook?"

"Well, I . . . okay. For Dan Reuben's sake. I'll probably be hitting Holliday Beach around noon."

"Good. How about the Surf House?"

"Fine. About noon, then. Maybe a little later."

With a relieved sigh, Conan hung up, then poured a fresh cup of coffee and went to the library. When he opened the drapes, the sun was just striking the breakers. He smiled as he surveyed the beach, empty of people now that the holiday was over, but the smile faded when the memory of kites on the wind came between him and this Monday vista.

He went to his desk and set up the phone answering machine for recording, then punched the number for the Duncan Investigation Service in San Francisco. Charlie Duncan was on the line almost as soon as Conan had identified himself.

"Damn, Conan, it's only eight-fifteen—in the *morning.*"

"You said you'd have those reports for me *early* Monday morning. I didn't want to keep you waiting."

"Sure. Well, if you figured on catching me empty-handed, too bad. I've got the files right here on my desk. You want a verbal report now?"

"Yes. I'm recording this. Any problem with that?"

"Never has been. Okay." A rustling of papers, then, "First, Jonas Benbow. I put Carl Berg on him."

"Good. I hope Carl enjoyed his trip to Phoenix."

Duncan laughed. "Enjoy? He wasn't enjoying; he was working. Damn hard and fast. I hope you appreciate that."

"Oh, I do, Charlie. So, what did he get?"

"Let's see, Jonas Benbow has lived in Phoenix for nearly six years. He's also worked for the same company, Southwestern Investment Company. It's a big real estate corporation: ten offices in Arizona, Nevada, and California."

Conan came upright in his chair. "Real estate?"

"Right. That surprise you?"

"Yes. But it makes sense. Go on."

"Well, Jonas is an accountant in the main office, makes about twenty-five thousand a year. Doesn't own a car; rents a small apartment five blocks from the SIC office. Landlady says he's quiet, keeps regular hours, usually pays the rent on time. She *was* a little worried about him, though. Seems he didn't pay his rent for November, and he left town about a week ago. She also said Jonas was keeping company with a 'nice, respectable lady' who works at SIC. Marie Clement."

"Beautiful. I assume Carl made her acquaintance."

"Carl's my specialist in nice, respectable ladies. He told her he was Jonas's long-lost nephew or something. Anyway, he found out that on November twenty-second, the boss called Jonas into his office. Very unusual, according to Marie. Mr. Belasco doesn't—"

"Wait a minute!" Conan smiled, remembering Jonas's unexplained phone call at the Blue Heron. "That's Jonas's employer— Belasco?"

"Yes. Harvey Belasco. Very big man in Phoenix, and according to Marie, he runs a tight ship."

"Why did he want to talk to Jonas?"

"Marie said Jonas told her he had a family emergency, and Belasco called him in to break the news to him. Carl thought that was a little weird. From what you said, nobody in his family even knew where he was."

Conan braced the phone on his shoulder while he lighted a cigarette. "I suppose Marie was happy with the story."

"Yeah. Well, there *was* some kind of emergency. Marie says Jonas was 'terribly upset' when he left Belasco's office, and he told her he had to go out of town for a week or so. A little while later, he gave his landlady the same story on his way out. Oh—he promised to settle up on the rent when he got back."

"Mm. Is Jonas still employed by Mr. Belasco?"

"Well, he seems to be. Marie says his desk has been left intact, and nobody's been hired to replace him. The official word is that he's on a leave of absence."

"Jonas intimated that it had to do with his health."

"I'll get to his health later. Or maybe you're not interested in the nice job of breaking and entering Carl did at Jonas's apartment."

Conan laughed and tilted his chair back. "I'm interested, Charlie."

"It's a furnished apartment, one bedroom and a kitchenette. Jonas has done a lot of traveling, but he wasn't much of a souvenir collector except for foreign stamps and currency. And he had a drawer full of menus from restaurants all over the world. Here's an item you'll be interested in: he subscribed to the Westport *Herald* —that's Westport, *Oregon*—under the name of J. B. Renbow. I don't know why he'd use an alias for that."

"You're a city boy, Charlie. Jonas didn't want any of the folks back home noticing his name on the subscription lists. Any idea how long he's been a subscriber?"

"Carl found a bunch of clippings from the *Herald* about Jonas's wife and son. The oldest went back eighteen years."

Conan frowned sourly. "I suppose those clippings included Kate's and Mark's obituaries."

"Everything. Graduations, a marriage, a birth, deaths."

"Was he interested in any other hometown news?"

"Let's see. Just something about Gabriel Benbow—his father?— and some big land development. Baysea Properties. Oh, yes, that ties in with some of the info Sean dug up. Anyway, Carl found some *other* travel mementos—matchbooks, hotel receipts—all fairly recent, and all from Las Vegas."

At that, Conan's frown shaded into a speculative smile. "Yes, Jonas had a weakness for Dame Luck."

"Well, he hasn't gotten over it. Most of the receipts were from the Sands, and it happens that I have a friend there: assistant manager for the casino. He remembered Jonas; says he spends a lot of weekends there. Likes blackjack and the slots. He's run up losses up to ten thou a few times, but my friend says Jonas never leaves town without paying his debts."

"Commendable. Did your friend say how good Jonas's luck is, or how often he ends up ten thou in the hole?"

"The house hasn't lost any money on Jonas. That's all he would tell me."

Conan turned his chair to face the windows, but the view was lost on him. "Maybe that's enough, Charlie. Twenty-seven years ago, Jonas got in over his head as a result of bad luck at cards, so he 'borrowed' about twenty thousand dollars from his employer— which happened to be Taft County."

"You figure he's been embezzling from Harvey Belasco?"

"It's a possibility. What did Carl get on Belasco?"

Duncan snorted. "You asked for Benbow—in three days over a holiday weekend. You expecting a two-for-one sale?"

"No, but I know Carl Berg. Don't tell me there's nothing in that file on Belasco."

Again, the sound of rustling papers. "Well, SIC is an old family firm; good, solid reputation. Belasco is in his sixties and, according to Marie Clement, tight-fisted. But he pays his employees well; lots of fringe benefits. Conan, if you figure Jonas was dipping into the till, and Belasco found out, how come he's supposedly still working for SIC?"

Unconsciously Conan shrugged. "Assuming Belasco did catch Jonas with his hand in the till, what are his options? If he turns Jonas over to the police, it means a trial and a lot of very bad publicity for the old family firm. If he simply fires Jonas, he's out however much he embezzled. But Jonas knew about Baysea, not only through the *Herald*, but through the real estate grapevine at SIC. He knew his father was on the verge of banking a few million, so maybe he promised Belasco he'd replace what he stole, and came home to 'make his peace' with Gabe."

Duncan didn't seem convinced. "Sure, but Belasco'd be nuts to let Jonas leave town."

"It's his only hope for recovering his money, and he's keeping a fairly tight rein on Jonas. I overheard a phone conversation yesterday. Jonas was talking to Belasco, and what he said makes sense if you assume Jonas has a schedule for checking in with his boss. Probably three or four times a day, and if Jonas doesn't check in on time, Belasco can call in the police, and they'd probably call in the FBI, since Jonas crossed a few state lines. I think Jonas will try his damnedest to replace the money before taking a chance on a long prison sentence. Did Carl check the NCIC files?"

"He didn't, but I've got a buddy with the SFPD. No, Jonas doesn't have a prison record."

"And I doubt he wants to acquire one at his age. Damn, I wish I had some idea how much he owes Belasco."

"*If* he owes him. I guess you could call Belasco."

Conan smiled at that. "I can think of better ways to waste my time. What did Carl find out about Jonas's health?"

"He seems to be in great shape. That's according to Marie. There weren't any bills from doctors or hospitals in his apartment. Carl checked all the hospitals in Phoenix, and Jonas isn't on record with any of them."

"At least Corey didn't quite fall for that scam." Then he frowned, reached for his cigarette. If Corey *had* fallen for it, she might still be alive.

"Conan, who's Corey?"

"She . . . she was a friend of mine."

"Was? I thought you wanted all this information just out of curiosity."

He squinted through an exhalation of smoke. "The situation has changed. Anything else on Jonas?"

"Not unless I missed something. I'll send the file—both of them —by messenger service. Should get to you tomorrow. So, now we come to Nina Gillies. Yes, I assigned Sean Kelly to her. Sean sends her love, by the way, and wants to know when you're coming down to San Francisco. She says you're going to mildew up there."

Conan smiled, and he had a clear image of Sean, red-haired and vivacious, with her intriguing, husky voice.

"Tell her she's my one and only wild Irish rose."

"Sure. Now, if we've got the blarney out of the way . . . Sean, bless her efficient little heart, typed up a summary herself. I'll read it to you. A lot of her information came from the morgues of the LA *Times* and assorted scandal sheets. She photocopied some of the clippings. Damn, Nina Gillies is one gorgeous woman. Or was, anyway."

"She's still gorgeous, Charlie. But as Miss Dobie always says, beauty is only—"

"Sure it is. You want to hear this thing?"

"Read on, Macduff."

"Okay, Sean picked up Nina's story about the time she came to California: 'In 1966, Nina Gillies, an ex-Miss Oregon, married Randall (Randy) Coburn, an All-America quarterback for the University of Oregon. He graduated that year and signed a contract with the LA Rams. Nina Coburn (she took back her maiden name after Randy died in 1975) signed up with a prestigious Hollywood talent agency. For two years they were Hollywood's storybook couple. Lots of clippings from this period and photos of Prince and Princess Charming with some very famous and important people. They spent money like water off a duck's back—' " Charlie had to stop for a laugh at that. "Conan, I'm just reading what Sean has here. Okay. 'But the fairy tale ended unhappily in 1968 when Randy was implicated in a big drug scandal. He was never prosecuted, but the Rams dropped him. Nina's film career never got off first base. She did a few TV commercials and two small parts in movies, but that's all. Her agent dropped her about the same time the Rams dropped Randy. After that they didn't show up in the papers except in the back pages under court cases. LAPD had a long file on Randy. He was picked up a few times on suspicion of drug dealing—no convictions—and he had a string of DUIs. He tried acting as Nina's agent for a while, but the best he could do for her was starring roles in porno movies. Randy also had a habit of occasionally beating Nina into a hospital.

" 'But Nina wasn't exactly being dragged along on this downhill roller coaster. Her father ran a successful contracting business in Portland, and he regularly sent her money and begged her to leave Randy and come home. She refused. In 1975, her father died, and her mother sold everything and went to live with a sister in Springfield, Missouri. At the time of her father's death, Nina was in the hospital again, thanks to Randy. This time she decided she'd had enough. She sued for divorce, got an injunction against him, and filed an assault charge. He was out on bail the next day. By then, Nina was out of the hospital and staying with a friend, Carla Henried. The day after Randy got out on bail, he was found in an alley, dead, shot with a small caliber handgun. The alley was about two blocks from Carla Henried's house, where Nina was hiding out. Long finger of coincidence. Carla swore that she and Nina were at a movie the night of the murder. Since Randy was shot in the back of the head, execution style, the police decided the killer was probably one of his friends in the drug business. Nina was questioned and released. The case is still open.

" 'Nina sank out of sight for the next five years, and when she came up, she was a new woman. She apparently did it all on her own, working days in a department store, going to business school at night, and spending whatever free time she had getting in shape physically at the YWCA. Later she studied for a real estate agent's license, and when she got that, she went to see Isaac Wines. She first met him back in the Cinderella years. He hired her to work in one of his real estate offices, then when she got her broker's license, he put her in charge of it. He liked her work, and at this point, she's sort of his right hand lady in real estate. And maybe in other places, too, but that's just raw insinuation and comes from Wines's personal secretary, Velma Logan. She doesn't seem to care much for Nina, but she does like martinis. According to her, Wines *loaned* Nina one hundred thousand dollars to set up her own agency in Holliday Beach. Her main objective was to acquire the land for the Baysea Properties development, and if she succeeded, he'd forget the loan, plus she'd collect a ten percent broker's fee, plus a four hundred thousand dollar bonus from Wines. Velma wasn't sure that would happen if Nina *didn't* succeed, but she said it wasn't likely that Nina would ever work in the real estate business again. Then there's that loan, of course. And I found another interesting facet on all this. Wines hired a new receptionist for his office in LA about a year ago: Carla Henried, Nina's old friend—the one who gave her an alibi for Randy's murder. I didn't have time for an in-depth on Carla, but judging by her car, her address, and her mink, receptionists are doing very well these days. Carla isn't being kept so nicely for her good looks, by the way; she's no ranting beauty, and Isaac Wines is a connoisseur.

" 'That's the gist of it. Details and sources follow. Also a transcript of a call to Nina's mother in Missouri. As far as she's concerned, Nina died with her father. Conan, when are you going to take me away from all this?' "

Conan, his train of thought abruptly derailed, had to laugh at that. "Charlie, I'll answer that question personally—and privately."

"Yeah, I figured you would. Okay, anything she didn't cover?"

Conan took a puff on his cigarette. "No, she covered everything very well. As usual. Damn, the story of Nina's life would make a movie, even if she could never land a starring role while she was in Hollywood."

"Right. From the top to the bottom and back again."

Conan thought about that arduous ascent from the depths. No one who made that climb would relish repeating it. And at the top of Nina's mountain, Isaac Wines apparently stood smiling, offering a glittering future in one hand, and in the other, disaster in the shape of a loan Nina could never repay, a career in shambles, and—

What about Carla Henried? Was she being kept so well as a potential witness to a murder that the Los Angeles police still considered an open case?

Nina was perhaps involved in a very high stakes game.

"Conan? You still there?"

"Mm? Yes, Charlie. You'd better send the reports to the bookshop. I won't be at home much tomorrow."

"You need any help up there? Anything I can do?"

Conan considered that, then with a long sigh, "No, I'm afraid not. But thanks. And tell Sean and Carl I appreciate the good work."

"I'll tell them. Okay, Conan, I hope your Irish luck comes through for you."

"So do I. Thanks, Charlie."

When he hung up, Conan went to the kitchen for a hot cup of coffee and on his return, stood for a while at the windows looking up at the whisps of cirrus clouds brushing the sky. At length, he returned to his desk. His next call went to the local office of the telephone company.

He asked for Joanie Dann and was instructed to hold. Then, after a full minute's wait, "Joanie, this is Conan. I have a favor to ask of you, and it's in a very good cause."

The voice sounded younger than its possessor. She laughed and retorted, "And very illegal?"

"For a PI, yes. But it's also very important."

"Why?"

Conan's mouth tightened. "It's confidential."

"Don't you trust me, Conan?"

"Don't you trust *me?*"

"More or less. Okay, what is it this time?"

"Can you find out if any long-distance calls have been made from Gabe Benbow's house since last Thursday?"

"Oh, probably, if I get old Jenny here working on it." "Jenny" was a computer, and Joanie and Jenny enjoyed a close relationship.

"I'll take you to dinner at the finest restaurant on the coast, Joanie. Anywhere you want to go. And I'll throw in a magnum of Mumm's, if you get that information to me before—say, eleven o'clock."

That brought on another laugh. "Okay, Conan, the Côte d'Azur in Westport, and forget the Mumm's. Make it a fifth of Glenlivet."

"You're on."

"No, I'm off—my rocker. Oh—where are you?"

"At home."

"Oh, yes, it's Monday. Bookshop's closed. Okay, I'll talk to you later."

Conan spent the next half hour replaying the tape from his call to Duncan and adding more notes to the legal pad. Motive. All he had was motive, he thought bitterly. Everyone at Gabe's house

Friday night had motive. The tape ended, and Conan had begun skimming his notes from the day before, when the phone rang. It was Joanie Dann.

"Okay, Conan, I've got what you wanted. Ready?"

He was poised with pen in hand. "Let's have it."

"On Thursday there was one call to Westport, 579-1086, and two to Phoenix, Arizona, both to 973-6800. Then Friday, another call to the same Westport number and . . . let's see, three calls to Phoenix, one to 973-6800—oh, that's the same number as Thursday—and two to 973-7303. On Saturday, the Westport number again, and four Phoenix calls, all to that first number. Yesterday—this is getting monotonous—one to the Westport number, and three to Phoenix, first number again. And that's all I could get for you."

Conan was smiling broadly as he wrote. "That's *all?* Joanie, you're wonderful. What was the billing on the calls?"

"Let's see, the Westport calls were direct dial. The Phoenix calls were all person-to-person collect."

"Which means operator assistance. Beautiful." That way, Belasco could ascertain from the operator the point of origin of the calls to make sure Jonas was still where he claimed to be. "But I wish you could give me the times."

"Conan, you can't have everything. You owe me a quarter, by the way, for *this* call. I didn't dare risk anybody in the office overhearing all this."

Conan laughed. "You'll get your quarter back, Joanie. Thanks for the information—and it *is* in a good cause."

"I know. Oh—give me a little warning before this night on the town so I can get my hair fixed."

"All right, but how can one 'fix' perfection? Take care, Joanie."

Conan impatiently pressed the cradle button, then called Directory Assistance. A few minutes later, he had verified two assumptions: the Westport number was the residence of Leonard Moskin; the Phoenix numbers were for the office of Southwestern Investment Company and the home of Harvey Belasco.

Did that also verify the hypothesis that Jonas had again indulged in embezzlement, that Belasco let him return to Oregon to acquire the money to repay what he had stolen, and that the frequent calls to Phoenix were Belasco's way of keeping track of Jonas? Conan tried to imagine another hypothesis that would explain the facts as well, when the phone rang, startling him. He snatched up the receiver. "Yes?"

"Flagg, this is Earl Kleber."

"Oh—yes, Chief, what can I do for you?" He asked the question warily; Kleber's use of Conan's first or last name was a fairly dependable barometer of his mood.

"I just got a call from a buddy of mine in the Forest Service. Yesterday evening, he was running a routine patrol on a logging road up the Sitka River, and he spotted a guy on a motorcycle."

Conan asked with some foreboding, "Spotted him doing what?"

"Nothing right then. Jerry flagged him down, and the guy stopped. No problem. The name on his drivers license was Lyndon B. Hatch. He's a friend of yours, isn't he?"

Conan's foreboding hadn't lessened. "Yes. Why did Jerry flag him down?"

"Because he was carrying a rifle, that's why, and it's a long time past hunting season. Jerry said it looked brand new—a Remington thirty-ought-six with a Leupold three by nine scope."

Conan closed his eyes wearily. "What did Lyn say?"

"Told Jerry he was just camping out and heard there'd been bear sighted around there. Flagg, nobody's seen any bear up the Sitka for years."

"What did Jerry do about him?"

Kleber snorted. "What *could* he do? Nothing. Told him the law on poaching deer and went on about his business. So, what do you know about it? What's Hatch up to?"

Conan replied irritably, "I don't know, Chief, nor do I know why you think he's *up* to anything. Maybe he just has a phobia about bears."

"Sure. Hatch was a friend of Corey's, too, wasn't he?"

"Yes, he was."

Kleber paused, then, "Does Hatch agree with you about Corey —that maybe she didn't die accidentally?"

"Chief, I am not telepathic."

Kleber laughed. "Okay, Conan. Just thought you'd like to know about this. Any luck with your investigation?"

Conan looked down at the mute hieroglyphics of his notes. "Nothing that would stand up in court so far, but the game's not over yet."

"Right, but you're getting into the fourth quarter if you're playing for an autopsy. The funeral's tomorrow. I called Ronson. He says he'll take care of the cremation this afternoon."

Conan stopped himself from looking at his watch, but time seemed to be piling up on him. He said grimly, "I'm trying for a field goal. I'm having lunch with Dr. Feingold. Chief, if you hear anything more about Lyn—"

"Yeah, I'll let you know."

CHAPTER 12

Conan arrived at the Surf House dining room in time to procure a table by the windows overlooking the beach and to enjoy a brief conversation with the proprietors, Tilda and Brian Tally, before the lunch rush drove Brian back into the kitchen, and Tilda resumed her duties as hostess, gracious and graceful as ever, despite the obvious fact of her pregnancy. It became her, Conan thought, and at least this was one child who would be cherished.

He watched the lace-patterned scallops of the waves sliding in over the sand, then sliding back to meet the next wave in a brown flurry, scouring the sand smooth for yet another wave. It was nearly twelve-thirty when Tilda came to his table and presented a young man with a plethora of dark, curly hair, rimless glasses saddling a nose of noble proportions, and an ingenuous smile. "Greg Feingold," he said, thrusting out a hand. "Sorry I'm late. You're Conan Flagg. Right, of course you are. That nice lady—where'd she go? Beautiful woman. Wonder if she's—well, I guess she *must* be married. Or something. I hope so, anyway. Mind if I sit down?"

Conan had had his mouth open to offer that invitation for some time, and now he got in a hurried, "Please do sit down, Dr. Feingold. Would you like a cocktail or—"

"Mm? Oh, no, thanks. Maybe wine with lunch. Call me Greg." As he spoke, he searched the pockets of his worn, corduroy blazer; at length, he came up with a pack of cigarettes. "Bother you if I smoke? Oh—you've got the habit too. Damn, I'm going to quit someday. You'd think I'd seen enough lungs . . ." He lighted a cigarette and let smoke out with a long sigh. "What's good for lunch here?"

Conan found himself smiling. "Almost anything. I'll have Tilda bring menus—"

"No, you don't need to. You eat here a lot? Why don't you order. Damn, what a view. Just look at that!"

Conan instead concentrated on attracting the attention of a waitress and ordering lunch: the specialty of the house, petrale sole stuffed with Dungeness crab. "And a bottle of Adelsheim Sauvignon Blanc. Anything else, Doctor?"

"Mm? Oh, no. That sounds great." And when the waitress departed, "I really prefer 'Greg.' Never have gotten used to that 'doctor.' You said you wanted to talk about the Benbow case. What —well, I was wondering . . ."

"What business is it of mine?" Conan nodded. "By the way, if you prefer a first name basis, make it mutual. As for Corey Benbow, she was a friend of mine, and there's more to her death than meets the eye." He paused for a puff on his cigarette, trying to gauge Feingold's response. So far, he seemed only mildly curious. "Greg, my first question is, why wasn't a full autopsy done?"

Feingold shrugged. "It was just a routine accident case, and the cause of death was obvious. If it hadn't been, sure, I'd have done a full autopsy."

"If this was such a routine case, why were you asked to do the examination on a Saturday? What was the rush?"

"It's not so unusual, actually, for me to work on weekends. But this—well, I guess it could've waited till today. Local mortuary had adequate cold-storage facilities. But Owen called me early Saturday morning and asked me to take care of it."

"That's Owen Culpepper, our estimable district attorney?"

Feingold sent Conan an oblique smile. "That's Owen. He said he knew the family, and they wanted the formalities taken care of as soon as possible. Something about a fiancé who might make trouble." He stopped, giving Conan a stricken look, then, "I hope—I mean, that's not *you*, is it?"

Conan smiled to reassure him. "No. Did Owen suggest that a full autopsy wouldn't be necessary?"

"No. That kind of decision isn't his to make."

And clearly it *was* Feingold's; there was a hint of defensiveness in his tone. The waitress brought the salads, and Conan welcomed the diversion. Feingold doused his salad with dressing and began enthusiastically masticating it. Around a mouthful of lettuce, he said, "Okay, Conan, you think I should've done a full autopsy, right?"

Conan hedged. "It's just that there are some unusual circumstances surrounding Corey's death, and I don't like to see the option of a full autopsy closed off, and it will be this afternoon. The body is going to be cremated."

Feingold frowned at that. "Maybe you'd better tell me about these 'unusual circumstances.'"

Conan outlined those circumstances, while Feingold demolished his salad. Conan found his appetite waning, and when the waitress cleared the table, his salad was virtually intact. He concluded his account with Kate Benbow's diary—its implications and its disappearance.

"Greg, there were six people at Gabe's house when Corey presented that diary, and all of them had compelling reasons to protect the Baysea sale."

Feingold leaned back, arms folded. "Okay, you've got a weird situation. You told the police all this?"

Conan laughed bitterly. "What can I tell them? I have no proof that any of the six were there—except Gabe, of course. But why were there no skid marks? Why would a perfectly healthy young woman drive down that hill and over a cliff without hitting the brakes?"

"Without . . . ?" Feingold's thick eyebrows went up. "Nobody told me there weren't any skid marks."

"Did you talk to Sergeant Roddy? State Police?"

"No, I got a report from the sheriff." He grimaced sourly, then, "Well, it wasn't a DUI, that's for sure. Blood alcohol level was only point-oh-six percent. What you call subclinical intoxication. Not enough to keep a person from reacting to a dangerous situation, if they saw it coming."

"Did you run any other blood tests?"

"Just for barbiturates. Negative. Hey, that looks marvelous!" That was for the waitress and the entrée.

Conan waited with as much patience as he could muster while she performed the small ceremony of serving the wine. At length, when she had departed, Conan said, "I'm not doubting your findings, Greg; I'm not doubting that 'craniocerebral trauma and/or drowning' might have been the immediate cause of death. I just want to know why Corey went off that cliff without trying to stop the car."

Feingold seemed to be concentrating on buttering a roll. "The trouble with a situation like this is you have more than one thing happening to the victim at once, any of them potentially fatal. That blow to the head—and by the way, there's no doubt how that happened: she hit the windshield. This sole is fantastic! What's this with the crab? Oh, black olives. There were microscopic glass fragments matching the windshield glass in the surface abrasion over the impact area. Linear fracture of the right frontal bone and supraorbital arch. That was enough to kill her, but there was also some water drainage from the mouth and nose. That could've been from antemortem inspiration of water or just postmortem immersion in thirty feet of saltwater. What I'm trying to say is, these things are hardly ever cut and dried. Now, the question you really should be asking me is, was the victim alive when the cranial trauma occurred?" He looked up over the rim of his wine glass and smiled benignly. "Or were you saving that question for the next course?"

"I *was* saving it," Conan admitted. "So, what's the answer?"

"Well, I'm not sure. There wasn't any indication of bleeding in the abraded area at the fracture site, but submersion in water fouls things up a lot. Even if I was sure there *hadn't* been any bleeding, it's still possible the trauma occurred during an antemortem agonal interval."

"So, you can't be sure whether she was alive or dead when she hit the windshield?" Conan reached for the wine bottle and re-filled their glasses.

"Thanks. That's a nice wine. Oregon? No, I can't be sure beyond a reasonable doubt, but if she wasn't alive at that moment, she hadn't been dead very long." He chewed vigorously for a while, squinting out at the beach. "It seemed so damned simple. I mean, her car took a dive off a cliff, there was a classic impact fracture with glass fragments from the windshield. It seemed so . . ."

"Cut and dried?"

Feingold looked at him sharply, then shrugged. "Yes. But I didn't just look at that fracture and take off my gloves. There were no other wounds on the body; not even a small laceration or contusion. Oh—except a bruised area about fifteen centimeters in diameter over the sternum between the fifth and sixth ribs."

Conan's eyes narrowed. "Antemortem?"

"Probably. Maybe. Reddish blue color. But that's a long way from a fatal injury, so if she wasn't alive when she hit the windshield, how did she die?"

"I assume that's a rhetorical question?"

Feingold was again frowning introspectively as he forked up a mouthful of fish. "Asphyxiation? I mean, like a pillow or soft gag blocking the nose and mouth? But there was no cyanosis. That made me a little skeptical of drowning *per se* as a cause of death. Besides, anybody who's being asphyxiated forcibly is going to fight like hell. That leaves marks, and there weren't any, except the contusion on the sternum, and that wasn't consistent with a struggle. And I don't know when it occurred, except probably within twenty-four hours of exitus."

Conan considered the word "exitus"; how coolly objective Latin was. "And that leaves drugs or poisons."

"Well, you can forget about your, so to speak, run-of-the-mill drugs or poisons. Barbiturates are out, and there was no odor of bitter almonds, oil of wintergreen, or garlic; no cherry-red coloring; no corrosion of the lips or mouth. Conan, there was absolutely no indication of drugs or poisons." He stabbed at the remains of his sole absently. "Are you sure about those . . . circumstances?"

Conan had given up any pretense of eating. He raised his wineglass; that, at least, he could still enjoy. "Yes. I'm also sure that Corey drank a total of about one full black russian. Kahlúa has a strong flavor; it could easily mask a foreign flavor, especially for someone who seldom drank and wouldn't be so likely to recognize it."

Feingold attacked his entrée again, got another mouthful down, then dropped his fork. "Well, you've got me worried. If I don't do an autopsy now, I'll always wonder. The body's still at the local mortuary?"

For a moment, Conan was too overwhelmed to speak. Feingold's acquiescence had come far more easily than he had anticipated.

"Uh—yes. Ronson's is handling the funeral service."

Feingold rose. "Is there a pay phone around here?"

Conan came to his feet, too. "There's one in the foyer, or I'm sure Tilda will let you use—"

"Pay phone's fine. I'll be back in a few minutes. Oh—don't let the waitress take away what's left of my lunch."

Conan sank back into his chair and reached for his wineglass. It was especially piquant now. And Earl Kleber didn't think it could be done, forcing a full autopsy. Conan lighted a cigarette, then silently toasted the rushing waves with his wine.

But by the time he crushed out the butt of the cigarette, Feingold still hadn't returned, and the wine began to have a sour taste. Conan lighted another cigarette and tried to resign himself to defeat, calling it a temporary setback; just the turn of the cards. That didn't help.

At length, Feingold returned and slumped wearily into his chair, shaking his head. "Too late."

Conan stared at him, anger surfacing. "What do you mean, too late? Al Ronson told Chief Kleber the cremation wouldn't take place until this afternoon."

"I talked to Ronson himself. They don't have the facilities for cremation here, so they take the bodies to a crematorium in Salem. Ronson took the Benbow remains in this morning. I called Salem, but . . . it was too late."

"Damn!" Conan closed his eyes, and it was a moment before he got his hands unfurled from their angry fists. "Why did Ronson have to be in such a hell of a hurry?"

"He said the guy who usually takes the bodies into Salem for him called in sick this morning. Ronson has a funeral at one today, so he went into Salem early to get back in time for that."

"Someone has had incredible luck in this!"

Feingold gazed out the window, but he didn't seem to take any pleasure in the view now. "You know, Dan Reuben told me once that sooner or later a case comes along where you foul up for one reason or another. He said, you're bound to make a mistake some day, and when you do, you'll have to live with it the rest of your life."

Conan emptied the wine bottle into their glasses. "Greg, you don't know whether you made a mistake or not, and you had no way of knowing about the events preceding Corey's death. At least you've eliminated a lot of possibilities. It's as important to know what isn't true as it is to know what *is* true." He smiled wryly and added, "I think that's something else Dan Reuben once said."

CHAPTER 13

Finding the wide driveway at France's and Moses' home empty, Conan cavalierly swept into it and parked near the steps to the front deck. The lady of the house was standing at a table on the deck, filling ceramic pots with soil from a plastic dishpan. She was attired for that task in a panama straw hat, safari slacks, and a smock boldly patterned in black and brown. Her work gloves, appliquéd with yellow flowers, were so fresh and crisp, he wondered if she didn't put on a new pair every time she worked in her garden. She rubbed them together to remove the loose soil, watching Conan silently as he approached.

The Benbows had a panoramic view of the ocean and Sitka Bay. The sky had a milky sheen, a halo of refracted light ringing the sun; the sea shone like molten metal, and the wind blew chill out of the northwest.

Conan said, "Looks like a change in the weather coming."

France's arched brows went up; she didn't so much as glance toward the ocean. "What do you want, Mr. Flagg?"

He smiled coolly. "I thought you might like to tell me *your* side of what happened Friday night at Gabe's."

Her Nefertiti eyes narrowed, then she pulled off her gloves and tossed them on the table. "I suppose you'll *hound* us until you *finally* get it through your head that what happened had nothing to do with Corella's death."

"Yes, I suppose I will."

She went to one of the deck chairs near the table, and although she didn't invite him to do so, he took the chair next to hers. Her apparent willingness to talk to him about Friday night didn't surprise him; no doubt by now the conspirators had compared notes and prepared a story for him.

Conan lighted a cigarette but didn't offer France one, nor did he seem to notice, when she took out one of her own, that she was waiting for a light.

"All right, France, what *did* happen at Gabe's?"

Her narrow nostrils flared. She found a lighter in the pocket of her smock and got her cigarette ignited. "Corey came to the house, of course, as you—"

"What time was it when she arrived?"

"Eight-thirty."

"Exactly?"

"I didn't mean exactly. *About* eight-thirty. All of us talked for a while, just small talk, and finally—"

"Didn't you fix her a black russian at Gabe's request?"

France took a quick puff on her cigarette. "Yes, I did. Anyway, she finally read that—that diary and threatened—no, it wasn't just a threat, it was *blackmail*, pure and simple!"

"Which rather annoyed you, I understand."

"Of *course*, it did! And, yes, I admit I . . . well, I lost my temper. I, uh, threw Corey's drink in her face. But she was so insufferably *smug* about that diary. She didn't care about us; she didn't care about anything but her . . ." France took another nervous puff, visibly getting herself under control. "Then Corey went to the ladies' room, and—"

"Where was everyone seated at this point?"

"Well, Gabe was in his chair at the end of the coffee table, and I was sitting next to him. I mean, on the couch to his right. Moses was next to me, and Nina was on the other side of Moses. Jonas was sitting nearest Gabe on the other couch, then Corey, with Leo at the other end."

Conan nodded. "What happened after Corey retreated to the ladies' room?"

Another nervous puff. "Well, Moses and I went to the kitchen to talk for a few minutes."

"How many minutes?"

"Oh, for God's sake, I don't know! Maybe—five minutes. Then Nina came into the kitchen and . . . suggested that I make another drink for Corey, but I was so—my *hands* were shaking. I started to fix the drink, then I . . . Moses and I went back to the living room."

"Was Corey in the living room when you returned?"

"Uh, no, I don't think—no, she wasn't. Nina had come out of the kitchen by the time Corey rejoined us."

"With Corey's drink? Where did she put it?"

"On the coffee table in front of the couch where Corey had been sitting."

"Didn't she also bring a drink for you?"

France replied frigidly, "I suppose she did."

"And Jonas and Leo were still on the couch on either side of Corey's place when you returned from the kitchen."

"Yes."

"Go on."

Her voice was edged with strain as she continued, "Well, when Corey came back, we tried to reach some sort of compromise. I should say, she laid down her *terms* to us."

"Did Corey drink any of that second black russian?"

"I . . . don't know. Anyway, Corey said she wasn't feeling well and decided to go home. She said we'd work out the details of her so-called compromise later."

Conan took time for a leisurely pull on his cigarette, looking out at the misted horizon. "Of course, you knew Corey had epilepsy."

He turned in time to see France's mouth open slackly, an enigmatic expression with elements of both surprise and relief fixing briefly on her face.

"No, I . . . I didn't know that."

Conan was simply trying to find out more about Corey's unexpected illness when he pulled the epilepsy ploy out of the air. Apparently he had struck a nerve.

He asked caustically, "You didn't know? And you Benbows are such a close-knit family."

Her rouged cheeks turned a deeper red. "We *are* a close-knit family, but Corella set *herself* apart. She betrayed all of us."

Conan studied France. A strong word, "betrayed." Then he put on a speculative frown. "If Corey had an epileptic seizure that night, it would clear up a lot of questions about the accident. Can you describe the symptoms?"

France took the bait. "Well, she seemed to have sort of a . . . fit, you know. Whatever you call it."

Conan nodded. "Convulsions?"

"I guess so. She began shaking and jerking, and she just pitched forward. Jonas caught her, and we got her down on the floor. Then

Nina said she had CPR training, and . . ." France hesitated, masking the lapse with another puff on her cigarette. "But Corey recovered then, of course. The whole thing only lasted a minute or so, then she—well, she seemed a little shaken, but otherwise quite recovered. At least, we thought—I mean, she *said* she was."

There were probably elements of truth in all that, Conan decided, but again the problem was sorting fact from fiction. CPR. If Nina *had* attempted CPR, that would explain the bruise on the sternum that had puzzled Feingold.

He asked, "Were there any warning symptoms of the seizure?"

France's short puffs had quickly burned her cigarette to the filter. She went to the table to crush out the butt in an ashtray. Her hands were trembling slightly.

"Warning symptoms? Well, she seemed to be having trouble breathing. She—she said her mouth and throat felt . . . numb."

That, at least, had the unequivocal ring of truth in it. It was too specific to come out of France's vague knowledge of epilepsy. Then Conan frowned as Moses' maroon Cadillac swung into view.

"Oh—here comes Moses," France said, her relief obvious, her cool aplomb restored. "Mr. Flagg, I hope you're *finally* satisfied. Now, if you'll excuse me, I have to go in and fix lunch for Moses."

Conan had some difficulty visualizing France as the cozy homemaker preparing hubby's lunch, but perhaps that failure of concept was his error. He went to the table and put out his cigarette. "One more question, France. Jonas said Gabe promised him three hundred thousand dollars out of the Baysea sale—in lieu of any future claim on Gabe's estate. Is that true?"

She replied archly, "That *certainly* has nothing to do with Corella, and it's none of your business."

"So little about this case seems to be my business. Was Jonas's forfeiture of his future inheritance Moses' idea?"

"What do you mean by that?"

Conan didn't have a chance to explain. A car door slammed, and Moses, dignified in a three-piece suit, approached at a brisk pace, his chill gaze fixed on Conan.

"Mr. Flagg, you must have the hide of a rhinocerous, or you wouldn't have come back here!"

Conan smiled at that. "Oh, I can be as thick-skinned as I have to be. France was telling me—"

She cut in, "I was answering his questions about Friday night. I know how you feel, Moses, but he *won't* leave us alone until he's satisfied."

Moses made a nice show of annoyed resignation. "You're probably right, dear. But, Mr. Flagg, I *don't* like you sneaking in here behind my back and bothering my wife, and I won't put up with it! *Good-bye,* Mr. Flagg!"

They worked well together, Conan thought; a good team. He shrugged and said, "I'm leaving, Moses. It was a relief to find out about Corey's epileptic seizure."

One thing about Moses' extraordinary self-control—when it faltered, it was particularly noticeable. Conan was treated to a virtual repeat performance of France's odd response of mixed surprise and relief.

But it was gone in the blink of an eye. Moses said coldly, "I'm glad you're relieved. *And* that you're leaving."

Conan started for his car, then turned. "Whose idea *was* it— Jonas's three hundred thousand dollars in *lieu* of inheritance? Yours, Moses? Good thinking. After all, Gabe has already lived well past his biblically ordained three-score and ten."

Moses flushed hotly. "Get *out,*. Flagg!"

Conan did, with no reluctance at all.

When Conan reached the Holliday Beach Book Shop, he had his choice of parking places, since all the other businesses were also closed on Monday, the resort sabbath. The bells on the front door echoed in the musty silence, and after he locked the door behind him, he paused to savor the unique odor of books—to him the headiest of perfumes.

Ostensibly, he had stopped at the shop today to be sure Miss Dobie had fed Meg. She had, of course. Conan went into his office, put a tape on the stereo, and turned the volume up, so that the elegant configurations of the Mendelssohn *Symphony in C Minor* accompanied him as he walked among the shelves. He found Meg upstairs in an old leather armchair facing one of the dormer windows. She greeted him perfunctorily, complaining when he picked her up and usurped her napping place. But she seemed satisfied with his lap as long as he provided a gentle back rub. Her rumbling purr softly underlined the Mendelssohn. Conan sighed, envying her capacity for instant repose.

"Duchess, I lost a major battle today. I wonder about the war."

He had learned a great deal since he had talked to Earl Kleber Saturday, yet there was still no *corpus delicti*, and now there would be no autopsy that might have provided that vital proof of the crime. Still, he had gleaned a few possibly dependable facts by checking Jonas's and Nina's stories against each other; they had had no opportunity for prior consultation. And France's story— well, discrepancies were always revealing, and there was the success of the epilepsy ploy. At least, he could now regard it as a strong possibility that Corey had displayed symptoms similar to an epileptic seizure.

Meg stirred and murmured a husky reminder for him to resume her massage. He did, but he was thinking about the odd response that both France and Moses had displayed to his suggestion that Corey had suffered from epilepsy. There had definitely been an element of relief in it. Relief because epilepsy would provide an explanation for a phenomenon they knew had quite a different cause?

He laughed silently. How he would relish being present when Moses and Frances learned that Corey had not had epilepsy. At any rate, he thought, still counting—or at least trying to find—his blessings, he could be sure of most of the information he had *about* —if not *from*—the six conspirators, especially the information from Charlie Duncan. But that only further elucidated motive for each of them.

Perhaps he should give more consideration to the other legs of the tripod: means and opportunity. Greg Feingold had thrown some light, in a backward fashion, on means. *If* Corey was not alive when her head met the windshield. Conan chose to assume she wasn't because of the missing skid marks. When she approached the curve at Reem's Rocks, she was either dead or heavily sedated. If the latter, barbiturates and alcohol were eliminated. If the former . . .

Feingold had ruled out some of the more obvious poisons, but that still left a wide range to choose from.

But for the killer to choose from? No, opportunity had to be considered here. None of the six people at Gabe's house that fateful night had expected Corey or the revelation of the diary. The murder had to be a spur of the moment thing and the means readily available.

"Meg, why am I thinking in terms of killer *singular?*"

She opened her sapphire eyes, gave him a vague glance, then lapsed into a deep, purrless sleep.

There were six people involved in this murder, yet he found it difficult to imagine these particular people reaching a consensus on anything as serious as murder in the short time available for discussion. That would be while Corey was in the bathroom after the dousing administered by France. Five to ten minutes, probably. And that motley group not only came to an agreement on committing a murder, but found the means at hand, and formulated a plan?

That he could not swallow. Of course, the time limit assumed that they wanted to keep their deliberations secret from their victim. But if they didn't, if Corey had any inkling of their plans, she would try to escape, and that would mean a struggle. Corey was physically strong and not easily cowed; she would fight fiercely, and that would inevitably leave marks of some sort. The bruise on the sternum? No, that could be explained by Nina's attempt at CPR.

If there wasn't time for a group decision, then it was an individual decision. One of the six had found the means at hand and had seized on the opportunity.

Yet afterward, when the killer had presented the others with a *fait accompli*, would they all willingly make themselves accessories to murder? Aside from the morality of it, would they risk the legal consequences of first-degree murder simply to protect the Baysea sale?

Yes. Conan recognized the answer with profound rage that found no immediate expression except for the painful tension of his jaw muscles.

And was the risk so great? What were the legal consequences that should strike fear into their hearts? So far, there were none. The law was, in this case, if not a ass, certainly impotent. Any one of those particular people would take that minimal risk without a moral qualm.

"Duchess, it looks like we have a visitor." Conan watched the Holliday Beach police car pull up to the curb behind the XK-E. Earl Kleber got out of the car and strode to the front door of the shop. While his knocks echoed through the building, Conan restored Meg to her original napping spot, then hurried downstairs to open the door.

"Come on in, Chief. You'll attract customers standing around out here."

Kleber gave a short laugh and stepped into the shop, looking around idly while Conan locked the door behind him.

"I saw your car out there, Conan."

"I just stopped in to check on Meg."

"Mm. That cat like music?"

"Well, she prefers Beethoven. Come into the office. I'll put on a pot of coffee."

Kleber followed him into the office and laid claim to one of the chairs in front of the desk. "Don't make any coffee for me. Can't stay that long."

Conan turned off the stereo and went to his chair. "I gather you were looking for me, Chief."

"Well, yes, I was. But this is *un*official. I had a call from Owen Culpepper a little while ago. He says Leo Moskin is talking about getting an injunction against you and maybe even pressing charges for harassment and invasion of privacy—his and the Benbows'."

Conan had his lighter and a pack of cigarettes out, but he tossed them angrily on the desk. "Harassment, for God's sake? And invasion of privacy? I haven't gotten past any of the Benbows' front doors, and when I did get past Leo's, I was very quickly ushered out."

Kleber nodded sourly. "Well, I figured you'd like to know what Leo was up to. Did you find out anything while you were doing all that harassing and invading?"

Conan retrieved his lighter and cigarettes and got one lighted. "Sure. I found out that six people were at Gabe's house Friday night when Corey arrived: Gabe, Jonas, France, Moses, Nina Gillies, and Leo Moskin. Corey read Kate's intriguing diary entry, and one of them poisoned and/or drugged her. The medium for the offending—and unidentified—substance was a black russian. And I know that each of the six people had very strong motives to kill Corey, and that all of them are at least accessories to murder."

Kleber's cleft of a mouth in a cliff of a jaw was tight. "And? Drop the other shoe, damn it."

Conan let his head rest against the back of his chair while he blew out a slow stream of smoke. "And? Well, the problem is, I can't *prove* any of it. Not one damned thing. Except motive. I'm knee-deep in motive."

Kleber sighed. "So, Leo Moskin was at Gabe's house. No wonder he's so worried about his privacy. I'll be damned."

"He won't, unfortunately, unless you believe in an afterlife that includes a good, hot hell." He paused, then with a shrug, "Well, I've 'harassed' three of the six into telling me their version of what happened. With some cross-checking, I've winnowed a few grains of truth from the chaff. Of course, they were so talkative with me only because they hoped I'd swallow their stories and leave them alone. But if you, or any other representative of the law, were to question them, all you'd get is a series of earnest denials."

"Which three talked?"

"Jonas, Nina, and France. I tried for Leo and Gabe. Moses . . . that would be a waste of time. I'd only get a rerun of France's story."

Kleber shifted restlessly, lacing his fingers across his black leather gunbelt. "You didn't get anything out of them we could use to dig up some *real* evidence?"

"No. By the way, did you know Corey's body was cremated this morning?"

"This *morning?"*

"Yes. *Before* I convinced Feingold that he should do a full autopsy. God, I'm surrounded by brick walls."

"You are? *I'm* cemented in!"

Conan looked at him, and that frustrated admission of defeat carried a chill weight beyond the mere words.

"Earl, there *must* be something we can do."

"What? There isn't even any proof a crime was committed. Even if you got a confession, you'd still have to get corroborating evidence for a conviction. That's the way the law works in this country."

A silence fell as Conan considered that pronoun. Kleber said "you," not "we," unconsciously. He wasn't shirking his responsibilities in this case; he was only recognizing his helplessness as an agent of the law.

Kleber said bitterly, "Hell, Conan, people get away with murder every day."

"Not Corey Benbow's murder."

The chief's eyes narrowed. "What are you going to do?"

"I don't know. See what I can 'harass' out of Leo and Gabe, I suppose. At least, Gabe. I think it's futile to try to breach Leo's internal and external security systems." Conan frowned thoughtfully. "I need a change in the emotional climate; something that will make Gabe more amenable to confession. Maybe I'd finally get a workable lead."

Kleber rose. "Well, there's going to be a change in the climate outside. Coast Guard called me to say there's one granddaddy of a storm headed our way. Already getting tidal waves and flooding in Hawaii."

Conan accompanied him to the front door and unlocked it. "When is this storm due to hit the coast?"

"They said probably Wednesday."

"On a spring tide. Tuesday's the full moon." Conan smiled obliquely and looked up into a sky patterned with chatoyant mackerel clouds. "Should be interesting."

"Interesting? Sure. By the way, you heard from Hatch lately?"

"No. Have you heard any more about him?"

"Not yet." Kleber started for his car, then turned. "Conan, don't . . . well, I'd sure as hell hate to see you on the wrong side of the bars in *my* jail."

Conan nodded. "So would I, Chief."

CHAPTER 14

Only a few remnant islands of old-growth timber survived in the dense secondary forests of the Coast Range. One of those groves surrounded Crestview Cemetery on a gentle slope above Holliday Beach. The cemetery, with its winter-gray grasses, at first seemed simply an open meadow studded with unnaturally shaped marble and granite boulders. The ancient Sitka spruce, massive trunks commanding each its span of space and claiming the earth beneath with unseen, grasping sinews, tolerated the false meadow as they tolerated all things, even time. There seemed some basic affinity between them and the monuments of stone.

Conan heard without listening the drone of Reverend Abel's litany. "Earth to earth, ashes to ashes, dust to dust . . ." And what had that small, bronzed urn to do with Corey Benbow?

> Go and dig me a hole in the meadow,
> A hole in the cold, cold ground,
> Go and dig me a hole in the meadow,
> Just to lay darlin' Corey down.

On this winter afternoon, the sky garbed itself in gray, clouds moving swiftly with the west wind, just out of reach of the top branches of the trees. A marble obelisk was inscribed simply "Benbow." Three smaller marble blocks stood in its lee: Grace Edmonds Benbow; Katharine Donovan Benbow; Mark Benbow. There was no marker yet for Corella Danner Benbow; only a small hole in this artificial meadow.

Reverend Abel, prayer book open, its pages fluttering in the wind, stood at one end of that raw gouge in the earth. On his right, Gabe Benbow, with his seamed and craggy face, was the essence of solemnity—hands clasped, staring at the urn within the earthen cavity as if he found it an affront. Perhaps he did; Gabe didn't approve of cremation. Or so he had always maintained.

Standing next to Gabe, Moses and France also gazed down into the grave, Moses in a dark brown suit, France fashionably funereal in a black, veiled hat and black fur coat; the coat was sealskin. Jonas also stared into the grave, but with such bleary fixity, Conan doubted his sobriety.

Nina Gillies was not among the mourners, but, surprisingly, Leonard Moskin was, dressed in somber hues that did not diminish his massive presence. He had earlier made it clear that he was here simply as a friend of the family. His gaze was more mobile than the others', and several times during the ceremony, Conan found those hooded eyes fixed on him. There was no hint of sympathy in them.

Across the rift the grave seemed to create, Conan stood beside Diane Monteil. She was dressed in white: a muslin dress with a heavy knit shawl against the chill of the wind that tossed her pewter-gold hair. She seemed the only light in this bleak scene. At her side, protected from the wind, she held the white kite with the bluebird in the rainbow circle. Kit held the spool. He wore a gray suit and tie, and perhaps he was expected to be a little man today; grief was an adult experience. His sea-colored eyes quested constantly, seeking answers he would not find here. His free hand was clasped in Melissa's. She was dressed in white, like her mother, and she seemed to be searching for answers too, and near tears because she found none.

Encircling the divided "families," more mourners looked on: three Earth Conservancy officers from Portland and at least thirty townspeople. Among them, Conan saw Chief Earl Kleber and his daughter Caroline. Many of the mourners were young people, like Jory Rankin, who had undoubtedly cut classes to be here.

But there was one ominous absence, one mourner who above all should be present. Lyndon Hatch. Conan had convinced himself that Lyn would—must—finally come out of the woods, figuratively and literally, for Corey's funeral. He hadn't.

". . . we consecrate the immortal soul of our sister unto thy everlasting mercy, O Lord. Amen."

The reverend's resonant drone at last ceased. Gabe leaned down, picked up a handful of dirt, and cast it upon the urn with the words, "'When the dead is at rest, let his remembrance rest. . . .'"

And that, Conan thought, was an odd but perhaps indicative choice of a quote. Let his *remembrance* rest. . . .

Diane said quietly, "All right, Kit . . . now."

She held the bluebird kite up by its bridle, the wind tugging at it. It was Jory Rankin whose soft, tenor voice began the song "Amazing Grace," and a small chorus of mourners added their voices to his. And Conan, who in the best of times found that song hard to listen to, because it struck resonances within his mind of old griefs, listened and found it beautiful, even in this ragged, unpolished rendition. The wind claimed the bluebird kite; it seemed to leap toward the clouds, and Kit, with the spool spinning in his hands, watched its retreat longingly.

The end of the string was not fixed to the spool, and Kit knew it. The rainbow and bluebird were only a patch of color against the gray clouds when the string spun out to the end. With a wordless cry, Kit caught the loose string and clung to it. Diane knelt beside him, one arm enfolding him. "Kit, let it go. You have to let it go."

At length he did. The kite pulled away, tumbling erratically, and the wind swept it out of sight beyond the trees.

With a collective sigh, the mourners began moving away down the grassy aisles between the markers toward the parking area north of the cemetery. The Benbows and Moskin, Conan noted, had left well before the ceremony of freeing the kite was concluded.

Conan walked with Diane and the children toward his Vanagon; they had ridden to the cemetery with him. No one spoke for some time, until finally Diane began, "Norman has arranged a private hearing today with the judge on the custody case. He thinks we can—"

She stopped, silenced by a reverberating crack—a sound instantly recognizable, despite its incongruity here.

A rifle shot.

Screams and shouts were punctuated by another shot, then a third.

Like almost everyone else in the cemetery, Conan was on the ground, and if Kit and Melissa sustained any injury from the fusillade, it could only be the result of protective crushing by two adults.

There were no more shots, and after a tense wait, Conan got to his feet. "Are you all right?"

The children nodded, wide-eyed. Diane whispered her assent as Conan helped her up, then grabbing Kit's hand, he snapped, "Come on, Di—let's get out of here!"

Chief Kleber had taken command, his shouted orders averting total chaos. Conan led Diane and the children at a run around the center of confusion, grateful that he had parked the Vanagon near the exit. He noted in passing that Caroline Kleber was in her father's police car, calmly using the radio to call for assistance.

The focus of attention was Gabe Benbow's Continental. Two of its side windows were shattered, but all the Benbows seemed to be present and accounted for, and Gabe was already bellowing demands for police protection at a red-faced Kleber. Conan didn't envy the chief, but neither did he stay to assist him; Kleber could manage.

Kit and Melissa piled into the back seat of the Vanagon, and Conan wondered if he weren't underestimating their resiliency; they both seemed stimulated, more than frightened, by all the excitement. Diane got in the front seat, and when Conan started the motor, she leaned toward him, keeping her voice down so that the children couldn't hear. "It was *Lyn*, wasn't it?" Then when Conan didn't immediately respond, "He was shooting at the Benbows, Conan. Or probably just Gabe. They were all right there by his car when the shots started."

Conan drove down the road in second gear, in no great hurry now and mindful of the police cars that would soon be barreling toward the cemetery. Then he smiled, and the smile erupted into a laugh.

"Conan, what's so funny?" Diane asked irritably.

"I was just thinking about all the Benbows hitting the dirt at once. All of them in their funereal best."

After a moment, she was laughing too. "Well, as Gabe would say, 'Whoso diggeth a pit shall fall therein.'"

"At least this might provide the change in emotional climate I was hoping for. Gabe might be thinking seriously about the wages of sin now."

Diane's smile faded. "What are you going to do, Conan?"

"Just talk to him, Di. Don't worry."

"What about Lyn?"

Conan braked at a stop sign, then turned left onto Foothills Boulevard Road. "There's not much I can do about Lyn until he decides to come out of the woods. I just hope Kleber doesn't bring him out forcibly. Are you going back to Dundee after the hearing?"

She glanced into the back seat. "Yes. I think a few more days with Mom and Dad will be good for the kids. And me. Conan, we haven't had a chance to talk about—well, about your investigation."

"Call me this evening when you're free to talk for a while. Anytime before . . . oh, about midnight."

"Do you turn into a pumpkin then?"

He laughed. "The less you know about my nocturnal metamorphoses, the better."

Conan managed to stay out of reach of a telephone for most of the remainder of the afternoon by the expedient of having a long, leisurely lunch at the Surf House, where he could watch the breakers at high tide. He might have whiled away the time with a walk on the beach, but on this afternoon there *was* no beach; it was submerged under roiling cascades of white water. There was no rain yet, and this storm was not following the usual scenario, which in itself was ominous. Gulls milled restlessly, spiraling ever higher until they were only tiny gray dots against the gray sky.

Finally, at four o'clock, he returned to his house, where he only had time to put on a pot of coffee before the phone rang. He took the call on the kitchen phone; it was Chief Earl Kleber.

"Where the hell have you been, Flagg?"

Conan smiled faintly. "Out to lunch, Chief. Why?"

"I've been trying to get hold of you for two hours. You sure pulled a fast disappearing act at the cemetery."

"I had Diane and the kids with me, and it seemed like a good idea to get them out of there. What happened, anyway? Some poacher mistake Gabe's Continental for a deer?"

Kleber replied irritably, "I don't know who did the shooting. We had twenty men from the sheriff's office, the State Patrol, and our department out in those woods. Turned up zilch."

"Did any of the Benbows sustain any damage—other than racking up a big cleaning bill?"

"This isn't funny, damn it! No, nobody was hurt. What I want to know from you is, where the hell is Lyndon Hatch?"

Conan put a cast of surprise in his tone. "Lyn Hatch? Chief, I told you I have no idea where he is. Why all this interest in Lyn?"

"Don't pull that innocent act on me. He was seen yesterday out in the woods with a rifle, and he never made a secret of how much he hates Gabe Benbow's guts."

"Is that according to Gabe Benbow? Chief, Lyn is a field representative for The Earth Conservancy, and he also has a tendency to say exactly what he thinks. So, I leave it to you to guess how Gabe feels about *him.*"

"Maybe. But what in God's name was he doing out in the woods? Answer me that!"

"I can't, except to say that Lyn has spent most of his life outdoors. Maybe it's therapy for him."

A long pause, then, "He was engaged to Corey, wasn't he?"

"Not to my knowledge. Is that from Gabe too?"

"Yeah. Oh, hell, I don't *need* all this hassle. Now I'm a man short because Gabe hollered so loud about police protection. And Giff Wills—he had Gabe convinced the sheriff's department's so shorthanded they can't spare even a stenographer, so it got dumped in *my* lap."

Conan's eyes narrowed. "I suppose nothing less than round-the-clock bodyguards will satisfy Gabe."

"Sure. All courtesy of the taxpayers of Holliday Beach. Conan, if you *do* happen to hear from Hatch . . ."

"I'll tell him you're worried about him."

When Conan hung up, he went to the windows. Beyond the pall of cloud, the sun had not yet set, but little of its light penetrated the gray veils. He felt none of the exhilaration with which he usually regarded the approach of a major storm. He was thinking about Lyn Hatch and Earl Kleber; of revenge and the law. And justice. Justice had somehow gotten lost between the two.

CHAPTER 15

At midnight, Conan reached the metal gate marking Gabe Benbow's property line. It was, as he anticipated, closed and padlocked. He parked the XK-E on the narrow shoulder of the road.

It wasn't the padlock on the gate that induced him to leave the car here; he'd opened it before *sans* key, and he had the necessary tools with him. In fact, he was the quintessential cat burglar tonight, his clothing all black, including the skin-thin leather gloves and the knit cap that doubled as a ski mask when he pulled it down over his face. He wore a wool jacket that didn't rustle with his movements, and in one pocket, he carried his special tool case and a pencil flash; in the other, a Mauser 9 mm semiautomatic.

He chose to leave the car here because he knew Gabe's house to be occupied, not only by Gabe and his prodigal son, but by his reluctantly provided police guard. The car lights, if observed, would betray his approach, and on this black night, driving without them would be impossible. At any rate, it was only a quarter of a mile to the house.

Conan vaulted the fence, and with the pencil flash as his only light, set off down the road at an easy trot. Above him, scudding clouds thinned occasionally to reveal a dim glow where the full moon should be. He felt now the exhilaration he had missed earlier as he crested the highest point of the road and began the descent toward Shearwater Spit. Here nothing shielded him from the wind or the pervading roar of the breakers. The air had a dry crackle to it and a scent he couldn't separate from pine and earth that enhanced them without revealing itself. The wind gusted hard out of the west, oddly warm and caressing.

The only light in the Benbow house was in the northwest-facing windows of the living room, and he didn't see it until he reached the parking area. He sprinted across the lawn to the deck, then pulled the ski mask over his face, staying close to the wall as he moved toward the windows. The drapes were partially open. When he finally took a cautious look into the room, he smiled.

Gabe's recliner was occupied, but not by its owner. Sergeant Billy Todd, youngest officer in the HBPD, and a native son. He was engrossed in a book, and Conan recognized the brown-paper jacket Miss Dobie put on all new rental books at the Holliday Beach Book Shop. Billy Todd had been a faithful bookshop customer since he was twelve years old.

Conan retreated off the deck and made his way around the back of the house to the east wing. He didn't know where Jonas was domiciled, but he did know the location of the master bedroom, and that was his objective. Two large, aluminum-framed windows met at the northeast corner, and the one on the north had a sliding panel; it was open a few inches. The screen was locked, but Conan jimmied it out of its frame in a few seconds. Apparently, Gabe considered the screen lock security enough; there was no rod in the track to stop the window from opening all the way. Conan boosted himself onto the sill, then dropped behind the curtains. Over the distant surf roar, he heard a sonorous snoring.

He extricated himself from the curtains and saw a night-light illuminating the bathroom to his right. Across the room from him, the door into the hall was open, a dim light reaching it from the living room. It was a long hallway, Conan knew; at least thirty feet. To his left he saw a semi-colonial bedstead, and that was the site of the snoring. The light from the hall fell softly on Gabe's craggy profile and open mouth, lips sunken over dentureless gums. If he suffered any qualms of conscience, it didn't affect his sleep.

Conan crossed silently to the door, listened for sounds of movement from the living room before he eased it closed, then went to the bed and felt for the switch on the lamp mounted on the headboard.

Gabe awoke with a glaring light in his eyes, a masked figure looming over him, a gloved hand covering his mouth, and a gun only inches from his forehead. His muffled cry turned into a wheezing gasp.

Conan said softly, "Behave yourself, Gabe, or by God I'll blow a hole in that incredibly hard head of yours."

Gabe's pale eyes were wide and glazed, and Conan had to admit that there was some satisfaction in the naked terror reflected in them. He took his hand away from Gabe's mouth slowly, and when no cries for help resulted, pulled off his mask-cap and thrust it in his jacket pocket.

Gabe croaked huskily, "Flagg! Why you goddamned—"

"Taking the name of the Lord in vain?" Then Conan pressed the barrel of the gun hard against the old man's temple. "Don't kid yourself, Gabe. I'm perfectly willing to kill you, especially after attending Corey's funeral today. And I'd get away with it. The graveyard sniper strikes again, and no one would even know *I* was here."

"I got—there's a policeman out in the living room! All I have to do is—"

"What makes you think Billy is still there to hear you?"

Gabe seemed to sink into himself with that, breath rattling, arthritic hands clutching the bedcovers under his chin like a frightened, grotesque child.

Conan sat down on the edge of the bed, keeping the gun close to Gabe's face. "I want to know what happened here Friday night, Gabe—the night Corey was murdered."

A hoarse whisper: "Murdered! No, she wasn't—it was a—a fit. Epilepsy! That's it, she had—"

"No, she didn't. That was just a little invention of mine. Corey was in perfect health. Now, begin at the beginning, when Corey arrived. What time was that?"

Gabe's lips worked aimlessly over toothless gums, then his eyes rolled toward the gun, and he began to make words of the incoherent sounds. "She . . . she came about eight-thirty, I think."

"And what happened, Gabe?"

"Well, at first we—all of us just . . . talked, you know, then she brought out that—" His fear momentarily gave way to remembered anger. "—that goddamned diary of Kate's!"

"You forgot something, Gabe: the first black russian."

"Oh . . ." His head went up and down in anxious affirmation. "France made it. When Corey first came. Then after she read the diary, that stupid woman threw it in her face. France, I mean. She threw—"

"I know, Gabe. Get on with it!"

Gabe's fingers twitched crablike on the sheets. "Well, then Corey went into the bathroom to clean up—"

"Where was everyone seated before this interruption?"

"I—I think . . . well, I was in my armchair, and on the couch to my right, it was France, then Moses, then Nina. Jonas was next to me on the other couch, then Corey, and then . . . Leo. Damn it, can't I even get my *teeth?*"

Conan smiled coldly. "You're doing fine without them, Gabe. What happened after Corey retired to the bathroom?"

Gabe's tongue darted out to moisten his lower lip. "That's when Moses took France out to the kitchen. Nina and Leo and me, we talked—tried to figure out what to do."

"Where was Jonas?"

"What? Well, he was—I guess he got up to see what Moses and France were doing."

"Did he go into the kitchen?"

"I—I don't know. He came back and sat down before Corey— wait a minute. Nina went to the kitchen too, then after a while, France and Moses came out, then Nina. She brought drinks. One for France and another for Corey."

"Where did she put Corey's drink?"

He assayed a shrug. "I guess . . . yes, right in front of where Corey was sitting. On the coffee table."

"And everyone was back in their original positions, with Leo and Jonas on either side of Corey? Were they drinking? Where were their glasses?"

"Damn it, I don't—on the table, I think."

"Near Corey's glass?" Then when Gabe nodded silently, "What about Leo? Did he remain seated all this time?"

"I guess so. I didn't see him move."

Conan leaned closer. "And you, Gabe? Did you move?"

"No!" He tried to draw away from Conan, head pressing deeper into the pillow. "I didn't get out of my chair once!"

"When Corey returned, what happened?"

"We . . . we talked for a while. Tried to figure out some way around—I mean, something—"

"Did Corey drink any of that second black russian?"

"I can't remember—wait. Yes. She said something about how she hoped we could come to a *peaceful* agreement. And Jonas picked up his glass and said, 'I'll drink to that.' Damn fool! And he *will* be damned, eternally damned, if—"

Conan shifted the barrel of the gun until it was only an inch from

Gabe's left eye. "Don't start preaching, Gabe—not you! Did Corey join in Jonas's toast?"

"Yes. I know she drank some then and probably later on. We talked for—it seemed like a long time. And then . . . then Corey, she kind of choked up. Said she couldn't breathe and her mouth and throat felt numb."

"Numb? That was the word she used?"

"I think so. Then she started shaking all over, and Jonas caught her before she fell over on the table. We got the table out of the way, and she just kept on shaking and jerking. . . ." Gabe was all but panting now, but he hesitated, eyes shifting past the gun to Conan's face. "Then she . . . well, she stopped shaking, and in a few minutes, she sat up and said she was all right again and— *ahhh!*"

That strangled cry came as Conan pulled him upright by his pajamas collar. "I've *heard* that story, Gabe, and I still don't believe it! The truth! I want the *truth!*"

Gabe husked, "Okay! Okay! I'll tell you—I'll . . . tell you the truth." When Conan loosened his grip on his collar, he sagged back limply. "She—she *did* stop shaking, but . . ."

"But *what*, Gabe?"

"She stopped breathing. Jonas tried to find a pulse. At first, he said he could feel something, then Nina—she said she had CPR training. She and Jonas . . ." Gabe's eyes squeezed shut. "As the Lord is my witness, they *tried.*"

Conan's breath came out in a long, aching sigh. "But she was dead."

Gabe nodded. "But it wasn't—nobody *killed* her! She died of— of natural causes! I swear it—that's the *truth!*"

Conan hissed, *"Natural causes?* Do you expect me to believe that? Do *you* believe it? You ignorant, arrogant bastard!" His finger tightened on the trigger. But after a moment, he drew away from Gabe. A good thing, perhaps, that this gun was not the lethal instrument it seemed right now.

"All right, Gabe, let's have the rest of the story."

Gabe swallowed audibly. "Well, Leo said we couldn't call the police. I mean, if anybody found out *he* was here—well, we figured it'd just be easier if, I mean since she . . . since I thought she died of natural causes, we figured she could just as well have died . . . someplace else."

"Like at the bottom of Sitka Bay? So, you took her body and car to the curve above Reem's Rocks, put her behind the steering wheel, and pushed the car down the hill." Gabe only nodded. "Did all of you take part in that?"

"Yes. All of us."

For a while, the only sounds were Gabe's strained breathing and the roar of the ocean. Then Conan asked, "Why are you suing for custody of Kit? Why in the name of anything reasonable or just do you want to take Kit away from Diane?"

There was life—and cantankerous defiance—in the old man yet. He replied hotly, "The boy's a *Benbow!* It's not right for him to be raised by strangers!"

Conan was nearly awestruck by that, and he almost missed the warning creak outside the door. A second later, the door banged open, and Sergeant Billy Todd loomed within the frame, his .38 police special extended in a two-handed grip.

"Freeze!"

Conan didn't quite freeze, but held his hands away from his body, the Mauser suspended by one finger through the trigger guard.

Todd's jaw dropped. "Conan?"

"Himself," Conan admitted, rising.

Gabe jerked upright, blinking like a flannel-pajamaed Lazarus. "Billy! He told me you—goddamn it, Flagg! Billy, you arrest that man! He tried to kill me!"

Sergeant Todd holstered his gun as he crossed to take Conan's. He checked it, frowning. "Where's the clip?"

Conan smiled. "Well, I must've left it at home."

"Billy, didn't you hear me?" Gabe threw back the blankets and surged out of bed. "That man tried to *kill* me!"

Todd gazed blankly at Gabe—thin hair flying, toothless gums making mush of his consonants. "Gabe," Todd said, holding up the Mauser, "Conan wasn't about to kill *any*body with this. No clip. No *bullets.*"

"I didn't know that! He *threatened* me—"

"Gabe, shut up," Conan said wearily, "and let Billy do his job. Now's your chance to get your teeth in."

To Conan's amazement, Gabe did shut up and did head for the bathroom, but perhaps that was due in part to the fact that he had acquired a case of hiccups.

Todd sighed. "Conan, what are you doing here?"

Conan glanced into the bathroom, where Gabe was downing a glass of water. "I came here to talk to Gabe about Corey Benbow's death. I had to put the fear of *something* in him. He wouldn't talk to me otherwise."

"Corey's death?" Todd's eyes narrowed.

"She didn't die accidentally, Billy. At this point, I still can't prove anything. I was just hoping . . ."

"Did Gabe have anything to say?"

Conan smiled crookedly. "Oh, yes. But you needn't bother to ask him what it was. He'll just develop amnesia. But there's one thing—if you'd just play along with me for a little while. I want to look around in the kitchen."

"I don't know, Conan. You've put me in a hell of a spot. Gabe could charge you with breaking and entering, and if I don't do something, it won't look good to Kleber."

Gabe came out of the bathroom, robed, his teeth and righteous self-possession restored. "Damn right, it won't look good, and Earl Kleber's going to hear about it if—"

Conan cut in, "Billy, only the three of us know what happened here tonight. If anyone asks, just say I came to the front door and knocked, and Gabe *graciously* invited me in to have a little chat about Corey Benbow. It'll be your word and mine against Gabe's. Two to one should be as good as *six* to one."

Todd obviously didn't understand that allusion, but it silenced Gabe. Todd studied him a moment, then nodded. "Well, that'd save a lot of paper work."

Conan smiled and started for the hall door. "I'm going to take a look at the kitchen, and Gabe—ever accommodating and cooperative—won't object at all. Will you, Gabe?"

"What? Now, *wait* a minute!"

Conan led the way down the hall, with Todd a pace behind, Gabe vociferously bringing up the rear. When Conan reached the living room, he stopped just inside the door. It was in a corner of the room in the wall where the two wings of the house met, and that gave the room some interesting angles. Otherwise, it had the bland consistency of a Hilton Hotel suite, with white walls, beige shag carpet, and drapes and upholstery in earthy, abstract prints. Gabe did not collect things, nor did he seem to have found any object encountered during his lifetime worthy of cherishing for sentimental reasons.

The hall's left-hand wall continued to form what Conan knew to be the kitchen wall, but he went first to the rectangular grouping of furniture at the center of the living room and stood behind one of the couches that formed the sides of the rectangle. He was facing the front door and windows; raindrops glinted on the glass. The rain had finally begun. To his left, Gabe's recliner closed one end of the rectangle, and the other end was closed, after a space of about four feet, by a fireplace faced in used brick. A fire blazed in the hearth, providing sterile heat, but no warmth; it was a gas fire-log. The coffee table between the couches was a lucite-encased slab of redwood, its beautiful color and grain made garish by the plastic.

And there, on the opposite couch, seated between Jonas and Moskin, Corey had drunk her death.

Conan turned abruptly and went around the corner into the kitchen, pushing through a pair of louvered, swinging doors, with Todd and Gabe still on his heels. The kitchen was relatively small, with sink, dishwasher, a long counter, and wall-hung cupboards on the right; refrigerator, electric range, microwave, and storage closet on the left. The aisle between ended in a closed door.

Conan's search was perfunctory—merely opening drawers and doors and glancing within—until he got to the cabinets under the sink. He studied the various household cleaning products, while Billy looked over his shoulder curiously, and Gabe stood at the swinging doors delivering a continuous tirade that Conan ignored exactly as he did the sound of the surf outside. It was amazing, he thought, how many poisonous substances were available in the average American home. None of these, however, could explain the symptoms. They were cumulative poisons, or carcinogens, or caustics.

He rose and went to the closed door. It was locked, but a twist of the knob opened it. He felt for a light switch, found it, then stepped inside. The back door of the house opened off the right-hand wall, and this room served as a utility room and storage for tools and garden equipment.

Conan felt his pulse quicken. He was getting close, and he had an inkling now of what he was looking for. "Gabe!"

The shout was unnecessary. Gabe was still right behind him. "What's the matter *now*, Flagg?"

"Was this door open Friday night?"

"Sure it was. I always keep it open when the heat's on in the house. These tools'd rust if I didn't keep it dry. Now, I'd like to know what business you got poking around in *here!*"

Conan didn't answer. On the open shelves to the right of the door, the array of garden chemicals included pesticides, herbicides, snail bait, phosphate, and fertilizers. He found what he sought at eye level at the front of the shelf: a brown glass bottle with its label divided into three horizontal stripes—red, white, and blue. On the white stripe, two skull-and-crossbones symbols bracketed the word "POISON."

Black Leaf 40. As the label attested, "The original nicotine sulphate solution."

The level of the liquid in the bottle was well below the top of the label, which was stained by pourings; the dark glass was powdered with dust, but the cap was clean.

Sergeant Todd asked uneasily, "Conan, what's wrong?"

That question Conan couldn't find the words to answer. He had what he was looking for. He *had* it, yet he had nothing. Black Leaf 40, a forty-percent solution of one of the deadliest poisons known; a few drops of straight nicotine sulfate could kill, and in this solution, less than a teaspoonful was known to be lethal.

"Gabe, where do you usually keep this Black Leaf Forty?"

"What? Oh, that. Right where it's sitting."

And that was only a few steps from the counter where Corey's last drink had been prepared.

"Listen, Flagg, I've had just about enough of your—"

"Is that Jonas?" He had heard the squeak of the swinging doors, and to his relief, Gabe went back into the kitchen to face his son's queries. Conan turned to Todd, keeping his voice low. "Billy, I think—I know—the poison that killed Corey came out of that bottle, but I can't prove it, and you can't do a damn thing about it. You don't have a search warrant, and you couldn't get one, when I don't even—"

"You're saying somebody poisoned Corey?" His skeptical gaze moved from Conan to the bottle and back.

"Yes. Now, I'm going to ask you to do something that may seem silly. Please do it, if you have any faith in me. Go get your jacket, then come back here. Then go out to your car. And just ignore Gabe's questions."

Todd sighed. "I'll probably regret this." But he was on his way out. Conan could hear Gabe and Jonas in a low-toned exchange that stopped as Todd passed them. Conan took the bottle from the shelf and slipped it in his jacket pocket. Todd returned a few seconds later in his visored cap and uniform jacket. He glanced at the empty space where the bottle had been, then with another sigh, turned and strode through the kitchen.

Gabe and Jonas were standing facing each other near the kitchen door. Gabe demanded of Todd, "Where do you think you're going?"

Todd's only response was, "I'll be right back." He didn't break pace.

"Well, Jonas, did we wake you?" Conan asked pleasantly as he sauntered out into the kitchen. Then with a glance at his watch, "Or did you have to get up anyway for your one-o'clock call to Phoenix?"

Jonas, looking rumpled and disgruntled, paled at that, and Todd's exit out the front door went unnoticed.

Gabe asked, "Phoenix? What are you talking about, Flagg?"

"Didn't Jonas tell you? He has to call Phoenix rather frequently to, uh, check in with *Doctor* Belasco. But don't worry; he's not charging the calls to your phone."

Gabe's head whipped around so that he could glower at Jonas. "What's this all about? You didn't tell me—"

Conan put in, "I'm sure he didn't want to worry his ever-solicitous father. Before Billy gets back, I have one more question, Gabe. What happened to the diary?"

It was amazing the way Gabe could suddenly look so blank. "I don't know what you're talking about."

"Oh, for God's sake," Jonas said irritably. "Pa, from what you told me, you've already spilled the whole goddamned bag of beans!" Then to Conan, "How did you know about . . . *Doctor* Belasco?"

"Let's just say I was concerned when I learned about your ill-health. Look, Billy's going to be back in a few minutes. *What happened to the diary?*"

Gabe replied staunchly, "We burned it! It's gone. Nothing but ashes."

Conan laughed. "You burned it? In that fake fireplace, no doubt. Or perhaps you microwaved it."

Jonas went to the refrigerator and as he peered into it said bitterly, "My old man, with all the wisdom of his years, gave the damn diary to Nina Gillies."

Gabe's face reddened ominously, but Conan ignored the new tirade that followed; he was wondering why Jonas had volunteered that information—and judging from Gabe's reaction, it was true. Was Jonas expressing gratitude to Conan for not telling Gabe about "Doctor" Belasco, or simply responding to the threat implied in that name? Or was he purposely pointing a finger at Nina?

Jonas found a can of beer, opened it, and smoothly lifted it to his mouth to catch the effervescent overflow. He said to Conan, "Nina promised she'd 'take care' of the diary. Pa figured she meant she'd destroy it."

Gabe insisted, "She will, too! She's got as much to lose in this as any of us."

"Or as much to gain?" Jonas took another swig of beer, eyeing his father skeptically.

And Gabe was atypically quiet, thinking, perhaps, as Conan was, of the potential for blackmail in that diary *after* the Baysea sale was concluded, *after* Nina had collected her commission and other fringe benefits.

The front door opened, and a gust of wind and rain heralded Billy Todd's return. There would be no more revelations from the Benbows, *père et fils*, Conan knew. He crossed to the door, keeping his voice down as he said, "Thanks, Billy. One more favor: try to keep Gabe occupied and away from a phone for—well, half an hour, if possible."

Todd should have told Conan to forget it, but he only sighed yet again and said, "I'll try."

Conan pulled on his cap as he went out the door into the wind-driven lash of rain. The quarter mile to his car seemed a long way now. He set off at a run.

CHAPTER 16

When Conan reached the XK-E, he didn't pause to catch his breath, only to tear off his rain-wet gloves. He backed and turned, hands slapping at the wheel, then the Jaguar leapt forward like its namesake, and he restrained it only out of consideration for the slick pavement.

It was inevitable that as soon as Gabe freed himself of Todd, he would call Nina to find out if she had destroyed the diary as promised. That would alert her to the fact that Conan knew she had the diary, and he wanted to see what, if anything, she did about it.

When he skidded to a halt at the stop sign marking the junction with Highway 101, he took a few seconds to look at his watch. Ten minutes since he left Gabe's house. He jammed the gearshift into first and screeched onto the highway. Traffic was nearly nonexistent at this hour, and the speedometer edged past eighty before he reached the Holliday Bay bridge. He geared down as he crossed it, counted off four streets to Douglas, then swung right. After the first block, he switched off his headlights, and when he neared the end of the second block, he turned right into an empty driveway and shut off the motor.

The driveway was cast in black shadow by a row of jack pines, and it was directly across the street from the parking area behind Nina's apartment building. Her car was still in the carport, and the one light inside the building was in her apartment.

Conan's breath came out in a sigh of relief as he adjusted the side mirror so he could watch the building. He waited with forced patience, while the wind whipped the trees and dashed rain and pine needles against the car. Nina might at this moment be on the phone talking to Gabe. If she still had the diary, it was undoubtedly in a place she considered safe. But safe from a private investigator whom she would now know to be capable of breaking and entering?

Finally the light in Nina's apartment winked out, but his only move was to check his watch. She might simply go back to bed, satisfied with her hiding place. *If* she still had the diary; *if* she hadn't in fact destroyed it.

Then he smiled, shifting to keep the rear entrance of the apartment building in the narrow field of the mirror. Nina emerged, wearing a hooded raincoat. He couldn't see her face, but he had no doubt of her identity—not when she went straight to the blue Cutlass. She backed out of the carport, and Conan ducked down until her headlights arced past him as she turned onto Douglas Street and sped west toward the highway. Conan backed out of the drive, but left his lights off. Nina's car stopped at the highway, then turned right and disappeared. When Conan reached the corner, he saw her taillights rapidly dwindling to the north.

He switched on his lights when he turned onto the highway, but remained a respectful distance behind Nina; the paucity of traffic made close tailing too risky. He was fairly sure of her destination: Pacific Futures Realty. There was a safe in her office, and if that's where she was keeping the diary, she'd be better off to leave it there. He'd had some training at opening safes without combinations, but it wasn't his forte. But Nina wouldn't know that, and the office, unguarded as it was, would seem vulnerable.

He checked the bookshop automatically as he passed, noting that the night-lights were on as they should be. Holliday Beach was as forlorn as a ghost town at this hour, streetlights casting bright pools in which nothing moved but the sheeting rain. At length, a block short of Pacific Futures, he pulled right into a side street and stopped, watching the red beacons of Nina's taillights. As he anticipated, she turned left and parked in front of the office. A few seconds later, a light went on inside the building.

Conan left the XK-E's motor running; Nina wouldn't be in the office long. And he was right. Within less than five minutes, the light went out in the office, and, dimly through the rain, he saw her return to her car. He waited until she turned south and headed down the highway toward him. He headed east, and there was some risk in that. He was assuming that she would return to her apartment, and by taking this cross street to Foothills Boulevard

Road, he could reach her apartment well before she did. But if he misjudged her destination . . .

He refused to think about that; keeping the car on the narrow, pot-holed road at high speed required too much concentration. But his assumption was borne out. When Nina drove into the carport, the XK-E was already parked in the driveway across the street. But Conan wasn't in it.

He was inside the rear door of the apartment building, looking out through the glass panel. And he was the cat burglar again: black gloves on, ski mask over his face. He had also taken the precaution of turning out the hall light.

The rain driving at the glass gave him a warped view of Nina hurrying toward the door. She had something rectangular and tan under her left arm. She didn't seem to notice that the light was off in the hall—not until she opened the door a scant foot.

Conan had only to reach out and pull her into the hall. She managed a startled cry before his hand closed over her mouth. With his free hand, he found the pressure point at the clavicle, and she went limp. He eased her to the floor, switched on the flash and picked up her parcel: a manila envelope sealed with a band of wide tape and marked in emphatic letters, "Personal." He didn't need to open it. The hard outline of its contents told him he had exactly what he wanted.

He ran across the street to his car and hastily left the scene of the crime, although he wasn't concerned that this mugging would ever be reported to the police.

But he felt no real satisfaction in the success of his evening's work. He was too tired, too wet, too thoroughly chilled, and it was three in the morning. Perhaps that was why, when he reached his house and waited for the Genie to lift the garage door, his first reaction to what he saw within wasn't relief, but annoyance verging on anger.

His headlights glinted on a red Honda motorcycle. A bedroll and backpack were lashed on the back, along with a zippered rifle sleeve.

CHAPTER 17

Lyn Hatch, clad in a sodden rain parka, blond hair and beard unkempt and wet, eyes ringed with dark shadows, stood inside the utility room door. He was the picture of weary dejection, but that didn't register with Conan—not when Lyn's first words to him were, "Where the hell have you *been?*"

Conan didn't answer. He stalked past Lyn and marched through the living room to the staircase. Lyn followed him, but at a little distance. He didn't speak again, nor did Conan until he was halfway up the stairs. He said curtly, "For God's sake, Lyn, it's like a refrigerator in here. Turn up the thermostat and get a fire going."

It was only when Conan was in his bedroom and nearly undressed that Lyn's miserable state finally came home to him. He went to the balcony and looked down into the living room, where Lyn was crouched over the hearth laying a fire.

Conan asked, "Lyn, how long have you been here?"

He snapped a strip of kindling over his knee. "I don't know. Since about midnight."

Conan sighed. He'd been here for three hours, but hadn't unpacked anything from his cycle, hadn't turned up the thermostat, hadn't even taken off his wet jacket. Did he expect to be thrown out by his unknowing host?

"Lyn, damn it, bring your backpack, or whatever, up to the guest room. I'm going to thaw out with a hot shower, and I'd advise you to do the same. Have you eaten lately?"

"Sure. Well, this morning, anyway."

"This morning. You mean *yesterday* morning. Get dry and warm first, then we'll take care of your stomach."

Lyn straightened, smiling tentatively. "Thanks, Conan."

Half an hour later, Lyn, wearing one of Conan's robes, sat cross-legged on the floor with his back to the fire, elbows on the coffee table, talking around a thick, roast beef sandwich. Conan, in a wool caftan, lounged on the couch, enjoying a cigarette and a snifter of Courvoisier.

"I've been a little crazy," Lyn admitted. "Like that damn rifle. After I talked to you on the phone Saturday, I went straight down to Westport and bought the gun. You know, you can buy a rifle at any sporting goods store and just walk out with it. No license, no waiting period—nothing."

Conan nodded, holding a sip of cognac on his tongue. "Of course. Only sane people with benign intent buy rifles. Where have you been hiding out all this time?"

He shrugged, chewing a mouthful before he answered. "Mostly in the woods south of Shearwater Spit."

"In sight of Gabe Benbow's house?" Lyn only nodded. "You were seen up the Sitka River."

"Yeah, that forest ranger. There's an old quarry above Cougar Creek. I went up there for some target practice. Just like riding a bicycle, you never forget. I'm still a damn good shot." He said that with no hint of pride.

"You missed when you fired at Gabe at the cemetery."

"I didn't miss." He put his sandwich down and wiped his mouth with his napkin. "I mean, I pulled my aim. Hell, I could've hit him. Conan, I was out in the woods with that gun for—what?—three days? I don't know how many times I had Gabe in my sights. But I kept telling myself I didn't have a clear shot for one reason or another. Then at the cemetery, I had the old bastard right in the cross hairs and . . . damn it, *I* couldn't kill him." Lyn shook his head, then with a barking laugh, "But I figured I could at least scare the hell out of him."

Conan nodded and raised his glass. "Oh, you did that. All the Benbows, in fact."

Lyn picked up his sandwich, studied it a moment, then, "You want to tell me about your—well, your investigation?"

Conan told him, step by step, and day by day, while Lyn finished his sandwich, then paced up and down in front of the hearth, and finally settled at the other end of the couch with the snifter of cognac that Conan insisted upon.

Lyn asked a few questions, although he had various colorful

comments, until Conan reached the point in his story at which he had discovered the Black Leaf 40. Lyn looked at the bottle that was now on the coffee table beside the manila envelope. "Is that it —the bottle you found?"

"Yes."

Lyn stared at it; his voice was tight. "Any one of them could have poisoned her!"

Conan didn't comment on that, but Lyn was wrong; only one person could have poisoned Corey. He went on to explain the ruse he'd perpetrated with Sergeant Todd's help. "I just wanted to let Gabe know that the Black Leaf 40 had been recognized as the poison. When he realizes the bottle is gone, I hope he thinks Billy took it—as evidence. No, I had no ulterior motive beyond making Gabe—and his fellow conspirators—nervous. Now, my last little adventure of the night . . ." He picked up the manila envelope, tore it open, and handed the diary to Lyn. "Nina was keeping this for future reference, apparently."

Lyn opened it to the November twenty-first entry, then his eyes squeezed shut, and he put the diary back on the table, asking huskily, "How did you get hold of it?"

"Outright robbery. I've had quite a career in crime tonight." He didn't elucidate on that, and for a time the only sounds were the whispers of fire and rain and the roar of the surf, a sound so continuous, the mind disregarded it for more immediate stimuli. But now when Conan stopped to listen to it, he heard the ominous undertone in it.

Lyn asked, "Is that all there is to it? You said the law doesn't even recognize the fact that a crime was committed. Is that the end of it?"

"For the law, yes."

"But there's got to be—I mean, *you* found out what happened. Why can't the police?"

"I found out because I'm *not* the police. The conspirators thought it was safe to talk to me. Not one of them is going to break —count on that, Lyn. And even if one *did* confess, the others would deny it. Besides, a confession isn't worth a damn legally without evidence to back it up."

"But what about the Black Leaf Forty? Maybe there were fingerprints—something . . ."

Conan closed his eyes. Lyn had to ask the questions, but that didn't make the answers easier. "Of course there were finger-prints on it. But there is no legally acceptable proof that it had anything to do with Corey's death."

Lyn made a strangled sound, his glass coming down hard on the table. "*Legally* acceptable! Corey Benbow—remember her? Remember the way she laughed, the way she . . . danced through life? Corey was *murdered* and the law is *blind?*"

Conan let those words fall into a silence, then he said quietly, "It's justice that's blind in our symbology. It means justice is disin-terested. Not *un*interested." He leaned forward to get his ciga-rettes from the table. "I've been thinking a lot about justice lately. It comes from the Latin—what else?—and it has to do with what is lawful, or right, or fair. I've never known a human being who didn't have strong feelings about justice. I suppose that's because we're such social creatures; a concept of justice seems to be essen-tial to any society."

"Conan, for God's sake!"

Lyn was staring at him, anger flashing in his eyes. Conan nodded as he lit a cigarette. "What would satisfy *you*, Lyn? What would you call justice in this case, given that the law is impotent here?"

"I don't *know* what I'd call justice. I just don't think it's right for anybody to take another person's life—and what do we have that's more precious than that—and get away with it!"

"Or profit by it in any way? Or continue their lives as if nothing had happened?"

"Yes!"

Conan smiled fleetingly at that berserker's fervor. It wasn't for-eign to his thinking. He said, "I'm glad you came out of the woods. I'll need your help."

Lyn came to his feet, hands in muscular, brown fists. "You've got it. What do you want me to do?"

Conan looked at his watch, drained his glass of the last of the cognac, then rose. "Right now, the first thing on the agenda is to get some sleep."

Lyn frowned, distracted, as a blast of wind slapped the rain hard against the windows. "Any of those windows ever blow out?"

"No. They've withstood winds above a hundred and ten miles an hour. How far above, I don't know. I lost my wind gauge on that one. I have braces for them. We'll put them up tomorrow morning.

By the way, at four-seventeen tomorrow afternoon, there'll be a ten-foot high tide; the highest of the year."

"With this storm behind it? Damn."

Conan listened to the rumbling throb, mouth shadowed with a smile. "Yes. And the wind is still holding west."

CHAPTER 18

Conan came down from the ladder after inserting the last of the two-inch-wide, hardwood braces in the brass mounts in the window frames. He'd had little sleep in the early hours of this day; the raging of the storm had wakened him repeatedly, and in the hours since the dawn's pale advent, the storm had intensified. He pressed the palm of his hand against the window, feeling the chill of it, the vibrations of rain torrents smashing against the glass, and in the span of his hand, he made contact with powers that stretched his imagination to comprehend.

The window might as well have been opaque for all he could see beyond it. He went to the sliding glass door near the fireplace, took a deep breath, as if he were about to dive into cold water, and stepped out onto the deck. The wind tore at his hair and clothing, sodden within seconds; his skin tingled with every chilling pulse of rain. He held on to the deck railing, palms again measuring the frequencies of power; these transmitted from the rock on which this house was built—rock that was a tuning fork for the pounding cadences of the breakers.

It was a veiled world, its tumultuous, ever-changing shapes all gray and white; yet within that narrow spectrum existed endless ephemeral subtleties of hue. There was no horizon; the sea had only one perceptible margin: here where it met and did titanic battle with the land. Four hours before high tide, yet the breakers were already hitting the seawall; the beach was visible only in the nadirs of the surges.

The swells had been forecast at thirty to forty feet, but measurements were meaningless. Mountains of water took shape beyond the distant limits of vision, moved in ranked ranges toward the shore, at length toppling in white avalanches. The freed water spilled shoreward faster than any human being could run, smashing into rocks and seawalls in blizzards of atomized water and fragmented foam. Logs and stumps, the accumulation of years that had rested stolidly on the sand, felt the tug of the receding waves, moved out with them, rolling and bobbing in an elephantine fugue, raw tons of timber floating like kindling on the ebbing waters until they were stranded on the sand, waiting for the next racing flood to pick them up and hurl them at the shore with a sound like thunder.

This staggering display of power was a psychic catharsis that cleared the mind and put life and death in perspective. Even Corey's death fit into this tumultuous perspective in some sense Conan couldn't verbalize. He wasn't surprised, nor did it seem an invasion of a private experience, when Lyn Hatch joined him on the deck. This was something the two of them could share, just as —or perhaps, because—they shared the experience of grief.

At length, Conan went back into the living room, and Lyn followed, his hair and beard flecked with snowflakes of foam. He laughed in wondering exuberance. "My God, it's beautiful!"

Conan nodded as he pushed his wet hair back from his forehead. Then, reluctantly, he turned away from the windows and crossed to the stairs. "Beautiful, but incredibly wet. You'd better get into some dry clothes."

Lyn sobered. "Yes, I guess so. Conan, what . . . well, when do we get started?"

Conan paused at the top of the stairs. "Soon. I have a phone call to make, then some shopping to do."

A short while later, Conan sat at his desk in the library, while Lyn stood at the windows, mesmerized by the storm that provided a rumbling undercurrent to every word and thought. Conan pulled the phone toward him and punched a number. It was Jonas who answered finally with a cautious, "Hello?"

"This is Conan Flagg, Jonas, and I want Gabe. Before you tell me he won't talk to me, give him this message: I have Kate Benbow's diary. The original."

Jonas hesitated only a few seconds. "I'll go get him."

Conan waited patiently until at length Gabe initiated the conversation with, "Flagg, you son of a bitch! The original? I'll believe that when I *see* it!"

Conan laughed. "I'll have it with me this afternoon."

That elicited a long silence, followed by a suspicious, "This afternoon?"

"I think a reunion of sorts is called for to discuss this turn of events. I mean, the fact that I have the diary now. Of course, I'm not as naïve as Corey was. I have photographs of the diary and the pertinent passage in a safe place, and if anything happens to me—an unfortunate *accident*, for instance—the photographs will find their way into the hands of the DA. And in case Owen Culpepper absentmindedly forgets them, copies will go to the state attorney general and the commissioner of the Real Estate Board."

When at length Gabe responded, his voice was husky with tension. "What do you *want*, Flagg?"

"Justice. But that's rather an abstract concept. What I want is an opportunity to talk to all the conspirators. That means you, Jonas, Moses, France, Nina, and Leo. Today, Gabe. At your house, let's say . . . three-thirty."

Gabe spluttered incoherently, finally making his exasperation intelligible. "Today! At *my* house! Flagg, you're crazy, and so's anybody else who'd be out in this storm. We'll be lucky to have any power on. Lights've been going on and off all day, and I—"

"*Today*, Gabe. Get out some candles."

"But I can't—well, *Leo* sure won't drive all the way up here in this—"

"He'd damn well better chance it! I want him there, Gabe." Conan paused, his tone almost honeyed now. "It might be worth the trip. My father—ol' Henry Flagg—was a born horse trader, and maybe a little of it rubbed off on me."

"Horse trader? What do you mean?"

"I don't think I need to spell it out. By the way, if you're still entertaining a publicly funded bodyguard, get rid of him. What we have to talk about, you don't want him to hear. Three-thirty, Gabe. I'll expect all of you there." He gently cradled the phone, cutting off another spluttering volley, then looked up at Lyn, who was listening intently.

Lyn asked, "You think they'll come?"

Conan looked past Lyn to the rain-curtained windows. "They'll come. They all have too much at stake not to."

CHAPTER 19

Where the last of the jack pine, stunted by salt winds, offered a scant cover, Conan stopped the car and looked down at Gabe Benbow's house. The windshield wipers could clear the driving sheets of rain only for split seconds at every sweep. The usually quiet waters of Sitka Bay were ridged with white wave fronts, and to the west of the spit, foam-capped mountains rumbled one after another toward the beach, reached for the grassy spine of the spit, then slid back to meet the oncoming waves in running walls of water. The vast thundering was unrelenting.

Conan smiled obliquely as he recognized the cars in the parking area: Nina's Cutlass, France's and Moses' Cadillac, and Leo Moskin's Rolls. He checked his watch: 3:12. "Well, Lyn, we aren't the only ones who believe in early arrivals."

Like Conan, Lyn Hatch was attired in a hooded rain parka; at his knee, he held the rifle, still in its protective sleeve. He had to raise his voice against the wind and rain pounding at the car. "Conan, don't leave me standing outside the back door too long. I might blow into the bay."

Conan nodded. "Five minutes, Lyn. If somebody hasn't opened the door for you by then, open it yourself, even if you have to shoot off the lock. And, Lyn . . ." Conan studied him a moment, then, "Be careful."

Lyn only laughed at that as he opened the door. The car shuddered when he slammed it behind him, and within seconds, he had disappeared into the undergrowth.

Conan drove toward the house, gripping the wheel hard to keep the car on the road. There were no lights visible in the house, but most of Taft County had been without electricity for nearly an hour. He parked beside the Rolls, then took his Mauser out of the glove box and slipped it into the pocket of the jacket under his parka. For a moment, he watched the voracious waves battering the spit.

For Corey; for justice.

He got out of the car, flinching at the blast of cold rain, went to the trunk and took out a paper sack; the bottles clinked together until he got the sack tucked firmly under his left arm. The parka flapped noisily as he ran up the flagged walk; he was all but blinded by the rain, and he felt nakedly vulnerable. A howitzer could be aimed at him from the darkened house, and he wouldn't be able to see it.

But it would have to be behind the closed drapes, he realized when he reached the front deck. There was no movement in the drapes, but he had no doubt that his arrival had been closely observed. Observation from the windows was, fortunately, precluded once he reached the front door. He put the sack down and rang the doorbell, then stood hunched against the wind, giving anyone inside ample time to identify him through the peephole, but when the knob began to turn, he quickly stepped to one side of the door. When it opened, he was for a vital moment invisible.

It was Gabe Benbow who flung open the door to greet his visitor with an old .38 revolver in hand. Gabe let out a hoarse cry at the chop across his wrist that paralyzed his hand. Conan caught the gun, then jabbed it hard against the old man's chest. "Inside, Gabe!"

Gabe retreated as ordered, his mouth slack, yet he seemed affronted more than fearful. Conan put the sack inside the door, then kicked the door shut behind him and surveyed the room. Two kerosene lamps on the mantel, a cluster of candles on a tray in the center of the coffee table, and the blue glow of the gas flames in the fireplace provided a wan light that cast irrational shadows. Jonas had been standing near the door on Conan's right, but he withdrew toward the couches, hands raised. Moses' retreat from the other side of the door was equally expeditious. He stopped beside his wife, who stood near the fireplace, hugging a brown wool *mantilla* around her shoulders.

To her left, in front of the hearth, Leo Moskin balanced his considerable weight evenly on both feet, his chin down like a wary bull. Nina stood behind the farthest couch, her hands resting on the back, green eyes narrowed. A purse was in the seat in front of her, its clasp open.

Conan stayed near the door, the revolver moving in a slow arc. "I would advise all of you not to make a move. A thirty-eight bullet can do a great deal of damage. You, Gabe—sit down. There, in your usual chair." Gabe started to protest, then clamped his jaw tight and went to his chair to sit glowering at him.

Conan caught an aborted movement. "No, Nina. Don't try it. Bring it here—the purse. Carefully."

She snapped the purse shut, then brought it to him. Her slacks were too well fitted to conceal a gun or any other weapon, Conan noted, nor were her walking shoes suitable for hiding places, nor the soft sweater and cardigan.

She thrust the purse at him, then, cold eyes mocking, held her arms out from her body and asked, "Do you want to frisk me? Get your kicks for the day?"

He opened the purse and took his eyes off her only long enough to look inside. The chrome-plated, Saturday night special gleamed in the dim light. "Sorry, Nina, no body search will be necessary. Go sit down. On the couch, exactly where you were Friday night."

She lifted her chin, then strode back to the far couch, where she sat with her arms folded, mouth a harsh, compressed line. Conan shifted his attention to France. "Your purse, France—and take off the shawl."

France glanced at Moses and at his nod, irritably pulled off the *mantilla* and tossed it over the back of the couch nearest her, then picked up the leather shoulder-strap purse on the seat. She took the purse to Conan without a word, then retreated to her husband's side. Like Nina, she wore slacks, and there seemed no potential hiding place in them, nor in her tailored blouse.

Conan opened the purse, frowning as he shifted its contents. "Jonas, you'd better go open the back door."

Jonas stared at him, nonplussed. "What?"

"The back door. And be sensible; no heroics."

Jonas shared the look of alarm that flashed from one conspirator to another, then with a sigh, he picked up a candle from the coffee table and headed for the kitchen.

Conan dropped France's purse on the floor beside Nina's. There was no weapon in it, except a canister of tear gas on a key chain. "Sit down, France. Yes, exactly where you sat Friday night."

She complied, turning nervously at the sound of voices and footsteps from the kitchen. Jonas emerged first, hands in the air, and behind him, with the barrel of the Remington against Jonas's spine, Lyn Hatch made an effective entrance that stunned the conspirators into open-mouthed silence.

Conan said casually, "I'm sure you all remember Lyndon Hatch. Yes, apparently you do. Lyn, you'd better search Jonas. I've already found two guns in this friendly group."

Lyn conducted a businesslike body search, while Jonas stood rigid. Finally Lyn shook his head. "Nothing, Conan."

"I'm glad to hear that. Jonas, sit down." He didn't have to tell him to go to his seat of Friday night. "Moses, you're next."

Moses' hands went into small fists. "This is an outrage, and I'll have nothing more to do with it! Come on, France, we're leaving!" And with that he started toward the door.

In one smooth movement, Lyn raised the rifle and fired, the reverberations of the explosion numbing. A vase on a shelf beyond Moses shattered into shrapnel shards, and France screamed, red-nailed hands pressed to her cheeks. The double slide and snap of the rifle's bolt punctuated the silence as Moses, half crouched, stared first at the small hole in the wall where the vase had been, then at Lyn. *"You could've killed me!"*

Conan laughed as he crossed to Moses and searched him. "Yes, Moses, he could have, so keep that in mind. Well, it's a relief to find you didn't come forearmed. Certainly you're now forewarned. Go sit down."

Moses did, next to his white-faced wife, while Conan turned to Moskin. Without a word, Moskin raised his left hand in a placating gesture, then reached into his tweed jacket, removed a slim .32 automatic from an underarm holster, and offered it, butt first, to Conan.

Conan took it, meeting his cool, hooded gaze; there was no hint of fear in it. "Leo, I'm glad to see the spirit of cooperation isn't entirely dead here. Sit down."

Moskin moved toward the nearest couch with a contemptuous, "Yes, I know—where I was sitting Friday night."

Conan pulled out the .32's clip and emptied the shells, then tossed the gun on the floor by the purses. He also emptied Nina's .22, then after a glance at Lyn to make sure he had the conspirators covered—he did, looking like a battle-weary soldier in his drenched parka—Conan emptied Gabe's revolver, dropped it with the others, then took off his own parka and crossed to the hearth. There he made a point of bringing out the Mauser and snapping a shell into the chamber.

"Lyn, would you mind taking care of the, uh, groceries?"

"Sure." He picked up the sack by the front door and carried it with him to the kitchen. He remained there for several minutes, during which time Conan studied the intent, questioning faces, masklike in the wavering candlelight. Rain battered at the windows, and the incessant throb of the ocean was something felt as much as heard.

Nina found a pack of cigarettes on the table in front of her and lighted one. Her hands were shaking. Moses, on her left, leaned back with one arm on the back of the couch, his hand resting on France's shoulder, the candles multiplying themselves on the lenses of his glasses. Perhaps France found some reassurance in her husband's hand on her shoulder; if so, she seemed to need it. Her thin face was pale, every muscle taut.

Gabe still maintained his affronted silence, glaring at Conan fixedly. Yet it struck Conan that Gabe had never seemed so old, despite the dim light that softened the years of lines.

Jonas had aged too in the last few minutes, and at this moment, Conan could believe he *was* ill; there was a decidedly gray cast to his skin, and his constantly shifting eyes were bloodshot.

Only Leo Moskin seemed quite unimpressed with what was going on around him, offering a facade of monumental boredom as he casually lighted a cigar, puffing out an acrid fog of smoke. But he was the first to hear Lyn return from the kitchen. He watched suspiciously as Lyn—unarmed for the moment so that his hands were free to carry a small tray—came around to Conan's left and put the tray on the table.

On the tray was an empty rocks glass, a shot glass, a fifth of Kahlúa, another of vodka, and the Black Leaf 40 bottle.

"My God . . ." The words were barely audible, and they came from France. But Moses' hand tightened on her shoulder, and she said nothing more. Nor did anyone else. Lyn retrieved his rifle from the kitchen and took up a position behind and to Gabe's left, where he could keep all of them in sight.

Conan returned the Mauser to his jacket pocket with the observation, "Lyn is an excellent shot, by the way; he doesn't miss at close range unless he intends to. And there's something else you should know about Lyn: He was deeply in love with Corey Benbow."

Gabe rasped, "So, what's he going to do? Shoot us all? Is that what this—this damnable game of yours is about?"

Conan laughed harshly. "Gabe, *you* were the one who came to the front door with a thirty-eight in hand. And get one thing very clear in your mind—all of you! This is not by any stretch of the imagination a game!"

A strained wail from France as she pressed her hands to her temples: "Oh, dear God, what do you *want?*"

"Justice," Conan replied. "That's all, France." Then he picked up the Kahlúa bottle and opened it. Silence held sway while he measured a shot into the glass, then added two shots of vodka. "Tell me, Gabe, since you're such a religious man—or make such a point of being a church-going man—what does your God have to say about justice?"

Gabe spoke in solemn tones: " 'Vengeance is *mine;* I will repay, saith the *Lord.*' "

"Ah. And vengeance belongs to no one but the Lord? The God of Moses, Gabe. Exodus. 'Eye for eye, tooth for tooth, hand for hand, foot for foot, burning for burning, wound for wound, stripe for stripe . . . Thou shalt give life for life.' "

Moskin, his facade of nonchalance finally cracking, took his cigar out of his mouth to demand, "What in the hell is going on here?"

France shrilled, "He thinks we—we murdered Corey! That's why he—"

Gabe snorted in disgust. "Shut up, France. Flagg, you're crazy! Nobody *murdered* Corey. I *told* you that."

Conan folded his arms, eyes slitted. "A young woman in perfect health suddenly goes into convulsions and dies—only a short time after delivering what all of you recognized as a potentially fatal blow to the Baysea development *and* after consuming part of a cocktail prepared in this kitchen—and you still insist no one murdered her? You're not that naïve, Gabe. We will begin with Corey's murder taken as an established fact."

Gabe shifted forward in his chair. "Begin what? You and your hotshot friend over here going to kill all of us? I said it before, Flagg: you're crazy! You figure you'd ever get away with something like that?"

"Are you so sure it matters to me—since I'm crazy?" He smiled coldly, meeting Gabe's baleful glare. "Apparently one can't get away with group murders. Right? But single murders are another matter."

Gabe spluttered, "So, what're you—you're saying you're just going to murder *one* of us? With five witnesses, you—"

"There were five witnesses to Corey's murder, and her killer got away with it! Which of you will run to the police with your story, knowing that if you do, the *whole* story will come out? Five witnesses made themselves accessories to one murder to protect the Baysea sale—what makes you think they won't become accessories again? *Sit down, Gabe!*"

Lyn emphasized that order by shifting the rifle into firing position, and Gabe, who had risen in anger, sank suddenly back into his chair.

Jonas, after glancing apprehensively over his shoulder at Lyn, ventured, "What . . . the stuff on the tray—what's that for?"

Conan replied levelly, "I'll get to that later, Jonas." He paused, and the creak of timbers in the house punctuated the hiatus. Then he reached into his breast pocket and took out Kate Benbow's diary.

Nina lunged for it. "Goddamn you! I *knew* it was you!" But when Lyn again raised his rifle, she subsided.

Moses blurted, "Nina, you said you destroyed it!"

"No recriminations, friends," Conan interposed. "It's too late for that. Jonas, you can examine this; make sure it's the original, and that it's your wife's handwriting."

Jonas rose, his hand trembling as he reached for the diary. He remained standing while he leafed through it, stopping toward the end of the book, undoubtedly at the entry for November twenty-first. Then he nodded and returned the book to Conan. "That's it." And with that affirmation, he hurriedly sat down.

Conan put the diary on the coffee table by the tray. "The price of justice can be high. I'm well aware of that. You have all joined in a conspiracy to subvert justice—legal justice—in the murder of Corey Benbow. A very successful conspiracy. But *legal* justice isn't the only kind of justice."

France hunched forward, crying, "Will you for God's sake tell us what—what you're asking of us?"

"One of you murdered Corey Benbow. Eye for eye. I want that person to pay for Corey's life."

Moskin croaked, "You—you mean . . . you've got to be joking!"

Conan turned on him. "This is no more a joke than it is a game. Someone I loved is dead, and if the law is helpless, *I* am *not!*"

"*I* didn't kill her!" Moskin insisted.

"And *I* didn't either!" Nina chimed in, and, over a chorus of disclaimers, she added, "You've got no right to hold us here, to threaten us and—"

Conan only laughed at that. "I have a right. Lyn is holding it in his hands. So, be quiet and listen—all of you. Now, there was a time when nothing was more important to me than keeping Sitka Bay and Shearwater Spit out of the hands of developers. But Corey's death has altered my priorities. So, there's Kate's diary; there's the time bomb that could blow all your avaricious hopes to atoms. On the other side of the scales is a murderer; the one person among you who poisoned Corey Benbow. And at the fulcrum—Lyn and I, who have come here for justice. Simple, isn't it?"

Covert glances of speculation passed from one conspirator to another. Only Jonas frowned as if he were confused, then looked directly at Conan with dawning comprehension that made his mouth sag open.

"Who?" Jonas asked the question, and it seemed to catch in his throat. "Who are you . . . accusing of murder?"

Conan raised an eyebrow. "I haven't accused anyone, have I, Jonas? But if you'll all think about it, I'm sure you'll reach a consensus."

Moses demanded, "What do you mean? Draw straws or something for your scapegoat?"

"Scapegoat? No, Moses. I want the person who is actually guilty. So, perhaps the first order of business is to decide who that person is, and we might as well begin with the classic motive/means/opportunity triad. Motive?" He laughed bitterly at that. "*All* of you had motive: money, power, self-preservation, et cetera. Corey was a threat to each of you. So, we'll go on to the next leg of the triad." Darkness was accumulating in the room with the almost perceptible fading of the outside light. He looked around the candle-studded table, thinking how like a macabre séance it seemed.

"Means. Well, after talking to Dr. Feingold, I knew every possibility was eliminated except poisoning, and the descriptions of Corey's symptoms bore that out. And since none of you could have anticipated Corey's arrival or the revelation in Kate's diary, that meant the poison was a substance readily available in this house. Last night I found just such a substance—and Gabe can confirm that."

Gabe's chin jutted belligerently. "All you found was a bottle of insecticide that's been sitting on that shelf for months."

"Exactly." Conan picked up the Black Leaf 40 bottle and read aloud, " 'The original nicotine sulphate solution.' And here it's spelled out with the usual skull-and-crossbones symbols: 'Poison.' But, of course, any gardener could tell you about Black Leaf Forty." He paused, watching France turn even paler, then, "Yes, Gabe, it had been sitting on that shelf for months. *What* shelf?"

"The shelf—the one in the utility room . . ."

"The one just to the right of the kitchen door—which was open Friday night." Conan put the bottle back on the tray. "And the symptoms of acute nicotine poisoning include shortness of breath, a sensation of numbness in the mouth and throat, convulsions, and unconsciousness. Which brings us to the third leg of the triad: opportunity." Another blast of wind lashed at the house, and the candle flames wavered. Somewhere, a rain gutter, torn from its moorings, began banging insensately.

"By opportunity," Conan continued, "I mean the opportunity to lace Corey's second black russian with Black Leaf Forty."

France stuttered out, "You can't—you can't blame *me* for that! We had—all of you, you *know* we had b-black russians before! We had them all the *time*, and you—"

"France, be quiet!" That curt admonition from Moses.

Conan said agreeably, "Yes, France, I realize you can't be blamed for the choice of drinks served that night. That was simply a piece of luck, wasn't it?"

"I don't know what you're—"

"But you *were* responsible for the fact that a *second* drink for Corey—one prepared *after* she presented the diary—was necessary. You disposed of her first drink by the expedient of throwing it in her face."

"No! I didn't—I mean, that wasn't on *purpose*—"

"Then why didn't you empty your own glass on her?"

Cheeks glowing hectically, France snapped, "Because my glass was already . . . empty."

Moses cut in, "Damn it, Flagg, if you're accusing France—by *God*, I've never seen such a cruel and mindless farce in my life!"

"I have accused no one," Conan replied mildly.

Moses surged to his feet, but any rebuttal he planned was quashed when he found the Remington again aimed at him.

"Moses . . . please!" France tugged at his arm, and finally, glaring at Lyn, then at Conan, he sank back to the couch. Conan caught Jonas's longing look at the vodka bottle and knew he was heartily wishing for a stiff drink.

Conan thrust his hands in his pockets. "I've heard several accounts of what happened here Friday night, not all of them in agreement. The question is, who mixed Corey's last drink—or who had access to it *and* the poison in the utility room. Leo—" Moskin started, as if an electric shock accompanied his name. "Leo, when were you in the kitchen?"

"I wasn't *in* the kitchen—not at *any* time Friday night!"

"Jonas, can you verify that?"

"Yes. He didn't even get off this couch."

"Gabe? Did you see Leo go into the kitchen?"

"No! And *I* didn't go in there either."

"Jonas, can you and Leo vouch for Gabe?"

They both nodded, and Conan said, "Well, at least Leo and Gabe can be eliminated from our considerations." He smiled faintly as Moskin breathed an audible sigh of relief. Gabe seemed vaguely surprised that he had been under suspicion at all. Conan turned to Jonas. "But you *did* leave the couch after France showered Corey with her first drink."

Jonas had to clear his throat before he could speak. "Well, yes, I . . . I got up for a while. But I didn't set foot in the kitchen!"

"Moses, you were in the kitchen, weren't you? Can you vouch for Jonas?"

For a long time, Moses only stared at his brother, his eyes unreadable behind the lights reflected in his glasses. Jonas seemed on the verge of pleading, when Moses said flatly, "I can vouch for him."

With anger edging her voice, Nina said, "*Sure*, you can vouch for him! He's your brother!"

"Which has no bearing," Moses retorted, "on this situation, and it's something I'd prefer not to be reminded of."

"I don't believe that!" Nina's face was only inches from Moses'. "You goddamned Benbows! Blood is thicker than water—right? I know what you're doing, and you can't—"

"Oh, shut up, Nina!" Moskin snapped. "*I* saw Jonas. He got up and just stood around for a while, then he went over toward the kitchen door. I could see him from here, and he didn't go *inside* the kitchen. Hell, I don't like him either, but that's the truth."

Before Nina could get out a rejoinder, Conan cut in, "Wait your turn, Nina. We still have Moses and France to consider. Notice how the names always go together as a unit? They're a good team. According to the accounts I heard, after France disposed of Corey's first drink in a fit of temper, Moses took her into the kitchen. True?"

France blurted, "Yes, but you make it sound like—"

"So defensive?" Conan asked in mocking surprise. "But if the story you told me Monday is true, you and Moses weren't alone in the kitchen."

France's eyes gleamed with triumph that turned cold and vicious as she focused on Nina. "No, we weren't the only ones in the kitchen! Nina was there—when was it, Moses? She came in just a few minutes after we did, didn't she?"

That unleashed a barrage of bitter charges and counter charges between Nina, France, and Moses, with the others joining in the shouting match until Conan took out his gun and fired a shot into the ceiling. France screamed as she ducked into the dubious protection of Moses' embrace, then quiet was restored, and the banging of the unmoored gutter could be heard providing an arhythmic percussion for the broad chords of wind and sea.

Conan put the gun back in his pocket and continued, "The question at this point is, who mixed Corey's last drink? France, you told me you *began* mixing it. Is that true?"

"Yes, but I didn't—"

"Moses, did you see France begin mixing a black russian?"

Moses glanced warily at Lyn; the rifle was lowered, but Moses didn't seem inclined to test Lyn's reflexes. "I . . . yes, she started it, but she *didn't* finish—"

"Did she go into the utility room?"

"No!"

"Nina? You were in the kitchen at that point. Did you see either France or Moses go into the utility room?"

Nina replied acidly, "Yes! I saw her go into—"

That threatened a new onslaught of argument, but Conan managed to quell it with another question. "Nina, when France went into the utility room, did she have the glass with her?"

"I don't . . . no."

"She brought the Black Leaf Forty bottle out to the counter?"

Now Nina turned cautious. "I don't know. I left the kitchen then."

France lunged at her, long nails reaching for her face, shrilling, "You bitch! *You* didn't leave—*we* left then!"

Moses restrained her in an unaffectionate bear hug. "That's the truth!" he shouted, then, "France, damn it, be still!"

When she subsided, Nina was prepared to launch a verbal counterattack, but Conan cut in, "It's quite possible that any one of you three—or all of you in conspiracy—might have put the Black Leaf Forty in Corey's drink, but first I want to clear up another matter. I'm afraid, Nina, that of the four versions of the events of Friday night I heard, three of them agreed that you left the kitchen last. Since one of those versions was France's, I'll discount it. That still leaves two to one. Leo? I didn't hear from you."

Moskin was staring at Nina; he didn't seem to realize he was being addressed at first. "What?"

"Which of the three left the kitchen last?"

"Nina." He said it with no hint of emotion.

"Was she carrying anything?"

France put in, "Yes, she was—"

"Be quiet," Conan snapped. "Leo?"

He pulled in a deep breath, his gaze still fixed on Nina. "She was carrying two glasses. Two black russians. She put one on the table in front of where Corey had been sitting, then she handed the other glass to France. Said something like, 'Have another drink—not that you need it.'"

Nina could restrain herself no longer. "All right! Maybe I did bring the drinks in, but France *mixed* them—"

"No, I didn't!" France insisted. "I only started to mix *one*—"

"So what? If you put poison in one of them, *I* didn't know it!"

Conan gave that a curt laugh. "Good point, Nina. I understand that when Corey returned from the bathroom, you all had a friendly discussion about possible compromises and that sort of thing. Does anyone take exception to that?" Six heads moved back and forth almost in unison. "And I understand that during that discussion you all drank from your respective glasses; you even had a toast to your agreement. Jonas, during this peaceful interlude, did France consume any of *her* cocktail?"

Jonas looked up, uncomfortable at suddenly becoming the center of attention. "Sure she did. I remember thinking—sorry, France—that she should've stopped a couple of drinks back."

Conan turned to Moskin. "Leo, do you agree? I mean, that France consumed part of her drink. I'm not interested in her state of sobriety."

"Yes, she *consumed* it, all right."

"Gabe?"

Sitting his chair like an elderly Solomon, Gabe pronounced, " 'Be sure your sin will find you out.' Yes, she drank it. Spirits are the very blood of Satan, but she was never one to turn her lips aside."

France retorted, "Gabe, I don't need a sermon on the evils of—"

"None of us do," Conan interposed, "but in this case, France, be grateful for your predilection for the 'wine that maketh glad the heart of man.' Or woman. Nina insists it was you who laced Corey's drink with nicotine sulphate, and that she was *not* aware of it. That's possible except for one thing: Nina mixed another drink for you. Why? Well, it wasn't out of the goodness of your heart, was it, Nina?" He didn't expect, nor did he get an answer to that. "Perhaps you enjoyed playing to France's weakness. At any rate, you came back from the kitchen with *two* drinks. How was France to know which was the poisoned drink? Jonas, was there any difference in the glasses?"

"No, they're all part of the same set. Just like . . . like that one on the tray."

"Yet France accepted one of those two cocktails and blithely drank it, knowing she had a fifty-fifty chance of dying as a result? I find that hard to believe. Nina, you were the only one who knew which of the glasses to put at Corey's place. You were the only one who knew that one of the drinks was poisoned."

Nina pressed back into the cushions, eyes shifting warily from one conspirator to another, but she had no time for a rebuttal. Gabe, his face nearly purple, surged out of his chair. "You goddamned, stupid *fool!* We could've worked out of this somehow! *Now* look what you've done! You messed up the whole damn—"

"You *bastard!*"

"*Lyn!*" Conan shouted the name, because Lyn again had the rifle raised, but not to fire—rather to crack Gabe's skull with the stock. Gabe cowered, hands coming up to protect his head, and Lyn, face wrenched with grief-fed rage, seemed to teeter like a boulder on the edge of a cliff.

Then he took a step backward, all expression leaving his face as he lowered the rifle. He said curtly, "Sit down, Gabe, and shut up." And Gabe did, staring resentfully up at him.

Conan read the silent apology in Lyn's eyes and nodded, then reached down for the Black Leaf 40 bottle.

"I find it difficult to believe that none of you recognized the truth earlier; recognized the killer among you. But none of you really cared, did you? You saw no evil, heard no evil, and certainly spoke no evil—not to any representative of the law. You're all guilty. Even in the eyes of the law, an accessory is as guilty as the actual killer. As for the eyes of God—well, perhaps you should ask your resident expert in godliness about that. Neither Lyn nor I care how you work that out in your own minds. As I said, we're here for one reason: we want justice." He opened the bottle and poured the inch of dark liquid remaining in it into the glass on the tray. He heard a gasp from several members of the party, but nothing more.

Conan picked up the glass, speaking quietly so that they had to strain to hear him against the incessant roar of the storm. "Corey Benbow was a vital, loving human being. She left behind an orphaned child who must learn grief before he's old enough to comprehend it. She left behind friends and people who loved her; people who can never fill the vacuum her death created in their lives. Corey was thirty-two years old. She was robbed of all the years that should have been left to her to live and love and dream. Why?" He looked around at the faces caught in the candlelight, finding fear more evident in them than regret. Except Lyn. He stood slumped under the weight of his grief, eyes closed.

Conan continued, "Corey Benbow died for greed. Nothing more. Her only crime was her concern for the world in which her son must grow up. Her only failing was naïveté. It didn't occur to her when she came here alone with the diary that anyone would be willing to sacrifice a human life—*her* life—for greed. All of you are accessories to her murder, but only one of you poured the poison into her drink. So, consider again the metaphor of the scales. On one side, the diary. I will give it up willingly for justice." He picked up the diary and held it in his left hand, balancing the glass in his right hand. "On the other side of the scales is a murderer."

He turned then and thrust the glass toward Nina.

"Your cocktail, Nina—for justice."

She jerked back, trembling, staring at the glass. "You—you're out of your mind! I'm not going to drink that—for God's sake, did you think I *would?*"

Conan didn't answer, and no one else so much as moved; they waited in frozen silence, and when Nina managed a harsh, uncertain laugh, no one seemed to recognize any humor in the situation.

"What *is* this? Some sort of weird joke? You—none of you expect me to *drink* that! You lousy bastards! You're crazy—all of you! You're *sick!*"

Still, none of them moved; they only stared at her, and perhaps she realized then that not one of them would try to stop her if she *did* choose to drink the contents of the glass.

"Oh, my *God . . .*" The words ended with a muffled moan as Nina pressed a hand to her mouth.

Conan waited a few seconds more, then he said bitterly, "So much for justice," and put the glass down on the tray. He slipped the diary into his breast pocket as he started for the door. "Come on, Lyn."

It was Moskin who lurched to his feet and cried, "Wait! The diary!"

Conan turned and demanded, "Why should I give it to you now? It's too late, Leo." He picked up his parka and put it on, while Lyn backed toward the door, the rifle at ready.

That might have been the end of it, if Nina had remained motionless and silent. The emotional charge would have spent itself in a few more seconds.

She moved with no apparent conscious thought, acting under the spur of fear. She tried to kick the glass off the table, but her heel caught on the edge, and she only succeeded in jarring the glass.

That abortive movement was a catalyst.

France shrieked, straining forward to catch the glass, barely getting her feet under her when the couch toppled, unbalanced by Nina's attempt to escape over the back. Moses and Moskin lunged for her, all three tumbling to the floor, her screams stifled by the weight of their bodies. The coffee table crashed onto its side, candles flying in a shower of flame and wax, and Gabe plunged into the fray with bellowed orders. "Hold on to her! Grab her legs!"

France clambered over the fallen couch, the glass held high, shrilling, "Her nose! Hold her nose so she can't breathe!"

Nina kicked and scratched and bit in a thrashing frenzy, the gas flames and the lamps on the mantel providing a wan, equivocal light for the heaving struggle. Gabe bawled, "*Give* me that glass!"

A yelp of pain from Moskin, then, "Drink it, you rotten bitch!"

The roiling bodies thudded against the wall, grunts and cries of pain counterpointed by muffled expletives. Nina's legs were pinioned under Moskin's sprawled mass, and Moses clung to her like an ungainly beast of prey, while he twisted her arms behind her back. France held her head with a clawlike hand in her hair, the other hand clamped over her nose, and Gabe was on his knees with the glass, prying at Nina's clenched teeth with bloody fingers.

"Stop it! For God's sake—stop it!"

That voice crying in this dark wilderness was Jonas's. He held on to the back of his father's chair, again and again repeating his plea, but it went unheard and unheeded.

A raucous chorus of triumphant shouts. Nina, on the edge of unconsciousness, swallowed and coughed; dark liquid ran out of her mouth. The sound of her surrender was a whimpering sob.

That sound seemed to send out pulses of silence. The wind beat at the house, the sea throbbed unremittingly at the nether limits of human hearing, yet for a span of time, silence held all motion in abeyance in this room.

Conan took one of the lamps from the mantel and carried its circle of yellow light with him as he approached the erstwhile battleground. When the light struck them, the panting combatants drew away from Nina. Moskin had to use the wall to help him to his feet; his hand left red prints.

France huddled against the fallen couch, black hair a Medusa tangle, face streaked with mascara and blood from her slashed cheek. And tears. Moses, on his hands and knees, searched for his glasses, found them finally, and tried to fit the bent frames over his ears with shaking hands. One sleeve of his sweater was torn and sagging down his arm; his mouth was smeared with red.

Gabe might have had to literally crawl away, if Jonas hadn't helped him to his feet and into his chair. His head sagged with every labored breath, as if his neck muscles were too weak to hold it erect.

Conan glanced behind him and saw that Lyn was only a pace away, dark eyes haunted as he surveyed the combatants. Conan handed him the lamp, then knelt beside Nina.

She seemed small and fragile, like a bird that had been flung roughly to the ground. Her breath came hard, each inhalation accompanied by a soft moan; her perfect face was bruised and cut, her golden hair sticky with blood. She stared up at him, one eye nearly swollen shut, her mouth working aimlessly.

He said, "There must have been a moment when Corey realized she'd been poisoned, even though she wasn't expecting it. One terrible moment when she knew she was dying. You feel it now, don't you, Nina? Your mouth is numb, you can't breathe, and you're waiting for the convulsions to begin."

Nina cried out, an inarticulate sound so full of terror, Conan felt the hackles rising at the back of his neck, and the beating undercurrent of the storm seemed a projection of her fear.

Conan took a deep breath. "Nina, do you really think I'd let you die as a memorial to one of the gentlest people I've ever known? No. I only wanted you to understand—to *feel*—the enormity of your crime. All I put in that drink was food coloring and oil of cloves. That accounts for the odd taste and the sensation of numbness. You're going to live, Nina. I don't know what you'll do, or where you'll hide—Isaac Wines is not tolerant of failure, and the case on Randy Coburn's murder is still open—but you'll live."

At first, she only stared at him, then her swollen features contorted with rage, and she spat out, *"You bastard!"*

Conan smiled coldly, then rose and looked around at the incredulous conspirators. "I'll leave vengeance to the Lord now. I can ask no more in the way of justice. Nina will live, and you have not collectively committed murder. But no one can say you didn't try. Except for Jonas—the prodigal son you so despised—you have all looked upon this woman to lust after her death, and you have committed murder in your hearts. Gabe, think about that next

Sunday as you sit in your accustomed pew at church—and every Sunday afterward."

Lyn said irreverently, "Amen." Then he put the lamp on the mantel, haggard features bronzed in its light. "Conan, let's get out of here."

Conan nodded and followed Lyn to the door, and it was only then that Gabe, rising shakily, found somewhere within him the audacity to demand, "The diary—you said you'd give it back!"

"I don't believe it," Lyn said dully.

Conan laughed. "Gabe, I'm grateful for that. It gives me an opportunity to remind you of something you said to Corey on Thanksgiving Day. Remember? *Promises are cheap.*"

Gabe strode angrily toward Conan, but Jonas restrained him. "Let it alone, Pa—please."

Gabe's forward motion stopped, but his anger didn't abate. "What're you going to do with the goddamned thing?"

Conan replied, "Take it to court, Gabe!"

Nina began sobbing. "Why didn't you just kill me? Why didn't you . . . why . . . why . . ."

Lyn opened the door, and the rush of wind drowned out her voice. The door jerked out of his hand and crashed against the wall, and the roar of the surf was a primordial sound evincing power of such proportions that the only possible human response to it was heart-pounding fear.

Lyn pushed against the wind onto the deck, parka flapping around him, then shouted, "Conan! Oh, sweet Jesus, look! Just look at it!"

Conan stood beside him, blinking into the rain. The light was nearly gone, shrouded by clouds and lashing curtains of rain, but the white mountains of waves caught the remnants of the day, and as Conan watched, a luminescent avalanche thundered toward the crest of the spit, then swept on inexorably over the top. The spit simply disappeared, until at length the wave front, its power spent, its waters divided, drained into ocean and bay, leaving behind a honed surface of sand studded with stranded drift.

Conan laughed aloud, throwing his head back to the rain, while a new wave front massed for another assault. He turned to call for Gabe, but Gabe was already standing beside him, grimacing into the deluge, sparse hair plastered back, his clothing rippling in the wind.

"Oh, Lord . . . stop! *Stop!*"

Jonas came to the door just as Gabe bolted toward the spit, waving his hands frantically, shouting, *"Stop! Stop!"*

"Pa! What are you . . ." Jonas fell silent, staring at the spit as another wave rolled over it. He spluttered, "The spit! It—it's *gone!*"

Conan shook his head. "It's still there. This isn't the first time it's been flooded. But it'll be a long time before anyone's foolish enough to build a house on it. Maybe I won't have to go to court after all. Jonas, you better go get King Canute before he drowns himself."

"Oh, damn. *Pa!*" Jonas leapt off the deck and ran after his father, who was slogging down the sandy slope toward the spit, still railing at the sea.

Conan started for the car. "Come on, Lyn. Let's go." But he paused for one last look at the spit as it emerged from the last onslaught. He smiled and said, " 'The Lord gave and the Lord hath taken away; blessed be the name of the Lord.' "